Mr. Flirt

KARICE BOLTON

Edited by Valorie Clifton

DEDICATION

Thank you to my readers!

Chapter One

Daring Disaster

Shep

The man never misses a dare or a bet.
He will never grow up.
It must feel great to be a manwhore, Sheppy.
You'll never settle down.

These are all the things I'd heard over the years, usually from females, but my friends sometimes teased me too.

For some reason, that last one was the dig that stung the most.

Some might think it would be the manwhore comment that would make me pause, but it wasn't. I knew I'd earned that title, even if it had happened accidentally. Well, many accidents.

But I didn't want it to look like I'd been stringing anyone along. Ever.

I always thought my intentions were clear, and I liked the women I'd wound up dating over the years. But truthfully, more times than not, they were the ones who broke it off with me. And if you glance over the character traits briefly once more, you might see why.

And now my mug was plastered on the front cover of our local magazine's Most Eligible Bachelor issue. However, that was no accident. I had a knack for staying solidly in my bachelor lane.

At an early age, I'd learned that I was good at getting the girl. I was just horrible at keeping her. I never wanted to be perceived as playing with someone's heart. I had a sister. I knew what lousy love could do to a girl's world, and I'd never want to do that to a single soul. My younger brother Colton felt the same way.

However, I could proudly say that I'd never cheated. I'd been cheated on, but I would never do that to someone I loved.

Shoot! I wouldn't do that to someone I hated, either.

I'd seen the devastation to our family when my father did it to my mom. And how I could never look at him the same.

So, why did I feel like reflecting on my life's worth tonight, of all nights?

It went back to character flaw number two.

I'd accepted a dare to attend this colossal matchmaking event in Seattle, but not as Shep.

Tonight, I was Perry. Perry Bartholomew. I pretended to be a college dropout, who enjoyed couch surfing with the best of them, without a goal in sight. I was more of a wanderer, if you would.

My mission tonight was simple. I needed to prove to my best friends, Mike and Brendan, that with this kind of bum résumé, my looks couldn't help me get a girl. My best friends felt that I would indeed have a win tonight with the female persuasion, but I knew better. These types of functions were for serious lookers. They'd be able to see through me immediately. A grand was at stake.

Honestly, I hadn't given the dare a second thought until I wandered into the hotel ballroom tonight with tables as far as the eye could see, with men and women nervously fidgeting and looking around the room like their future selves depended on tonight.

Now, I felt like a jerk.

A royal jerk.

But they'd slapped a nametag on my sweatshirt so

quickly and pushed me toward the first empty table that I couldn't actually get out of the jam that I could thank my best buds for getting me into.

Okay, it wasn't their fault. I could have declined the dare.

See character flaw number two.

Anyway, I knew I'd made a gigantic mistake when I stumbled to the first table.

Actually, it wasn't a huge mistake.

It was a disaster of epic proportions.

I'd found the woman of my dreams while I was in the middle of my worst nightmare.

I was looking into the most beautiful green eyes I'd ever seen in the world, and I'd seen many of them.

And her smile.

My knees wobbled the moment the curl touched her lips.

It was like someone stabbed me in the heart.

She motioned for the chair, which I quickly pulled out and sat in like a puppy dog on his first training day.

Her beautiful gaze dropped to my name tag as her gorgeous mouth rounded into the name *Perry*.

The woman's eyes turned quizzical for a split second, and she repeated the name. "Perry."

When I realized that was me, I nearly choked over my words. I shook my head but nodded and then shook my head again when my gaze dropped to her nametag. I was a mess.

"Lucy, I'm sorry. Unfortunately, there's been a mistake."

She bit her lip in the most deliciously sexy way before taking a sip of the red wine she had in front of her.

Damn. That had always been my kryptonite.

A gorgeous smile.

That and raven hair, which she had cascading down her bare shoulders. The thin straps of her pink camisole left little to the imagination.

Lucy was drop-dead gorgeous.

And her curves.

I had to confess to her.

I needed to tell her this was all a ruse.

"God, I hate these things," she muttered with a blush creeping over her cheeks. "My sister signed me up for my birthday present. Lucky me. Thanks, sister. At least you're normal."

"You hope." I snickered and shook my head. "Well, I can't imagine that you have any problems in the dating area. You're gorgeous."

She grinned and winked at me. "And I'm smart."

5

"I don't doubt it."

"But I don't have much time, so I find myself entering relationships of convenience as long as the convenience lasts like a weekend at the most."

My ears perked up, and a charge ran between us.

Not into lasting relationships? There is a God, and I wasn't about to ruin my version of heaven.

I needed to tell her the truth.

She shrugged, and it was hard to keep my gaze from her lovely shoulders.

"You know, I can't imagine you have a hard time getting dates."

I smiled wider. "Yet, here we both are."

"Ah, touché." She leaned over the table. "So, tell me. What do you do for a living?"

Ah, shit.

I'm about to catfish my future wife.

I was tapping out. This would be the first dare I'd fail, and I'd gladly take the loss.

"Uh, so I—" I started.

Her brows rose as her gaze stayed on mine. "Yeah?"

"I…"

Lucy glanced at the digital timer they'd hung on the wall. "I don't mean to rush you, but we've only got three more minutes. So you'd better make it count. Sell me."

My eyes dropped to the blue, low-pile rug beneath us in the ballroom, and I swallowed hard.

"Well, I think we just figured out why you're at an event like this." She chuckled. "You choke on the conversation part of the relationship thing."

I laughed and brought my eyes back to hers, and my pulse immediately jumped. There was something just so gorgeously intimidating about her. And it was only a plus that she didn't recognize me from the magazine or any accidental shenanigans I'd become known for in the female population of Seattle.

"I own my own business. Started as a software salesman."

She nodded, narrowing her eyes at me. "You own your own business as in the IRS gives you x years of failure before you give it up or…"

Lucy's words smacked me in the face, and I couldn't help but burst into laughter.

"Nah. Like a really solid business, Lucy."

Her shoulders relaxed slightly. "That's good. I don't think that kind of thing is all that important as long as there is direction or something, but I was just checking." Lucy's tongue slowly slid along her bottom lip, and I drew a breath.

"I don't feel like being a sugar mama."

This woman was too good to be true. The directness left me unhinged. I had to tell her the truth.

"Okay." She grinned wider. "Next question. Are you close with your family?"

"Absolutely. My sister is my best friend. Actually, some of her BFFs are my BFFs."

She chuckled. "BFFs?"

I nodded, unable to rip my gaze from Lucy's. "And I love my parents, but they aren't together. But they didn't divorce until we were older. My sister and brother were still in high school." Not wanting to elaborate, I cleared my throat and smiled. The woman in front of me didn't need to hear about my dad's midlife crisis, cheating escapades, and fateful decisions that destroyed his happy family. Nope. She didn't need to hear about that.

"Interesting." She folded her hands together, sliding them to her lap.

"You?"

She smiled, and happiness flitted through her gaze. "I have a younger sister. Her name is Mae. I love her to death. I basically raised her because my parents had a nasty divorce, and my mom had to work all the time and…" Lucy stopped herself, but I didn't want her to ever stop. "Sorry. TMI."

I shook my head slowly. "Not at all. I want to hear more."

She cocked her head slightly. "You do?"

I nodded.

"Most men tune out before I even say I have a sister."

"I'm not most men."

No, you're worse than most men, a little voice taunted.

I gritted my teeth and looked at Lucy. I knew I had to tell her.

The timer buzzed, and Lucy locked her gaze on mine. "You're going to get excellent marks."

I laughed and let out a slow breath. "Lucy, I like you, but I need to tell you one thing."

"Yeah?"

"I was here on a dare. My name's not Perry."

Rage flashed through her beautiful green eyes as she popped up from her seat and reached over the table to grab me.

Red wine spilled everywhere, and the room full of singles gasped in unison as all eyes turned to the screeching female in front of me.

I spun around, narrowly missing her hands of fury, and took that as my exit.

I knew that tonight was officially the last dare I'd ever accept again.

Maybe.

Chapter Two

Here Comes Baby

Lucy

Today had been a day, and it was far from over.

Between listening to two attorneys go at it all afternoon in the office next to mine, and I didn't mean debating, and being stuck behind the longest beagle parade in the history of beagle parades, I was positive that today was out to get me.

I needed to drop off my sister's birthday present at one of Seattle's swankiest bars before hightailing it to the hospital to help my best friend, Danni, give birth.

Why not skip dropping off my sister's present?

Because I didn't have that kind of sister; the word *forgive* never managed to wiggle its way into her vocabulary.

At times, it felt like she was the one who should be a divorce lawyer—not me.

Instead, she ogled over men and sent me to dating events. A shiver ran through me when my mind flashed back to the last one. The personal fiasco even wound up in the local gossip column in our paper. Thankfully, there weren't any names reported. Just a precious little anecdote about dating in the age of smart phones with my rear end up in the air, sprawled over the table in my missed attempt to strangle my match.

But back to why I was in the middle of the city when my best friend was about to give birth.

My sister turned the big 3-0 today, and I'd never hear the end of it if I didn't drop off her present.

I'd like to believe it was because my sister loved me so much and she just had to see a friendly face on her big day, but the truth was much darker. I gave good gifts, and my sister enjoyed receiving them. It was a perk of going to law school.

As I pushed into the overcrowded and overpriced bar, I immediately spotted my sister and her friends. They'd obviously been there for a while, considering just how loud their voices rang in the air.

The bar was one of those swanky places with exposed beams overhead, fancy wrought-iron chandeliers, brick facades, and drinks that cost a small fortune, with men in suits slurping them up.

My sister saw me, flung her hands up, and frantically waved as I walked over. I saw a few male glances in my direction and tried not to roll my eyes at them. I felt like a pork chop they wanted to gnaw on before tossing the bone away.

Did I mention I was a divorce lawyer?

Fact. This was the worst place to meet a guy, and I certainly didn't have time for an awkward hello. It was bad enough that slippery, snaky men surrounded me at work. I didn't need to mingle with them in my off-hours.

Not to mention I was still scarred by a man named Perry, who looked like a buff Viking warrior trapped in the throngs of hipster nation. It just proved to me that I wasn't cut out for the opposite sex. Or, more to the point, I didn't feel like thawing my heart anytime soon.

I slid a Chanel gift bag under the table, making my sister's eyes light up as I went in for another hug.

"Hey, Mae. Happy Birthday." I squeezed her extra hard before slipping into the chair reserved for me.

She beamed. "Thank you. I hoped you'd make it."

I smiled, noticing her eyeing the bag under the table. "I'd never miss your birthday."

Mae was my younger sister by four years, but when

our parents divorced, she was twelve and I was sixteen. Since my mom suddenly got thrust back into the working world, I took care of Mae more often than my mom. Rather than being best friends like some sisters, our relationship turned maternal. I had this incessant need to take care of her.

"Did you have a good day at the firm?" my sister asked, taking a sip of her pink drink. "You look more stressed than usual."

I had less than thirty minutes to wish my sister a happy birthday, dash out to my car parked a block away, drive to the hospital at the other end of Seattle, find parking in a cramped garage, and race to the labor and delivery unit.

I nodded. "Just another day in paradise, and Danni is about to pop," I teased, glancing around the bar. "Sorry I'm late. I got stuck behind the Beagle Parade."

Seattle seemed to have a parade for everything.

Mae laughed and held up her martini glass. "I didn't even notice. Plus, whatever is inside that bag makes up for it, I'm sure."

"Oh, Mae. Who is this sexy hunk coming our way?" one of her friends gushed.

"You mean the Greek God with blond hair and sapphire blue eyes that make me want to—"

I tuned out the other friend and grinned as anxiety

inched through my system. I'd barely warmed the seat, but I had to go. I could not miss the birth of my BFF's first child.

My sister hiccuped in response, and I knew now was my time to exit.

When I saw a bartender start this way with a tray full of drinks, I grabbed my purse and blew my sister a kiss. She batted her lashes at me.

"Off to deliver a baby."

"From law school to doula." Mae laughed without taking her eyes off the bartender. "Not bad for an older sister. Make sure she has her baby tonight, and then we can be birthday twins."

"I'll try to have her work on that," I teased. "Happy Birthday."

The moment I stepped outside and felt the chilly air blast my cheeks, I got a sudden surge of adrenaline. Today felt like a whirlwind, and the crazy part hadn't even happened yet.

I could do this.

My best friend needed me, and I was honored to be part of the biggest day in her life.

And since her husband took off with the neighbor's wife six weeks ago, there wasn't a way in the world I was going to let my girl go at this alone.

After Danielle walked in on her husband in the

laundry room with someone who wasn't her, I was shocked that Danni didn't go into immediate labor. However, she managed to smack the ironing board on his head before she waddled out of the room and up the stairs to her bedroom, where she collapsed on the bed and cried herself to sleep.

The thought of my best friend having that happen to her at such a delicate time made me look askance at any man in a bar, grocery store, or sporting event.

As I climbed into my car and pulled onto the road taking me to Danni, I thought about what was ahead. Not just in the here and now for Danni, but once her little one was born. Since she'd married Bill, she'd quit working and played the perfect housewife, and now I had no idea what she was going to do.

I clutched the steering wheel as I thought about what I'd like to do to the guy if I saw him, but thankfully, I represented Danni in her upcoming divorce. I was confident she wouldn't have to worry about finances just yet. We lived in a community property state, and I would make Bill pay in ways he'd never dreamed.

The thought made me so tickled that I almost drove by the hospital's entrance and had to make a hard turn. I glanced at the radio and saw that I had less than ten minutes to get to her.

"Come on, Lucy," I whispered to myself. "You can do this."

My luck suddenly changed for the day, and a parking spot opened right up by the elevator.

Within minutes, I was checked in at security for the labor and delivery ward and flew down the corridor, hearing distant moans and groans.

My uterus went into shock as screeching wrapped around me when I found Danni's room. I breathed a sigh of relief when I knocked on the door and heard a faint hello from inside.

I stepped into the room and opened the curtain to see my best friend looking like she was ready to pull the baby out herself, and I knew I was in for it.

"We got this, Danni."

Her eyes met mine, and a smile crept onto her lips. "Yeah? You think so?"

"I know so." I set my bag down and made my way toward my best friend. "Have you heard from your ex?"

She rubbed her belly and let out a deep sigh. "No. I texted him that I was in labor."

"Your mom was going to handle that."

"I know. I guess I just..." her voice trailed off, and my heart ached for my best friend.

17

I rubbed her back and shook my head. "You just hoped he'd turn into a decent human being again?"

She drew a deep breath and nodded. "Pretty much."

"Well, I may not have a beard like his, but I'm here now."

Danni snickered as the nurse stepped in. "Have you looked in the mirror recently, Lucy?"

My hand instinctively went to my chin, and I chuckled.

Danni sucked in a deep breath, and her eyes widened like she'd just seen a unicorn prance by. "It's coming."

"It's not an *it*, dear," the nurse hummed as she reached for the oxygen. "It's a baby."

Danni and I traded a glance as another unicorn pranced in front of her, and she reached for my hand and let out a scream.

Chapter Three

Disaster Strikes Again

Shep

"There is only one thing in life that I'm sure of, and that, my friend, is that I will never fall in love." I raised my beer to toast my best friend, Mike, as our bottles clanked amid the bustling sound of the bar.

"Whatever you say, man." Mike took a swig of his beer and pointed at a group of females huddling near the bartender. "But don't you think you're kind of old to be playing the part of the guy who won't ever be tied down? I mean, you've even been put up as the poster boy for Seattle. When's enough going to be enough? Do you want ten more years of magazine covers declaring your availability to the world?"

I laughed and let out a blissful sigh.

Why blissful?

Because I hadn't fallen for the trap that Mike fell for.

Just a few months ago, he'd felt like I did. There was too much in the world to do and see without being weighed down by love.

And then something happened to him.

It's like his wires crossed, and the next thing I knew, I was the best man at his wedding.

I'd gladly stay a best man for eternity. I didn't want to have to check in with anyone. I wanted to merely exist in my happy place, which at the moment was my favorite bar across the street from my condo.

I'd had a long week already.

And after being mesmerized by a scintillating raven-haired beauty at a dare-turned-dating-disaster several months ago, I solemnly vowed never to get serious. I had my chance that fateful night, and she came after me with claws out.

Lucy.

Ah, Lucy.

"Come on. Do you think if I had a wife, I'd be at the bar with you, talking about whatever the heck came to mind without a care in the world?"

Mike shrugged. "I'm here, and I've found the one.

And might I add, once you find your person, life becomes easy."

I spotted Brendan, my other best friend, making his way over with a drink. He gave a quick wave and arrived just in time to hear me explain some things to Mike.

"Yeah . . . well, first of all, you're in your honeymoon phase. It's all a trick. Sorcery."

Mike rolled his eyes, and Brendan laughed. "Is he going on about it again?"

Mike laughed and nodded, but I continued.

"I bet you have a time you're supposed to be home by and a lot of things you shouldn't do tonight."

Mike scratched his chin and looked perplexed. "Not really. I mean, apart from being a decent human being, I can't think of much."

"Oh, just a decent guy?" Brendan teased. "That doesn't seem too hard."

I shrugged and took a sip of beer. "You can't tell me there aren't some rules involved with your going out without her."

Mike laughed. "Not really. Just common-sense stuff."

Brendan nodded. "I have to agree with Shep on this one. Women tend to change after you walk down the aisle."

Mike shook his head. "And you know this, how?"

"Purely observation." Brendan's smile grew tenfold as he raised his drink to cheer me.

"Skylar is different," Mike muttered.

"If you say so." I didn't buy it for a second. Never once had I been in a relationship and didn't get bombarded with a million rules.

It would start simple, like I couldn't meet a friend for dinner or I had to call when I left the office, but then it would evolve to not being allowed to swing by the store on the way home or change plans at the last minute to go see a ballgame with a buddy.

Which was precisely why I prided myself on just not bothering. It was all too complicated and messy.

But Mike.

Mike got fooled. He fell for a pretty woman with an amazing personality, but soon, the real Skylar would show her true colors, and I'd be there to pick up the pieces of my best bud's heart.

Mike patted my shoulder as he took another sip of beer. I knew it because I'd lived it.

He looked me square in my eyes and grinned. "You know what's weird about you?"

I smirked. "Enlighten me."

"You're the happiest guy I know—successful, kind,

and funny. You've got the biggest heart I've ever experienced."

I chuckled. "Are you asking me out on a date?"

Brendan glanced at Mike. "Sure sounds like it."

Mike grinned wider. "I'm not done yet. You're all that good rolled up into a great big, giant ball of tenderness until the topic turns to love. That's when you turn into a real downer, a cynic, the Grinch on steroids." He took another swig. "I have to confess. You're not fun to be around when you start picking on love. Just because you haven't found the one doesn't mean she doesn't exist."

Ah, Lucy. The one who got away. The one who wanted to kill me.

Good times.

"Psh." I shook my head and glanced around the packed bar with extravagant chandeliers dangling from the ceiling, fancy stone floors sprawling in every direction, and expensive booze pouring freely from the bartenders' hands. "The place is filled with pretty women, and I guarantee you, not one of them is a perfect fit for Sheppy."

Mike grimaced and shook his head. "Uh, yeah. Especially if you refer to yourself in the third person."

"All I'm saying is that if I'm this old, and I can't find the perfect someone in a sea of eligible women, it's obviously not meant to be." I shrugged. "And I'm okay with that. I'd rather have fun than hurt feelings. You know, keep it light."

Brendan nodded. "Mike has a point. At least, I'm not vehemently against settling down one day. I'd love to find the perfect woman. But Shep, you're really a downer on love."

The double doors opened with a gust of electricity, and a woman walked into the bar.

Her dark hair flowed past her shoulders, and sparkling green eyes lit up when her gaze landed on someone at the table over from us.

Lucy!

It was like my world stopped as she glided to the table next to us. I quickly scanned the other women sitting at the table and couldn't help but smile. There wasn't any male waiting for her, but she hadn't noticed me in the slightest.

"As you were saying?" Mike elbowed me, and Brendan snickered.

I flashed them a quick scowl before turning my attention to the beauty who'd already taken a seat with her friends.

Mike leaned over. "So, what are you going to do about it?"

My scowl deepened. "About what?"

Brendan only laughed as I glanced in Lucy's

direction.

The truth was that Mike knew nothing about Lucy. I paid him a grand just to avoid questions from that fateful night.

And now karma was here to kick me in the chops.

I didn't believe in love at first sight or any of that, but I firmly believed in lust at first sight, and I couldn't tear my eyes away from her for the second time in my life.

She was even more dazzling than I remembered and judging by the stares from all the men around, I wasn't the only one who knew how special she was.

But the moment Lucy's laugh echoed into the room, I was done for. It wasn't some odd cackle or a deep hack or a nasally snicker . . . no, her laugh was enchanting and inviting and . . .

I called myself Perry and catfished what could have been the love of my life.

Except that I didn't buy into all of that.

Wouldn't buy into all that.

"You going to be okay, Shep? You're probably making that table of females extremely uncomfortable." Brendan eyed the table not too far from ours.

I tore my gaze away and laughed as Mike pressed his lips into a fine line.

I recognized the look Mike threw at me. It was the same tricky expression since college whenever a bright idea popped into his head. But through no fault of his own, they usually weren't very bright and often involved a dare . . . like the one that got me in so much trouble a mere few months ago. He whipped out his phone and pulled me into the camera frame, grinning, and hit *Play* before speaking into the camera.

"I've got a proposition for you," he began.

He always did.

My brows arched in anticipation. "Yeah?"

"I'll bet you five hundred bucks that if you go over to that table and introduce yourself, the new arrival will ignore you. She won't give you the time of day."

I straightened. "Ignore me? Like flat out turn her head in the other direction?"

"Something like that."

If there was one thing Lucy would do to me, I highly doubted it would be to ignore me. Throw a punch and finish the job, maybe. But that wouldn't lose me the bet.

I laughed. "Wow. Such faith in your buddy."

Mike shrugged and took a sip. "Just a hunch. Do you accept the bet?"

I shook my head. "Your hunch is that the most beautiful woman in the bar wants nothing to do with your best friend? Tell me how you really feel."

Mike smiled.

"Fine. The bet's on, and I won't accept a payment plan. I guarantee you that she won't ignore me."

There might be a few things she'll swing in my direction, but pretending not to see me won't be one of them.

So much for never accepting another dare.

He winked at me. "Not a problem, my friend. You're not the only one with a few bills in the bank. I'm good for it. Oh, and if you can get her to sleep with you, I'll pay you double."

Mike sat back, looking far too sure of himself, while I stood and walked over to the bartender to order a round of drinks for the ladies.

As the bartender followed me over to the table, I spotted Mike continuing with the video, which only made me up my game.

The truth was that I rarely struck out. Had I used my real name at the matchmaking event, maybe life would be different and I would have eloped with Lucy in Vegas.

I walked over to Lucy's side of the table as the bartender stood with a tray full of drinks. As I was about to kneel down, Lucy shot up from her chair, grabbed her purse, and darted toward the door as Mike stood up and began clapping.

I suppose there was a first for everything, and I couldn't thank Mike enough for capturing it for all eternity on his phone.

Chapter Four

Oh, Baby

Lucy

"Oh, Lucy. I don't want you to think like that," Danni whispered, smiling down at her little bundle of joy named Blair. "If I had never met Bill, I would never have had the best thing in my life happen to me."

Her words sank deep into my soul as I watched my best friend nuzzling her nose alongside her precious baby's cheek, and I couldn't help but smile.

Danni's eyes connected with mine. "Don't give up on men. They aren't all snakes."

I laughed and nodded, wishing I believed that, but I was a family lawyer specializing in divorce. Boxes of tissue were among my biggest expenses.

Not to mention my one-and-done at a local matchmaking event. Just the thought of that man made my fingers tingle with a desire to get in a boxing ring with him.

Granted, I could have been disbarred if I'd managed to dig my fingers into him liked I'd hoped. So things always work out for the best.

"Okay, but enough of that." I grinned, running my fingers along Danni's loose bun.

A person would never know she'd just given birth, but that was how Danni was. She'd always pick herself up and carry on, regardless of the situation.

"My mom should be here any second," she informed me. "She's still upset that she missed the birth."

I chuckled, knowing Danni's mom was a handful, to say the least. "She's the one who booked the cruise a week before your due date."

Danni laughed. "Exactly."

"How are you feeling?"

"Sore and exhausted but extremely grateful that everything went so smoothly."

I hid a smile as I thought about her labor that went on all night and into the early morning hours.

She turned to me just as the nurse came in. "You should go home. I know you probably have stacks of paper to go through or whatever it is you do as a hotshot attorney."

I rolled my eyes. "Code for get outta here. I'm exhausted anyway."

She smiled. "Something like that."

One of the many things that had made our friendship so strong over the years was the brutally honest tone we'd struck with one another.

"Besides, I don't want you to have to deal with my mom," she added.

"Oh, right." I nodded.

Danni's mom thought that her daughter should take one for the team and look the other way, pretend none of the cheating happened, or the lying, or anything else that may have undone their relationship.

Never mind the fact that Bill had seemingly moved on. It was never said between Danni and me, but even if she wanted to go that route, he didn't.

I noticed my jaw had clenched at the mere thought of him.

How could he not even be here for his daughter's birth?

I pushed down the anger and plastered a smile on my face.

"Love ya, and you two get some rest. Call me when

you want me back."

The nurse rolled over the baby's bassinet, which looked more like a plastic bin, and I wandered out of the hospital room.

Being there for the birth of Blair was something I'd never forget, and Danni asking me to be her godmother was such a blessing. The topper was Danni using Lucy as Blair's middle name. I was on cloud nine, and I didn't have to do any of the hard work.

But by the time I'd gotten on the elevator and walked all the way to the parking garage, I was exhausted.

I'd been going and going since yesterday, and it all finally all hit me.

Today was Saturday, and I felt like collapsing.

When Danni had drifted off after she gave birth, I tried to do the same on the awkward leather recliner, but between all the call bells and announcements coming over the hallway speakers, it was a lost cause.

As I slipped into the car, I saw a message from my sister slide over.

Hey, when you left, some super-hot guy asked for your information. He said you brushed him off, but he was so hot that I couldn't imagine any woman in her right mind doing that. I even tried to convince him to treat me to a little birthday surprise, but he didn't take me up on it. Anyway, he has your number. His name is Ship or Shep or Chip. I don't know.

My eyes widened at the words sitting on my phone screen. Brushed off some guy at the bar? I shook my head. I didn't even see any interested guy, let alone brush one off.

I scowled at the phone and started typing back.

Why would you give a complete stranger my phone number?

She quickly replied.

He was hot.

I rolled my eyes and texted back. My sister was so predictable.

Yeah. You mentioned that. Yet, you don't even know if his name is Chip, Ship, or Shep.

Another text tolled over.

Quit being such a lawyer and live a little. Besides, he might not reach out.

My scowl deepened. Why wouldn't he reach out?

Fine. Whatever. Did you want me to tell you about the birth of Danni's little girl?

I snickered to myself, already knowing the answer. I really didn't know how we could be sisters.

I'm sure it went just fine.

I smiled and groaned. Where was this girl's curiosity? Compassion?

How was the rest of your birthday?

She wrote back.

Amazing. Thanks for the Chanel bag. I love it, and I'm going to use it tonight.

I quickly typed back.

Tonight? Where are you going?

Mae replied.

Out with a guy I met last night.

Of course. I should have guessed. I shook my head and told her I loved her just as my phone rang. It wasn't a number I recognized, but that wasn't too unusual.

"This is Lucy," I answered flatly.

"Hey, Lucy. This is Shep Jensen. The guy you nearly elbowed out of the way last night."

My frown resurfaced. "Umm. I don't really remember that."

He whistled. "Oh, one too many, huh?"

I gasped and shook my head. The nerve of this guy. "No, actually. I had zero to drink and wasn't at the bar for more than ten minutes, so I think you're mistaken."

"Oh, I'm not mistaken." The guy's voice was cute. There was no doubt about that, and his confidence was refreshing, but that was where this would end.

"I'm sorry. You said your name was Ship or Chip

or—"

"It's Shep."

"Short for?" I prompted. "Shepherd?"

He laughed. "You know what they say about people who assume."

I couldn't help but laugh. "Seriously. Is this how you try to pick up all the women?"

"No, actually." He laughed some more. "It's usually pretty easy, so that's why I'm calling."

"Ah." I nodded to myself. "So, you just don't like being told no."

"Technically, you didn't say no," he corrected, and his voice sounded vaguely familiar.

"True, because I have absolutely no recollection of you."

"Ouch."

I snickered, nearly picturing him holding his chest.

If his looks matched his voice, I was in trouble.

"Listen. To be fair, my best friend just gave birth. I only stopped at the bar to give my sister her birthday present, so if I happened to ignore you, I'm sorry. It wasn't personal."

"It's always personal."

"Only to men who think they're God's gift to women," I muttered.

"Wow. Been scorned recently?"

I laughed, feeling this man's confidence oozing through the phone. "No, but my best friend's husband just cheated on her, and he didn't even have the decency to show for the birth of his own daughter."

Shep's tone turned serious. "Wow. That's really, really horrible."

"Isn't it?"

"It is, and I'm so sorry to be making light of everything."

"You didn't know," I assured him.

"Yeah, but still." He cleared his throat. "You probably think I'm a complete—"

I laughed, interrupting him. "It's not just you, but I'm pretty much not the woman you'd want to take out on a date."

"Yeah?" his voice softened. "Why's that?"

"I'm a divorce lawyer."

Shep's laughter rolled over the phone, and I couldn't help but smile.

"You don't scare me," he offered.

"That's too bad."

I could feel his smile over the phone.

"So, how about it? Will you have dinner with me?"

Chapter Five

Mr. Coffee

Shep

Did it hurt that I got downgraded from dinner with Lucy to coffee? Yeah, it hurt a bit. I clutched my chest at the thought as I stared intently at the door of the coffee shop, willing it to swing open any second, except that it didn't.

I glanced at my phone. Lucy was ten minutes late, and I didn't know if I should save face and book or wait it out for another ten. Had she figured out who I was?

Perry from the dating disaster?

Or Shep Jensen, Seattle's most eligible bachelor?

Tapping my finger on the table, I glanced around the place. It was a coffee shop that Lucy picked out, which I'd never been to before. There were rows of books at the far end where a gas fireplace made for a perfect reading nook.

Several people were reading papers and drinking their coffees out of porcelain mugs. I was surprised some of them weren't wearing ascots and plaid.

God forbid she'd pick a coffee shop that served the brown liquid in a paper cup. It intrigued me, and I knew it shouldn't, but this place screamed intellectual snob, and Lucy didn't strike me like that at all.

I thought back to her demeanor on the phone and couldn't help but hear her glorious giggles. She did laugh at my jokes, so maybe I wasn't being stood up. As her giggles wrapped around me, I realized they weren't coming from my head.

Lucy had somehow swept into the coffee shop without me noticing and was legit flirting with the male barista behind the counter.

No wonder she wanted to come here. She's got the hots for the tattooed foam maker. I rolled my eyes. If that were her taste, I was doomed. There wasn't an ounce of ink on my flesh. I had blue eyes, dirty blond hair, and for living in Seattle, I'd managed to maintain a tan.

And the fact that I was even listing off my attributes to myself while waiting for a woman who was completely baffling and hated my guts told me I was in trouble.

I didn't need to wind up like my best bud and his new

wife, Skylar. Dating was a slippery slope. It was great to have fun and get to know the other person, but it should be about the journey, not the destination, which to most women I met meant marriage.

The destination was always marriage.

But maybe Lucy would be so infuriated with me, she'd decide to sleep with me out of anger and...no, that didn't make any sense.

Watching Lucy swoop her hands into the air, laughing and swinging her hair around as she reached for her latte from the barista made my chest tighten a little. Would I ever be able to get a reaction like that out of her? I scowled at myself.

Why did I care?

She spun around with the cup in her hand as I stood to wave her down. When her eyes connected with mine, her carefree expression dropped, but she didn't charge out of the coffeeshop. Instead, she tore toward me, and the only thing shielding me was the table.

I held my head up high and started to pull out a chair for her.

"Off to a great start," I mumbled to myself.

"It's okay. I got it." She nearly ripped the chair away from me as she simultaneously set her cup down on the table.

Lucy folded her arms over her chest and glared at me.

"What are you doing here?"

I scratched my head and eyed her as she brought the white mug to her mouth. A little edge of foam traced her lips, and I briefly thought about what it might be like to kiss her. I ripped my gaze away from her mouth as her eyes landed on mine.

"I'm glad you didn't throw the coffee on me." I grimaced.

"I'm a lawyer. I know better."

"I never did get the red wine out of my shirt from that night."

Lucy continued to stare at me as the sound of a coffee grinder buzzed through the air. When it stopped, I continued.

"Glad you could make it." I looked around the place.

"I've been tricked." She licked the foam from her mouth but refused to remove her gaze from mine.

It was a challenge. Lucy was warning me.

I glanced around the space. "I've never heard of this spot."

Lucy smiled, and I about fell off my chair. Her smile was disarming yet enchanting. "That doesn't surprise me."

A grin slid across my face. "What does that mean? You don't think I fit their typical clientele?"

She ignored my question. "I always hung out here

when I was in law school, and the place stuck. It feels like home." She pointed toward the fireplace. "I can't even begin to tell you how many briefs I read in that chair the weird-looking guy is in."

My gaze found the person she was talking about, and I hid a smile. The guy looked like he could be my brother, minus the outfit. I was more of a jeans kind of guy, and that one over there liked to dress up.

"It's not very nice to call someone weird-looking." I smiled, and she tightened her eyes at me in a challenge.

"It's the middle of winter, and the guy looks like he hits a tanning bed every morning before sunup. His teeth are so white, they are translucent, and I'm surprised glitter isn't falling out of his eyes since they're so sparkly." She shrugged. "Plus, his tie matches his socks."

My gaze ran along the stranger's pant legs, and sure enough, his socks did match his tie, and I would imagine finding purple paisley socks to match your purple paisley tie wasn't easy.

"I'll try to remember not to be too matchy-matchy around you if I want to impress you." I grinned, and she cocked her head slightly.

Lucy chuckled and shook her head. "There's no impressing me, Perry. You dug your own grave."

"Then why didn't you turn around and leave when you saw me?" I asked, genuinely curious.

The look in her eyes was almost challenging. I couldn't help but grin wider.

"I wasn't going to waste a perfectly good cup of coffee." Her lips pursed together. "And I'm debating what best to do to you."

I laughed and shook my head. "You're in a precarious situation. Most things you're probably dreaming of doing to me would get you kicked out of the bar association."

She snickered and nodded. "You're right about that."

"I figured as much." I swallowed and took a deep breath. I knew what I had to do.

"Lucy, I'm hoping enough time has passed since—"

Her hand flew up. "Don't say it. I don't want to hear it."

"Give me a shot."

"Fine. Why would you care about impressing me?"

"The same reason I invited you to dinner." I sat back in the chair. "You intrigue me."

"And yet here we are at a coffee spot." It was Lucy's turn to smile. "But really, do I only intrigue you because I'm the first woman to turn you down?"

It wasn't really a question.

I laughed and shook my head. "You didn't turn me down."

She parted her mouth and ran her tongue along her lips. "That's right. I just ignored you."

"So, the truth comes out." I took a sip of my Americano.

Lucy laughed and shook her head. "I'm only teasing. I swear I didn't see you."

I nodded, choosing to believe that. "How's your friend?"

She looked surprised that I asked. "Danni?"

"It's the only friend I know about so far."

Lucy smiled and nodded slowly. "She's doing really well. Her daughter is an absolute angel. Obviously gets it from her mom and not her dad."

"You know, you won't be able to do that someday."

Her eyes widened. "Do what?"

"Insult her dad." I watched her carefully as she shook her head.

"I didn't even realize I had. You're absolutely right." Lucy bit her bottom lip as she contemplated something. "It's interesting you pointed that out."

"Don't get me wrong. He sounds like a complete dirtbag, but if there's any hope for the little girl to know her dad…" my voice trailed off.

Lucy cocked her head slightly. "You're very observant, Perry."

The name stung as a not-so-gentle reminder of the prank I'd played.

"I'm beyond sorry about that night. I take full responsibility."

Her brows furrowed. "Of course, you would. No one was making you do anything."

"Technically, a large sum of money was on the line."

She showed me a death stare. "And that's reason enough to make fun of people? Mess with their hearts?"

I straightened and kept my eyes on hers. "I don't recall making fun of anyone, and I'm certain I didn't mess with anyone's heart."

"You don't know that." She pressed her lips into a thin line.

"If I hurt your heart, I'm sorry."

Her expression softened slightly. "Not mine."

"You were the only one I met that night, and same for you."

"You are far too observant for your own good."

"I also like to think I'm a good listener."

Lucy's expression softened even more. "What does

your company do?"

"Apparently, you're a good listener too." I smiled, remembering our call. "It's a gaming company."

Maybe she'd forget about the details of the matchmaking event and accept my apology.

"What kind of games? Board games?"

I shook my head. "Video games."

"Do you design them?"

"I have a team for that," I offered simply. I wasn't sure she really wanted the specifics.

"Then what do you do? Why do you own a gaming company? What's your added value?" Her brows shot up.

I was wrong. The woman liked details.

"Well, back in college, I came up with a killer concept for a game. I had the storyline sketched out in my head, and I knew it would be extremely popular. But I wound up working in sales for a software company. I knew if I tried to develop it, the game would flop. I understood enough to know I needed a good team to help me develop my vision." I leaned forward. "I waited to quit until I could fully execute my dream. The game has done extremely well."

She studied me for a quick second. "So, are you a one-hit wonder?"

I laughed and shook my head. "Our last three games

have been voted best console game of the year upon release."

"You don't strike me as a gamer." She glanced at the barista. "Do you like video games?"

Ah, she thinks someone like the flirty barista is a gamer, but not the guy sitting in front of her.

I smiled. "Do you do this on all your dates?"

"Do what?"

"Interrogate them like they're on a witness stand."

Chapter Six

A bit of Trickery

Lucy

I stared at the smirking man in front of me as his words hit me like a ton of bricks. What I didn't like about this entire conversation was that I knew the answer to his question.

Shep's smirk only grew, and I had to admit it was kind of cute.

And he was kind of right.

I had a terrible habit of bathing my dates in nonstop questions, turning rigid when things got romantic and ending things if they did.

"I'm guessing the answer is…" He nodded slowly, keeping his eyes on mine.

A supercharged rush of hormones sizzled through my veins as his beautiful blues stayed locked on me. I sat still, hoping the sensation would leave as quickly as it came, but then his smirk turned to a sweet smile.

Just like the first night I'd met him.

Shep seemed so genuine and caring.

And that was how so many women got tricked on their way to divorce court.

I'd told myself over the last few months that the chemistry I'd felt with the cocky, lying stranger was all made up. I'd fooled myself into believing that he wasn't as sexy or funny as I'd remembered.

And now, there was no denying it.

He was all that and a bag of pickle chips.

"You're an interesting woman, Lucy." Shep sat back, letting his gaze fall to the table. "And I'll be honest. I don't know if this is a pity date, an experiment of some sort, or just something to fill your afternoon."

I had plenty to fill my day, judging by the stack of papers on my desk back at the firm. Most Saturdays, I spent my morning and most of my afternoon slogging through everything I didn't get through during the week, but today, I wanted to be different.

I just didn't expect to find a man who looked like God's gift to the world to have the moxie to trick me twice.

Don't get me wrong, I wasn't exactly a toad, but I

definitely felt I had some amphibian about me. My feet were bigger than most of my dates' appendages, my fingers longer and wider than an average bratwurst, thanks to my dad, and I rarely had time to put on an ounce of makeup.

Yes, I fully understood that women were enticing in our natural state. I get it. I went to law school and surrounded myself with intelligent men and women alike, and looks didn't matter, but I always tended to feel better about myself if I at least dabbed some mascara onto my already sparse lashes, which were a genetic gift from my mom.

And now I was sitting across from a man who enjoyed tricking women.

I brought my gaze back to Shep. "I don't have a lack of things to do, and I get paid well to do them, so I'm here because I want to be. Or I thought I wanted to be. Until I realized I'd been tricked again."

Shep smiled as a spark darted through his gaze. "You want to be here with me or that guy behind the counter?"

I followed Shep's gaze and snorted when I saw Thorn give a wave in our direction. "I don't think my best friend would be thrilled if I dated her uncle."

Surprise darted across Shep's features. "How old is your best friend? Twelve?"

Shep had a point. Danielle's uncle did look young for

his age, but he'd owned this place for nearly twenty years. It was how I'd met her.

I smiled and shook my head. "The whole family ages well."

"Wait. Is this the friend who just gave birth? Danni?"

I nodded. "We met here when I was in law school, and she was pining over her soon-to-be ex-dirtbag."

Shep wiggled his finger. "Remember…"

I laughed and rolled my eyes. "Right. Must not talk ill of the dirtbag in front of the child, but she's not here."

"I don't condone it. Don't get me wrong. There's nothing worse than seeing that kind of devastation, an entire family imploding based on a guy's lousy choices. I just feel so bad for their kid."

There was something so genuine about Shep's words. It made me wonder if he'd experienced the same growing up.

"I do need to work on it, and I'm sure over time after I rake him over the coals in court, I'll be less bitter on my friend's behalf."

Shep laughed and nodded. "Yeah, I'm sure that will happen."

"Do you enjoy what you do?" Shep asked, and heat suddenly swept over my cheeks.

It was all I'd ever done, so I assumed I enjoyed law.

I'd finally paid off the student loans, which made me enjoy it much more. I twisted my lips into a pout as I thought about it for a few more seconds. There were the long hours, the men who made partner all around me while I remained an associate partner, and the lack of a social life weren't the best.

But the pay was great.

I nodded quickly. "Yeah. I like it. I like what I can do for people, especially people who have been tricked."

"Are there a lot of you out there?"

I nodded. "Surprisingly so."

"Full selfish confession." He drew a breath. "You blow me away. The first night I saw you...the second night...and tonight. But I knew because of my stupid and very childish mistake that you wouldn't come out to see me for coffee tonight if I confessed."

"True."

"So, give me a chance?" His broody eyes stayed on mine. "I am truly sorry."

"I'll think about it." I took a drink.

"So, you love your job because of what you can do to help folks. Tell me more."

I hated that I wanted to.

"I can make things right in a situation that is very wrong." I squirmed in my chair.

I was an attorney used to tense situations and hostile courtrooms, but the way Shep watched me made me sweat. It was as if I didn't need to tell him the truth. He could read it. He was exactly who I'd never want on opposing counsel. I smiled. "Well, maybe not right, but I can make it more palatable, and that makes me feel good."

"That makes a lot of sense." He drew a deep breath and tapped his finger on the table. "Does your line of profession mean it's impossible to respect the opposite sex?"

His question jarred me back to something I'd been wondering as well. "I wouldn't say impossible to respect the opposite sex, but I would say it might be hard for me to understand or respect the institution of marriage." I clicked my tongue and shook my head. "And you certainly didn't do any favors for my male counterparts."

Shep nodded and crossed his arms over his chest. This was about the time most men fled the scene and labeled me as undateable.

He grinned. "I'm not much for the institution myself."

I laughed and shook my head. "Why does that not surprise me?"

"Well, I'm not jaded about it. I just don't think it's for me." His eyes connected with mine, and I felt a pulse of unexpected desire. Had I met my match?

I eyed him carefully, but all the annoying tingles swept over me. "Is that because you're a player? Enjoy a game, do you?"

Shep smirked and shook his head. "I don't like that word. I prefer totally upfront, noncommittal, fun guy."

I couldn't help but laugh. "A fun guy?"

He shrugged and looked immediately disarming. "Let's just say I have fun, and I'm sure my partner does too."

A smoldering heat flashed through me when I realized Shep wasn't just talking about a ride on Seattle's Ferris Wheel.

My eyes flashed, and my lips curled slightly as I thought back to all the wives crying in my office about their husbands with whom they'd spent years faking it.

I tapped my finger on the edge of my empty cup and brought my gaze back to his. "How can you be sure the women you sleep with are having fun too?"

"It's something I just know." He laughed and glanced around the coffee shop. "And this isn't exactly the kind of conversation I thought we'd be having."

"Is it too steamy for you?" I teased.

Shep's eyes sparkled with an intensity that slid fire over my skin.

"Not in the slightest."

I wiggled in my seat and watched him watching me. "Is that why you invited me out? To have fun?"

Shep's smile only widened. "Is that what you want?"

Chapter Seven

Dares Run in the Family

Shep

Dear Lord, this woman is setting me ablaze. Her eyes cooled as she poked at me like a lion caged in a zoo.

She ate men like me for an appetizer, and for some awful reason, I eagerly wanted to be forked.

Lucy contemplated my question, her eyes narrowed, and she let out a hiss. "I'll let you know after dinner."

"Dinner?" I blurted.

Her right brow rose sharply. "You've got plans?"

I shrugged and let out a sigh. "No plans, but this is just a sudden change. Is this a dare or something to teach me a lesson?"

Lucy furrowed her brows and smiled. "A dare?"

I laughed, realizing my sister and her friends had

really screwed with my sense of reality. "Crazy sister and friends. Long story." I waved my hands to dismiss it.

"I've got time. I just need to go to the office for a few hours while you decide where you want to take me."

Man, she was refreshing.

And confusing.

When I looked at her, the softness of her features and the gentle sway of her curves created a false vulnerability because the moment she opened her mouth, I wasn't sure what to expect.

And I loved it. I shouldn't have, but I did.

Which was probably why I was single. I liked to be tortured, and there were few who stood up to the challenge.

But a divorce lawyer?

Bingo.

"Do tell me about this sister of yours." She flashed a wicked grin that about did me in.

"Back in high school, she and her friends got together, as teenagers do, and swore to one another that they'd never date whoever their Mr. Wrongs were. They each made a list and promised they'd never date that type of guy. Flash forward to turning almost thirty, and they all decided to dig up their Mr. Wrongs and date them before they turned the big one."

Lucy looked completely intrigued. "The big one?"

I smiled. "Thirty."

She chuckled. "Been there, done that."

Hmm, not that it mattered, but I wondered how old she was. I would have guessed not quite thirty.

"The big one to me is turning forty, but I still have a ways." She smiled and let out a blissful sigh. "How did it work out for your sister and her friends?"

I nodded. "They are all married now."

"Happily?" she prodded as an attorney would.

"Extremely so." I nodded.

"That is quite an experiment." She whistled. "Maybe love is an equation, after all."

"Nothing else? Just plug in two willing participants, shake 'em up a bit, and voila." I didn't believe for a minute Lucy thought that. She knew feelings were involved—raw emotions that twisted the heart and made men piles of mush and women balls of fire. Those emotions equaled revenge, and Lucy was the conduit.

She shrugged, smiling. "Why not? I mean, the truth of it is that I have never met a spouse who didn't believe their marriage was going to be forever. They walked down that aisle with the best of them. They knew they'd beat the odds and—wham!" She punched her palm. "The husband flies off with the nanny, or the wife sneaks upstairs with the UPS man."

I choked on her words and slapped my knee. "No way. Your cases can't all be doom and gloom and full of soap opera antics."

She laughed, and the softness from earlier filled her gaze. "By the time it gets to me, it's usually pretty bad. Often couples start the divorce process with the best of intentions, and the untwisting of two lives begins, and that is when the secrets come out like old dust bunnies. They cling to every part of a person with such an elasticity that it colors and controls their behaviors. They can no longer see the good in the person. They just think of the most recent and sickest of situations."

"So amicable isn't really something you see a lot?" I felt a cold sweat tickle my neck. I knew I'd been right about not saying I do.

Lucy laughed and shook her head. "Rarely."

I had my own reasons for staying single. I didn't feel like I needed a partner to make me happy. I was already happy. But my goal in life was never to hurt a person I cared about. It didn't always work, but I gave it a valiant effort. To make life easier for me, it was best if I stuck to what I did best.

Flirting with a dash of fun on the side.

Then I didn't have to worry about emotions, hurting people, or creating some mess that I had to use Lucy to legally get me out of.

"It sounds like your sister lucked out." It was Lucy's attempt at assuring me that my sister's fate would be different than her clients.

"I'm sure of it. In fact, I'd bet my business on it."

Lucy sucked in a breath with a cute, puckered lip. "Ooh, don't do that."

I laughed and shook my head. "Nah. They are meant for one another. They equal each other out." Our eyes rested on one another, and a pulse of electricity bounced between us. On some weird cosmic level, it almost felt as if I were talking about Lucy and me. "Hey, have you ever played Jingle Berry Balls at Christmas?"

Lucy blushed and nodded. "It's my guilty pleasure. I play the game all year."

Pure happiness flitted through me. "That's one of our apps. We got into mobile gaming a few years back."

"You're kidding."

I pretended to crack my knuckles and kicked my feet out in front of me. "So, while you're busy kicking butt in the courtroom." I winked at her. "I'm busy coming up with ways to squash balls on Christmas."

Lucy giggled, and the same sweet innocence escaped her lips. That was the real Lucy. I just knew it. Being a lawyer and seeing the dirty side of love wasn't her, but it seemed to be defining her.

"I kind of feel like I met a rockstar just now," she gushed. "That game is so addictive, and it's such a stress reliever. It's like mind-numbing goodness."

I laughed and scratched my chin. "Well, I am an expert when it comes to mind-numbing pleasure."

"I said goodness."

"I know."

She smiled wider and nodded. "You are full of surprises."

"So are you."

She looked intrigued. How so?"

"After my failed shenanigans, I didn't think we'd still be sitting here with dinner on the horizon."

"Too bad I didn't make any dares with my BFFs." She winked at me. "I think I might have found my Mr. Wrong."

I scowled. "Yeah?"

She grinned. "Everyone knows an addict never dates the dealer, and that game is my drug."

I laughed and shook my head. "And I'm the dealer. Great. I should have kept my mouth shut."

"I bet you've got great tips and shortcuts."

"I'm feeling used," I teased.

"I just don't know how you're single." She shook her head. "I know why I am. I despise ceremony."

"Let's start with the fact that I show up to dating events as a man named Perry."

She laughed. "Well, there's that."

I brought my gaze to hers. "You're not going to have an easy go of finding love, are you?"

Lucy drew a deep breath and let it out slowly. "Probably for the best. I'm married to my work." She glanced at the door. "And speaking of, I do need to stop by the office before our date. I should probably head out now."

That's right, the date. The dinner date. The date I wasn't sure I could handle.

I smiled, watching her straighten her shoulders and glance around the coffeeshop. "Should I pick you up or meet you there?"

She stood with eyes pointedly on me. "With you, I should probably have my own way home. Text me the restaurant details."

"Really?" I grinned, feeling the charge roll off our bodies. "Why's that?"

"You're just that irresistible," she joked and gave a

quick wave as she walked out of the coffee shop, and I contemplated whether I was man enough to handle Lucy, the litigator.

Chapter Eight

To Shade or Not to Shade

Lucy

I stared at the photos in front of me and wondered if I'd doomed myself to stay single for all eternity. As I analyzed the woman in the photograph wearing dark shades, a scarf tied around her head, and a coat down to her ankles, I wondered what she got out of sleeping with a married man. Yet, with every question I posed, I had an answer.

Did she feel powerful by luring a man away?

If so, her sense of confidence was definitely in the gutter because it was never a compliment to be the other woman. No matter what the given excuse turned out to be, the man was an opportunist, and the same could be said of the woman.

Did the mistress think she was more desirable than

who he was with? In all my years practicing, I'd seldom met the *other woman* and thought she was a keeper.

Did the mistress truly believe she had more to offer? Nine times out of ten, she had less to offer and left the wife scratching her head.

I let out a sigh and zoomed in to see the husband of my client sitting in the car, waiting for his mistress. My teeth ground together, and I had to remind myself to relax with a quick massage of my jaw. What was wrong with these men? How could they do this? Granted, I'd also represented men in the same position. So, basically, why did these people cheat?

My mind drifted back to this particular client. She came into my office with dried tears shadowing her cheeks. She was lost, confused, and completely at his mercy. It was my job to fix that. By the time she came in the following week, the credit cards that had been frozen were restored, and she would receive twelve-thousand a month for the foreseeable future.

My heart pumped quicker at the thought of getting revenge on her husband. I would do for this woman what I planned on doing for my best friend. I would make these cheating scumbags pay. It was just a shame I couldn't go after the women they cheated with. Why in the world a mistress thought it was okay to be waiting in the wings was beyond me.

I clicked the file closed and logged off my computer. *Great!*

And now I signed myself up for a date with Mr. Flirt.

And I was in absolutely no mood to mingle. Seeing these photos only irritated the crap out of me.

Sure, Shep was sexier than sin and had eyes that melted me on the spot, but he was a male. A male who flirted so well, I was surprised he didn't offer classes on the subject. Not to mention, he pretended to be someone else the first time I met him.

What had I been thinking?

Right away, it was obvious he had no issues with bending the truth.

And in my profession, that was a red flag. It was like all those mistresses who waited for the husband to tell his wife, and every few months, there would be another excuse as to why he had to push the reveal date out yet again. It was so predictable.

But Shep wasn't professing his love for anyone. He merely wanted a good time, and maybe for once in my life, that was what I needed.

A smile touched my lips as I thought about Shep. He'd kept me on my toes during our conversation, and so far, he hadn't held back.

And neither had I.

For once.

Even better, he didn't seem the least bit threatened by my profession. In fact, it almost felt like he took it as a challenge.

I frowned, unsure of whether or not that was a good thing. I didn't have time to be someone's amusement.

Actually, I didn't have time for much of anything. Maybe being someone's entertainment was less time-consuming. It might be fun to have a fling and never look back.

Regardless, I had a date and needed to head out before I got even more annoyed at the opposite sex. I'd swung by my townhouse and picked up a royal blue silk dress with spaghetti straps and a pair of silver heels. I'd become an expert at changing in my office since my job often led to spur-of-the-moment dinner plans with clients.

Over the years, I'd noticed a pattern. Fresh off the breakup, a lot of women didn't want to go back to their empty house at night and would welcome any excuse to avoid it, even if that meant meeting with an attorney.

Granted, I'd represented both men and women over the years, but I was known for representing the good guy in the relationship. Sure, every side had its own version of the truth, but when there was infidelity or some other matter that spoiled any chances of reconciliation, it was easier to side with the victim.

The silk ran over my body as the dress fell into place. I slipped my shoes on and let out a deep breath.

Life wasn't all about doom and gloom. Maybe Shep's sister and friends had it right.

Maybe none of us truly knew who we should be dating, and we should rid ourselves of expectations.

Sounded easy enough.

Lower the bar.

Better yet—have no bar.

Just go with the flow and see who winds up in your bed.

I shivered at the last thought.

That was the one thing about me.

I had boundaries and very high expectations to go along with a very empty bed.

I snatched my purse and made my way down the elevator to the parking garage, where I unlocked my car and hopped in, all the while trying not to talk myself out of meeting Shep.

Just because he pulled pranks for fun didn't mean I

did. I was responsible and kind. Ish.

As I pulled out of the garage, I turned onto the street leading to the restaurant he chose.

The thought of Shep's amazing blue eyes made me smile, and the moment that happened, I had to brake hard to avoid an escaped ball bouncing from a park. Pulse-pounding, I waved at the mother and son, fetching the ball before moving on.

The moment I pulled into the parking lot, I let out a deep breath. I'd made it unscathed and could let him know this was going to be a one-and-done date.

But the moment I saw Shep stepping out of his Porsche, my heart fluttered, and my cheeks flushed.

He'd changed into a dark navy suit, and the way the pants fit around his waist and thighs left nothing to my imagination.

He gave a quick wave and smile as he walked over to the parking stall I pulled into.

My doors unlocked, and he opened the driver's side and helped me out.

"What a gentleman," I said.

He laughed and shook his head, still holding onto my hand. "You sound surprised."

I grinned. "Maybe a little."

When we stepped onto the sidewalk, he stopped walking and took a step back. "You're absolutely stunning, Lucy. Breathtaking."

Heat ran through me again, and I had to take a slow, deep breath without looking at him to regain control.

I glanced toward the flickering patio lights from the restaurant and knew I was in trouble.

"You're not so bad yourself. The suit looks nice."

Shep nodded. "I'll take that. It's better than getting downgraded to coffee."

I laughed as we walked into the restaurant. "But look where it landed you tonight. Dinner out."

He wiggled his brows, and his blue eyes sparkled. "Big time."

I studied him as he walked over to the hostess and gave her his last name for the reservations.

But as we took a step forward, she grinned and nodded.

"Right this way, Shep."

Chapter Nine

A Little Nookie

Shep

Lucy scowled as the hostess handed her the menu.

"Thank you," she muttered, and I tried not to laugh.

The woman was freaking gorgeous even when she was mad.

Mad about what, I hadn't the foggiest.

I looked out the window to see the sunset bouncing off Lake Union in various shades of pink and purple.

"Amazing night," I said softly, glancing at her staring at the menu.

"Sure is." She didn't look up.

I leaned over the table and started to whisper. "Is there something I need to know? Did you see an ex or…"

Her gaze snapped to mine. "I don't have any exes."

My brows shot up in surprise. "Not one?"

She shook her head. "Not, really, no."

I stayed quiet for a second as her gaze stayed on mine.

"But it doesn't look like you have a lack thereof." She kept watching me watching her.

I shook my head. "I don't think I'm following."

"Really? You gave the hostess you first name for reservations, yet she knew your last name? How many hostesses have you slept with around town?"

Shep's brows furrowed. "Wow. Geez. Give the woman some credit."

My response took her by surprise. Her shoulders relaxed, and she cocked her head.

"What do you mean *give her some credit*?"

She looked intrigued.

"I just don't think she'd love hearing that being friendly and remembering someone's name automatically puts her in bed with the person she's being friendly with."

She shrugged. "I thought it said more about you."

I shook my head. "No, it's insulting to her."

Lucy sighed. "I'm sorry. You're absolutely right. I'm an adult, and I shouldn't let my profession tarnish perfectly normal interactions. You probably just come here a lot."

I smiled and shook my head. "No, not really."

Her smile dropped back to a frown, and I had to admit that I loved seeing her riled up.

And I shouldn't. I was more mature than that.

Sort of.

I tapped my finger on the white tablecloth and waited for her gaze to reach mine again.

When it finally did, I smiled and cocked my head.

"But she's my cousin, so…" I shrugged, grinning. "I don't think she'd appreciate it if I forgot who she was."

The look on Lucy's face was priceless. Pure perfection.

A mixture of mortification and relief.

I was happy to see the relief.

It meant there was a shot.

That this lawyer didn't despise all men completely.

I had a shot.

Lucy's lip curled into the most intoxicating smile, and she let out a happy sigh.

"You've done an amazing job of schooling me." She kept the menu open.

I laughed. "It was never my intention to school you, but I have noticed that there isn't much slack given to the male population."

The server came over to take our drink order. I asked

if Lucy would like to share a bottle of wine with me, and she agreed. The server wandered off, and I brought my attention back to Lucy.

She closed the menu and slid it to the side. "I might as well just get this out of the way with you now."

"Yeah?" I asked. "Lay it on me."

"I know that I'm going to be single for the rest of my life or at least until I hit retirement age."

I leaned closer and tipped my head slightly. "And how do you know this?"

"I don't trust men or women to be in a relationship. I've seen one too many times when one of the two gets their life ripped away from them because their partner couldn't be trusted. All for a little nookie."

"Nookie?" I prompted.

"Nookie," she repeated.

"Is that a legal term or…"

Lucy chuckled. "It has made its way into my defense a time or two," she confessed.

"You feel really passionate about your clients," I said softly. "They're lucky to have you, even if it is to the detriment of your love life."

She shrugged. "I don't mind."

"That's too bad." I actually felt bad for Lucy and

wondered if she truly meant it.

"Well, I've seen quite a few marriages hit the thirty-year mark. No infidelity. Plenty of happiness. Lots of sexy times or, in legal speak, nookie."

She burst into laughter. "Did you just say sexy times and nookie while wiggling your brows?"

I frowned. "No, I didn't wiggle my brows."

Lucy's laughter was incredibly soft and everything I'd love to listen to late at night while curling up on a couch to watch a scary movie.

Okay, buddy. Hold up. Getting ahead of ourselves.

The server brought over our wine and poured. I sniffed, sipped, and nodded as he did our pours.

Lucy was watching a floatplane land, and she looked at peace. She'd obviously wound down from me riling her up earlier.

I felt kind of bad about it.

We placed our orders, and I waited for the server to leave.

"If you're pretty certain there's no love in your future, what made you come to dinner tonight?"

Lucy looked straight at me as her cheeks turned rosy. She took a sip of wine and smiled without saying a word.

"I told you." She grinned. "I'm addicted to the game

you developed. I need secrets, workarounds, you know…deets."

I laughed and shook my head. "And here I thought you were going to tell me you felt like a fling."

Her eyes widened. "A fling?"

I nodded. "Yeah."

"Why a fling?" she whispered, glancing around the dining room.

"You've made it very clear how you feel about relationships, so I figured a fling was my only shot."

"Do I look like the kind of girl who has flings?" She eyed me with heat rising behind her gaze.

I shook my head. "No, but then again, I don't make stereotypes a habit."

She licked her lips and let out a slow breath. It took everything I had not to watch the blue satin fabric rise and fall over her dazzling breasts with every bit of air she let fall from her lips.

"I want to hear about your sister and her friends," she said, completely taking me by surprise.

"Yeah?" I grinned. "Even though you don't buy into the happily-ever-after stories?"

"Convince me." Lucy took another sip of wine.

"Well, I have the best sister in the world. Her name is

Winter." I smiled, thinking back about my sweet little sister who'd always managed to strike out in the dating world until she went with her heart. "And her Mr. Wrong will make you think."

Lucy shook her head. "What do you mean?"

"She had sworn off clean-cut and well-dressed men who had any ounce of stability."

Lucy smiled, but she didn't laugh. "Why would she do that?"

Not wanting to reveal so much of myself through family revelations was getting extra tricky with the queen of questions in front of me. Like not wanting to tell her my little brother was a legal trainer on the road all the time just to avoid my father.

I let out a deep breath and brought my gaze to hers. "She wanted to date the exact opposite of our dad."

Lucy winced. "Ouch."

I nodded. "Yeah. So, she spent all of her twenties devoting her couch to men who never quite held down a job or men who needed a place to crash in between God knows what."

"It happens."

The server brought out our meals. I was never so happy to see a steak in my life. The way Lucy eyeballed her halibut made me think I was off the hook.

Until the server left.

"But why was she against dating someone like your dad, who sounds like he had his life together?"

I laughed and shook my head. "Well, he did to a point until he hit his fifties and had a mid-life crisis of some sort."

She thoughtfully dropped her gaze to her dinner and took a bite. After a minute or so of silence, I was happy to move onto a different topic.

Lucy's gaze met mine. "What kind of mid-life crisis?"

Damn.

I sucked on my bottom lip for a second as I debated how much to reveal.

"Fine." I took a bite of steak and enjoyed the flavors before swallowing. It had been fun dating Lucy for less than a day. "Our family always looked picture perfect, and Winter, Colton, and I knew we were privileged. You know, really lucky to have what we had growing up. No doubt."

"But?" Lucy prompted.

"Well, having boats and vacation homes made it easier for my dad to hide things. And he hid a lot." I shook my head, realizing how bad this made me look in light of the fact that I'd lied to her face at a matchmaking event. "He was cheating on our mom."

"I'm so sorry," she said softly.

"So, Winter being a teenager, decided that it was the wealth that warped our dad's brain and decided to only date men who were a bit rough around the edges. She wouldn't touch any guy who represented stability. My younger brother was a trainer for law firms, traveling from one to the next, never staying in the same state two weeks in a row. He's made a great career for himself. So good things can come out of rotten situations."

Lucy's brow rose. "And then? How'd it go for your sister?"

"She wound up falling for an amazing guy. He's a single dad who is super clean-cut and is a professor at the university."

"No, way." Lucy smiled. "That's awesome."

"It is." I nodded, watching her take another bite of halibut.

"It sounds like Winter has found her forever."

I patted my mouth with the cloth napkin and smiled. "So you think forever can exist?"

Lucy smiled. "I don't know, but my heart wants to believe even though my mind is smarter than that."

Chapter Ten

Just for the Sport of it

Lucy

Lord, help me. Shep's piercing blue eyes saw right through me.

He could see that I was genuinely happy for his sister, but deep down inside my cold, dead heart, I didn't believe it would last forever.

I glanced at my empty dessert plate and sighed.

Was I doomed to be anti-love for my entire life?

Wait. Was I anti-love?

No, I didn't think I was anti-love. Just maybe...

Hmm.

"I didn't mean to drop a bombshell on you," Shep said softly.

My eyes flew to his when I realized I hadn't heard a

thing he'd said for the last few minutes. I was lost in my own thoughts while eating a raspberry torte and staring at the lake.

I felt my cheeks flush and twisted my lips into a pout. "Don't hate me."

Shep cocked his head. "Why would I hate you?"

"Because I didn't hear what you just said."

Laughing, he took a sip of wine. "That's probably a good thing."

"Well, now I have to know what you said."

"Why's that?" His brows perked up, but his eyes stayed locked on mine.

The heat pummeling through me was intense. Just the way he looked at me made my decision-making skills go sideways.

"Because you regret what you said."

Shep chuckled. "I don't regret what I said. I seldom regret anything."

Surprise washed over me. "Oh, yeah? Spoken like a true flirt."

"A flirt?" His smile only widened as his eyes fell to my lips, lingering on my mouth for a beat too long.

I knew that smoldering look would melt panties across Seattle, and I refused to be a part of that whole scene.

"Your name really is Shep, right?" I teased. "It's not

Perry like when we first met, or Charles or something?"

He touched his chest. "Ooph. I deserve it. I do. My full name is Sheppard Sport Jenson."

I snickered. "Sport?"

"My dad was into the glory days of reliving his high school football career."

I shook my head. "I'm sorry."

He shrugged and laughed. "Could be worse."

"That's true. When you think things can't get worse, they always can. Your middle name could've been Perry."

Shep laughed. "Good one."

I smiled. "I thought so. But I do actually like the name Perry."

"So do I. It's why I picked it."

I watched Shep. "Now, tell me what it was you said earlier that you didn't regret since you rarely have regrets."

He laughed and shook his head, but he never took his eyes off me. "You're relentless."

"I am."

"I joked that maybe since we're both realists when it comes to love, maybe we ought to just have a little fun with it."

I nearly choked on the water I had just swallowed. "What do you mean?"

His gaze told me all I needed to know. "A fling or two?"

I straightened in my chair even though my body was trembling from the thought. I didn't do one-night stands.

Shep smiled and shook his head. "You could call me Perry."

There was something so endearing about this guy, and it was driving me nuts. Never in a million years would I go out on a second date with someone who pretended to be someone they weren't. Yet, here I was. There was something really boyish and innocent about Shep, even though I could see in his eyes that he was anything but innocent.

"Is your younger brother this flirty?" I asked.

Pride filled Shep's gaze. "No, he's far more mature. A great man."

I swallowed down my nerves and shrugged. His eyes dropped to the fabric of my dress before he pulled his gaze back to mine.

"I'll have to think about your offer, Perry."

Shep smiled, looking surprised. "Fair enough."

"Why do you look so shocked?" I asked.

"I thought you'd either throw a drink in my face or flee the scene." He glanced at another seaplane landing on the water.

"Yet, you took the risk."

He laughed, and I loved the sound.

I shouldn't have, but I did.

"I figured, what did I have to lose?" The look in his eyes made me want to kick every sensible thought to the curb and dive in.

"True." I nodded. "So, you're a risk taker."

"Indeed. It's how I built my business. I had a great job as a software salesman, but I went all in when I came up with game development."

I'd be lying to myself if I didn't admit that I thought that was a huge turn-on.

The server dropped the bill off, and Shep handed him his card before I even had a chance to react.

"My treat." He kept watching me.

"Thank you." I couldn't believe I was about to say the words begging to be spoken. "You're my Mr. Wrong."

"And here I thought you were my Miss Right."

The server returned with the slip to be signed. Shep squiggled quickly and returned to studying me.

A flush tumbled through my entire body, from my toes to my nose. Every part of me felt like it was on fire. I drew in a slow breath.

"Could you prove me wrong?" I asked.

Shep smiled slightly. "You want me to prove to you that I'm your Mr. Right?"

I nodded like a puppy dog waiting for a treat.

"I'm not sure I am." He kept watching me.

I smiled. "You said your sister and her best friends dated their Mr. Wrongs, and they were their Mr. Rights when all was said and done."

He smirked. "I did say that, and it's true."

"Well, I can assure you that you are my Mr. Wrong on every level."

"Is that so?"

I nodded. "You're cocky. You're a little scruffy with that blond hair on top of your head that's unruly. You aren't fond of the truth. You derive pleasure from one-night stands."

"Where'd you come up with that?"

I smiled and continued. "You're a committed bachelor for life, and you enjoy playing games."

Shock registered over Shep's face. "Same could be said of you."

I scowled and shook my head. "Absolutely not. I don't play games. I'm not cocky, unruly, or scruffy. I live for the truth, and I certainly don't derive pleasure from one-night stands."

Shep's eyes twinkled with some sort of mischief that

worried me. He laughed and shook his head, dropping his gaze to the table. "Life is one big game to you, Lucy. You get off on winning cases, making sure all your pieces to a puzzle fit better than your opponent's. You may not be scruffy, but you have the cutest dimples I've ever seen in my life. And your idea of the truth is only a version to boost your agenda. And lastly, you don't do relationships, so you obviously understand sleeping with someone without getting attached." He smiled. "We have more in common than you think."

I gasped a little and cleared my throat. "You're wrong. I don't do relationships, and I don't sleep with people either."

"Ever?" Shep leaned a little closer, and it felt like all the air was being sucked out of the room.

I shook my head and fidgeted with my napkin.

"Why's that?"

Heat crawled up my chest and neck, finally landing on my cheeks. I didn't even blush in a courtroom when I was seething with anger. But Shep pulled the reaction out of me. "I don't want to get attached."

Shep sat back in his chair and brought his index finger to his full lips as he thought about what I said.

"Even with all you've seen, you think you could still fall for someone?" he asked. "It didn't sound like you thought it was possible."

"The truth is that I'm a sensitive Sally. I feel my clients' pain with all my heart. I shed tears with them when no one is looking." I shivered. "And I'll be damned if I ever let myself go down that path. I may act like I'm heartless, but I do have a pulse."

Shep smiled. "So what you're telling me is that I have a shot?"

Chapter Eleven

A Bun in the Oven

Shep

Lucy was the most beautiful woman I'd ever met.

The smartest.

And the most confusing in history.

I smiled to myself as I glanced at my sister, Winter, who was happily hugging her husband in between eyeing me. We were sitting in their kitchen while they finished making breakfast. They'd invited me over for a late brunch, but I was pretty certain there were strings attached that came in the form of babysitting or dog sitting ... basically, some sort of responsibility that they wanted to throw my way.

Winter spun out of her husband's arms, caught my gaze, and narrowed hers. "Why do you look so suspicious?"

I winced. "Suspicious?"

Her hands whipped to her hips. "You heard me."

"I was trying to tally my chances on whether I could eat breakfast and bug out before you asked me to babysit or watch your dog."

She waggled her finger. "I know you better than that. What are you really thinking?"

"Seriously. That was it." I laughed and walked over to her husband, Brad, as he pulled a jug of orange juice out of the fridge. "Has she been getting more paranoid than usual?"

Brad laughed and poured the juice into several glasses. "I plead the fifth."

Winter barreled over and flung her arms around me. "You're just the best brother ever."

I chuckled, hugging her back. "Okay. Now I know you want something out of me."

She traded a mischievous glance with my brother-in-law as she let go of me. "Fine, if you won't tell me why you've been so quiet since you got here, I'll just make up reasons and start the rumors flying."

I helped Brad carry a platter of bacon and sausage to the table when their son came barreling toward us with their two dogs, Berry and Larry, right behind him.

"Hey, Uncle Shep," Hunter shouted.

"Hunter, my main little dude," I said, picking him up.

He'd just turned five and was full of energy, but nothing compared to their dogs.

"Did Mommy tell you?" he asked.

I put him back on the floor and grinned. I could always count on Hunter to reveal family secrets.

Cocking my head, I glanced at my sister, who rolled her eyes.

"No, they didn't tell me a thing. All I know is that I'm being fed like a king."

Hunter scowled and grabbed a piece of bacon. "A king? I eat like this every Saturday. Does that mean I'm a king?"

I chuckled. "I think it does."

Hunter wandered off toward the family room while I was left without answers.

"Wait a sec, Hunter. Didn't you want to tell me what Mommy was going to tell me?"

He crawled onto the couch and watched us while he snacked on the bacon. "Nope. I'll wait."

I groaned as my sister beamed.

She winked at me. "Looks like our Hunter is growing up and understands his alliances much better."

"Nuts. I always looked forward to hearing the dirt from him." I grinned, glancing at the glasses of juice.

I took the juice to the dining table and glanced at the beautiful view of the lake.

"I'll tell you what's going on with us if you tell me what's going on there." She tapped on her temple and then gasped. "Wait a second. It's a girl. You've met someone, haven't you?" My sister's eyes widened.

I glanced at Hunter, Winter, and Brad and shook my head. "Nah."

Winter chuckled. "You suck at lying."

Brad nodded in agreement. "You do."

Hunter climbed off the couch and wandered over to the table and sat down as the frittata was delivered.

"Uncle Shep is in love. Uncle Shep is in love." My nephew grinned at me.

I cleared my throat and found my seat next to Hunter.

He hummed with the piece of bacon sticking out of his mouth.

"Are you sucking on that?" I grimaced, not wanting to see what it looked like.

Hunter pulled out the bacon to reveal a pink and floppy mess with holes.

Winter laughed. "You set yourself up for that one."

I chuckled. "I suppose I did."

As we all piled the food on our plates, I spotted

Winter giving Brad a funny look.

"Okay. We all know that you only invite me over for food when you need me." I smirked. "So, let me have it."

"That's not true," Winter said, chuckling. "You come over on the holidays too."

"And to watch soccer," Brad added.

Hunter giggled and grabbed a spoon for the frittata his mom put on his plate.

I leaned over. "Wouldn't a fork work better, buddy?"

He shook his head.

"Okay, then." I glanced at my sister.

"What's her name?" she tried again.

"I don't know what you're talking about." I took a sip of orange juice.

Winter grinned. "You have a twinkle in your eyes."

I knew there was no getting out of this, so I set my napkin on the table and let out a groan.

"Mommy and Daddy said you were a manlore." Hunter happily ate his food as Winter snorted orange juice out of her nose.

"They did, did they?" My brows rose, but I couldn't help but laugh.

"All in good fun," Brad explained.

"Lore, huh?" I smiled and nodded.

My sister chuckled. "Gotta love kids. No private convos ever. And you know, rhymes with . . ."

I rolled my eyes, hoping to leave the manwhore discussion behind. "Her name is Lucy."

Winter shot up from her seat like she'd completed the winning shot. "I knew it. You finally found *the one*."

Hunter looked amused by his mom's outburst, and I quickly shook my head.

"Is she part of your lore?" Hunter asked innocently.

I patted his head and glanced at his mom, who took her seat.

"I've only been on one date with her, and she's more screwed up than I am when it comes to love," I confessed.

Winter frowned and shook her head. "That's too bad. Why's that?"

"She's a divorce lawyer."

Brad flinched and shook his head. "Yikes."

My sister laughed. "Too bad you didn't start dating her when Mom needed a good one. You would have saved us a fortune."

Hunter cocked his head. "Why's that?"

"Long story," I told him. "But it's been one date, and I highly doubt it will go much of anywhere. She doesn't trust men."

"And then she meets Shep Jensen. Ooooph. A one-two punch," my sister muttered.

"What's that supposed to mean?" I asked playfully. "I am a complete gentleman."

Winter eyed her son. "Want to go eat breakfast and watch cartoons?"

Hunter lit up as his mom got him over to the couch and situated in front of the television. She wandered back and sat down.

"Great parenting," I teased.

"You just wait. Now, spill the beans."

"I am a good boyfriend. I never cheat. Never have."

"You've never had a girlfriend that lasted longer than two weekends in a row." Winter snickered. "Of course, you haven't cheated. You can't make your relationships last longer than a bi-weekly paycheck."

I shook my head, knowing my sister was right. But I was always upfront and honest with the women I went out with.

"Lucy knows I'm not a relationship type of guy," I explained. "And she doesn't believe in the happily-ever-after, so . . ." I took a breath.

Brad laughed and shook his head. "So, it sounds like a match made in heaven."

"I'm obviously not doing a great job of selling the situation."

Winter's brows rose. "There's a situation?"

I shrugged. "Wrong word. But we've been on a few dates."

My sister's eyes looked like they were going to pop out of her head. "There's been more than one date? You just said you'd have one date. Now, it's a few?"

I took a bite of the frittata. "Delicious."

"Don't change the subject."

"Fine. Maybe it's not technically three dates, but it kind of is."

"That's pretty black and white." My sister glanced at her husband.

Brad laughed. "It's Shep. Nothing is ever black and white."

"Fine. I went to a matchmaking event on a dare."

"You did? That's so sweet."

"Except that I pretended to be a guy named Perry."

My sister groaned. "That sounds more like the guy I know."

"But I confessed right on the spot."

My sister and Brad looked surprised.

"And that worked?" Winter asked.

I shook my head. "No, she about jumped over the table to strangle me."

"Okay. I'm lost." she eyed me.

"Well, then I was at the bar with my buddy, and in walks Lucy. I knew it was meant to be. She completely ignored me and hung out with her sister for a birthday party for about fifteen minutes before leaving."

"Okay." Winter put more bacon on her plate. "Where's this leading?"

"I asked her sister for Lucy's number, which she gave me." I drew a breath. "So, I called her for a date."

"And let me guess. You didn't tell her you were Perry."

I scowled and laughed, knowing how awful it sounded. "Of course not. Anyway, she downgraded me from dinner to coffee. So, that was date two."

Brad laughed. "You counted the matchmaking event as a date?"

"It counts. Anyway, I won her over with my charming ways at coffee, and we wound up going out to dinner."

"So, that's how you got to three dates?" My sister grinned. "That's kind of pushing it."

I beamed. "Well, we're headed out to dinner tomorrow too. We both know it's not going anywhere, but it should be fun while it lasts."

Winter snickered. "Well, that's the spirit."

"Now, tell me why you invited me over."

Winter looked at Brad and then put her hand on her belly. "I'm pregnant."

Chapter Twelve

Another Castaway

Lucy

I didn't know what I was doing, agreeing to another dinner with Shep.

Okay. It didn't hurt that he was God's gift to women, and I'd been under a lot of stress lately. And maybe every little cell in my body felt like it was doing a dizzying disco dance whenever I was around him.

So, he seemed like an ideal type of guy to relieve some tension with if I didn't chicken out first.

But I always chickened out.

That was who I was to my very core. I lived, breathed, and ate divorce every single day of my life. If I weren't busy making a grown man give up half his pension for his cheating ways, I was busy having divorce parties to make the women feel better.

Only it left me feeling worse.

A lot worse.

I'd always prided myself on sticking up for people who got kicked around in relationships. But because I saw every dirty detail and rotten trick played, all in the name of a glorified side piece, it was extremely difficult to trust.

My doorbell rang, which was the perfect reason to get me out of my thinking zone. No good ever came from the lust spiral of forbidden fruit.

I wandered to the door to see my perky sister holding her new Chanel bag and wearing a sloppy grin.

"You okay?" I asked as I hung on the door.

She touched her chest and fluttered her eyelids. "I'm in love."

My eyes widened. "With life? With your purse!"

She giggled and let her hand slide away from her chest.

"With a bona fide male who wants to spoil me, marry me, and have my children."

I eyed her. "In that order?"

Mae rolled her eyes and wandered into my townhouse. I'd chosen the place because it was in a quiet, gated community where angry men were less likely to find me after I crushed their wallets in the courtroom.

"Don't be such a Negative Nelly." She patted my shoulder like I was ninety-nine years old and needed help at the crosswalk. "Just because you're not cut out for love doesn't mean the rest of us have to be miserable like you."

I scowled and shut the door behind us. "I'm not miserable. I love my life."

"Yeah?" She wandered over to my cream bouclé couch and slid down with a big sigh.

I'd been down this road many times before with my sister, and I knew what to expect. There'd be a few weeks of utter fascination, followed by a tad bit of skepticism before full-on loathing of not only the man she was dating but the entire male species.

I smiled. "Okay, tell me all about him."

She let out a happy squeak that I couldn't project if my life depended on it. My vocal cords refused to reach that pitch.

"He's got brown hair and brown eyes." She grinned. "And a body to die for."

I waited a few seconds that nearly turned to a minute or two before I realized that my sister was done.

She'd already summed up her soul mate in the simplest of terms. At this rate of description, I'd be able to pick him out of a lineup . . . say, never.

"Okay. What about his personality?" I prodded, heading to the kitchen. "And do you want a drink?"

"I'll take a vodka with a lemon twist." She stretched toward the ceiling. "He's got a great personality."

"Sure, he does," I muttered under my breath as I reached for a glass.

"What about you? What all is going on with that guy from the bar?"

I made her drink and grabbed a soda for myself.

"We are going out tonight."

It looked like my sister's eyes were about to pop out of her head.

"Are you serious?" She shook her head in disbelief. "You hate people."

I frowned. "I do not."

My sister looked skeptical.

"I just don't like what people are capable of when it comes to relationships."

"Mainly men. Not people," Mae was all too happy to point out.

I shrugged. "Men are people."

She took a sip of her drink, and I glanced at the clock.

Shep was going to be here in less than an hour. He

wouldn't tell me what we were doing or where we were going.

Being that I always liked to have a plan, it wasn't doing wonders for my well-being.

I studied my sister as she happily curled her legs under her and looked to be settling in for the duration.

"You'd make cute kids," my sister offered as I nearly choked on my drink.

"Kids?" I shook my head. "I doubt I'll see him again after tonight."

She smacked her knee and frowned. "Come on, Lucy. Live a little. Let him bend you over and—"

"And what, Mae? Spank me like the naughty lawyer that I am?"

She laughed and shrugged before taking a drink. "I was just going to say have a little fun with doggie style, but hey, to each their own."

I groaned and shook my head. "I was kidding, Mae. I'm not into that."

She put her hand in the air. "I'm not one to judge. I once dated a guy who could only get into the mood if he sniffed my feet."

I set my soda down. "Seriously? And you still dated him?"

She chuckled. "What was in store for me after that

made it all worth it."

I squirmed in my chair, realizing I'd never had anything nearly that gratifying. If I were to think back on any of my encounters, I would have preferred a good book with a side of brie and cranberries.

"What?" She leaned forward.

"Nothing."

"Tell me."

"Fine. I've never been sent into orbit by anyone I've ever been with."

My sister looked at me like I'd grown a third eye in the middle of my forehead.

"No way."

I smiled, getting a kick out of my sister's reaction.

"That has to change, and this guy from the bar . . ." She waggled her brows. "He's just the man to do it for you."

"How do you know?"

"It's a gift."

I chuckled and watched my sister. She was always so happy. Granted, I always tried to engineer her life like that growing up, and once she hit adulthood, I loved spoiling her. But maybe she was so happy in life because she'd had good sex, and it propelled her into happiness.

I wouldn't know whether getting your world rocked

was a mood lifter.

Shep's mischievous grin danced its way into my thoughts, along with the funny thing he'd mentioned about his sister.

"You know, he told me his sister and her friends all found their Mr. Rights by dating their Mr. Wrongs. It all started on a dare and went out of control."

"Yeah?"

I nodded. "Maybe that's what I need to do. Just date Shep, knowing he's completely wrong for me."

My sister shook her head and set her glass down. She'd only taken a few sips.

"Lucy, I'm going to be honest. You're overthinking things. Just sleep with him, and don't look at it as anything more than fulfilling a physical need."

I nodded, knowing that wasn't how my mind worked. That was the problem. I couldn't have a true physical connection unless I had an emotional one first, and that had yet to truly happen. How could I groan and moan and slosh around with someone if I couldn't trust them? If I didn't know their deepest secrets and their dreams?

I groaned and put my head in my hands. "I'm a lost cause."

Mae laughed as I straightened. "Your bar guy likes to

be challenged. I can tell. He'll probably reward you for making it more difficult."

I scowled. "I'm not a dog looking for treats for good behavior."

She smiled and let out a happy sigh. "You're a tough nut to crack, and I'm your sister. Imagine what these poor men feel like talking to you."

I chuckled. "Well, they don't. Most of the time."

But Shep did, and he didn't take crap from me. He could spin it around and make me laugh, whatever it was.

My doorbell rang, and I nearly shot from my seat.

"He's early. I'm not ready. The guards were supposed to call when Shep drove up."

"You look beautiful." She stood and stretched. "And the gatehouse was pretty packed when I went through. They probably just forgot."

I smoothed my hands over my jeans as Mae wandered to the door.

"Let's get this over with," I muttered, wishing I believed my words.

But the truth of it was that I was bouncing with excitement just thinking about seeing Shep again.

And that went against everything I stood for.

My sister swung open the door, and Shep smiled.

"Hey, good to see you again. Mae, right?" He smiled as she nodded.

He looked over my sister's shoulder, and his expression immediately changed. He went from happy-go-lucky to smoldering.

Or was it in my head?

"Good luck, pretty boy. My sister already doubts she'll see you after tonight." She winked at him and shut the door behind her while I stood frozen.

Why did she say that?

Shep smiled as my cheeks flamed. His gaze fastened onto mine.

I pretended to dust off a stack of design books on the table.

"Is that so?" His brows arched.

"That you're a pretty boy?" I smiled. "I think we've established that."

His smile turned into a smirk. "That you've already written me off?"

Chapter Thirteen

Return Policy

Shep

Seeing Lucy get flustered was a rare event, and for some strange reason, it was kind of fun to witness.

Dare I say a turn-on?

Her cheeks reddened, her jaw tightened, and her eyes became laser-focused on me.

Being the lawyer that she clearly was, she tilted her chin toward me and licked her lips slowly.

A calculating move to distract me while buying herself time. I could only imagine the dance she did in the courtroom if she could take back control right here.

After all, her sister had spilled the beans.

Let the cat out of the bag.

But as I watched Lucy carefully, I knew one thing for

certain. The truth did not set her free. It only riled her up. So, while she might have told her sister that I was as good as history, she didn't seem settled by the revelation. Hopefully, the little jump drive I grabbed from the office will help me win her over.

"I haven't written you off." She kept her eyes locked on mine, and I almost believed her words.

But wasn't that what she did for a living? Convince folks that her truth was the only truth?

"Your sister seemed rather emphatic about our state of affairs," I said flatly without my usual playfulness.

Was it horrible that I loved watching her squirm?

Her toe tapped impatiently, and I realized she wasn't even aware she was doing it.

Lucy folded her arms over her chest. "My sister was mistaken. She's never been a good listener."

I reached into my pocket, never taking my eyes off Lucy's, and waved a little device in front of her.

I winked at her. "Maybe this will change your mind."

She focused her eyes on the tiny piece of plastic that held something she'd love.

"If that's the size of your condom, we've got a problem."

My jaw dropped open into a speechless void of

nothingness.

"Cat got your tongue?" she teased, winking at me. "I already know you're good to go in that department. So, what is it?"

I stared at this enigma of a woman and tried to grab onto some sort of sentence fragment. "How do you know I'm good in that department?" That was it? That's what fell out of my mouth? I was worried about her impression of my size?

I wanted to groan.

Run.

Hide.

And then I realized I'd been played. I thought I was making her flustered, but she had the final move.

This girl was a hell of a lot of fun.

She smirked. "You wear fitted jeans."

Without saying another word on that subject, I shook my head and continued from where we were meant to start.

"This is the beta expansion of that little game you said you played." I grinned. "Actually, I think you said you're addicted to it."

Her mouth dropped into a cute pucker.

Damn.

Everything about this woman spoke to me, called to me, and made me fantasize about stripping her clothes off and sliding her onto a desk while she shoved a stack of papers to the floor.

Because I was that good.

And then the fantasy would end, and I'd come back to earth knowing that nothing about being with Lucy was going to be easy. Plus, she was far too organized to slide anything off her desk.

Orgasm be damned, she'd probably stop the moment to neatly stack the pile elsewhere.

Lucy took a step forward, and I snapped my fingers away and slid the jump drive back into my pocket.

"You have to tell me the truth first," I said softly.

Her arms dropped to her sides as I playfully took in the surroundings of her townhouse.

Everything was crisp, white, and peppered with neutral colors like tan and light sage. I imagined her space gave her the calm she needed after battling it out in the courtroom or with a prospective boyfriend.

I brought my eyes back to hers, and she was smiling.

"You play dirty." Her mouth quirked up, and it was tough not to scoop her into my arms and kiss her.

But I knew I couldn't rush anything with her.

"That's my only requirement, and then you can have access to the next several levels that normal people won't get to see until a year from now." I smiled. "All this scrumptious goodness for a simple exchange of the truth."

Lucy stomped her foot, clenched her fists, and grunted. "Fine. The truth is that my sister thinks she knows my history."

"History?"

She sucked on her bottom lip for a split second, but it was long enough to make my entire body come alive with desire.

"Dating history." She shrugged. "Mae thinks that I can love 'em and leave 'em because I see the shadier side of trusting someone. But that's never been me. I can't . . ." She stopped for a second. "Basically, being a divorce lawyer comes with its fair share of complications. I'm not trying to dump you because we haven't even started being something. I don't have anything to run from with you yet."

"Ah, but when you do, I have something to look forward to."

She laughed and shook her head. "I don't know. Is that where you see this going?"

"You mean building something together that you want to run away from?" My brows rose, and I chuckled. "Now that is a relationship goal to strive for."

Lucy laughed and moved a couple of steps toward me.

Her sweet and citrusy smell drifted toward me, and the scent was invigorating.

"I am so freaking not the person you should be trying to date." She pushed her fingers into her temples while looking at me.

"And yet here I am." I pointed behind me. "Should I grab the groceries from my car?"

She frowned, and I prayed I wasn't too presumptuous. "Groceries?"

"I thought I'd cook dinner here for us."

A few seconds of silence lingered as a smile slowly spread across her expression.

"That is so thoughtful."

I smiled and nodded. "We could always put something in the prenup about me having to make dinner. I'm a great cook."

She burst into laughter as I turned around to go out to my car to grab everything I'd picked up on the way over.

"Do you need any help?" she called after me.

"Nah. You stay here and try to figure out what else to tell me to convince me."

"About what? Prenups?"

"No. That your sister's words weren't true."

She groaned as I jogged to the trunk of my car and

reached in for the groceries.

A neighbor lady out walking her dog slowed as I started toward Lucy's door.

"Oh, are you Lucy's boyfriend?"

I looked behind me to see the lady bending over and picking up something her dog had left in the shared grass. I waited until she straightened, holding the doggie bag.

"Just a friend," I corrected.

"Well, that's a shame. She's a lovely girl, but we are all worried she's going to work herself into an early grave. I've never once seen a man over before, friend or not."

I smiled. "Is that so?"

The woman laughed. "You look like someone who isn't just a friend with that smile."

My smile widened. "Have you tried convincing Lucy to date? I'm just taking every day as it comes, but I'd be in heaven if she were my girlfriend."

"Well, just keep showing up with food, and you've probably got a better shot than most."

"I'll keep that in mind." I spun around to see Lucy leaning against the frame of her front door. Her smile told me she'd heard everything.

I walked up the steps with the food as she waved me inside.

113

"That rolled off your tongue easily," she chided as she grabbed a bag from me.

"And so did what you allegedly told your sister. The truth usually does." I winked at her.

"Oh, I see. Now, you're using the word *allegedly?*" She reached for a bag of groceries, and I followed her into the kitchen.

"I'm finding out quickly that I'd better adapt my verbiage to include legal jargon to avoid possible delays or disruptions in communication."

She chuckled as she placed the bag on the counter, and I slid mine next to hers.

"Fine." Lucy crossed her arms over her chest. "I might have hinted to my sister that I can't fathom this thing going anywhere between us because I don't date. I suck at dating."

"No, you don't." I shook my head and noticed her shoulders relax slightly. "You're amazing at it, actually. Every time I leave you, I want to come right back. To me, that's a sign of some good dates."

Lucy's arms fell to her sides, and she leaned against the kitchen counter. "My focus in life is my career. Before that, it was my education, and prior to that period, it was helping my mom raise Mae."

I nodded slowly, waiting for the *it's not you, it's me* spiel where I leave with my tail between my legs.

"I've liked having those things to focus on that didn't require any effort toward something that could fail. I knew I'd do a good job with Mae. I knew law school would be no big deal for me. I understood that I'd be a great attorney. But I know in my heart that what I've learned about life because of my experience is that dating might not go so well."

I took in a deep breath.

"And then I met you." She laughed. "At a dating event where you were pulling a practical joke."

Lucy's eyes drilled into me.

"Yeah. Sorry about that," I mumbled.

"Yet, here we are. Against my better judgment and every red flag waving vehemently in front of me, you're about to cook me a fabulous dinner and make mad, passionate love to me the rest of the night."

"Come again?"

She laughed. "I hope so."

"I find it hard to believe you don't date much." My eyes focused on hers as her lips quirked into a playful grin. "Those lines just roll right off your lips."

Lucy pushed herself from the counter and started toward me. "So, how about it?"

"Dinner?"

She stood in front of me and laughed. "Yeah, dinner."

"I'll get right on it."

But I didn't move.

Lucy wrapped her arms around my waist and looked into my eyes.

"You say you are terrible at dating," I nearly whispered. The sound of my voice was gravelly with need.

Lucy nodded and looked up into my eyes. "Yeah."

"Then how about we spend our time undating?"

She chuckled and tightened her arms around my waist. "What does that even mean?"

"Whatever we want it to mean. We hang out without any expectations. Maybe we travel a little bit? We enjoy one another's company without worrying about failure."

Lucy kept her eyes on mine while silence sat between us.

"You've already said I'm not your type, and there are a ton of red flags, especially considering how we first met. Essentially, I'm your Mr. Wrong."

"I suppose."

"So, let's take a hint from my sister and her friends. Try me out, and maybe you'll be pleasantly surprised."

"What's the return policy?" she teased, her eyes

softening with each passing second.

"When and if you decide to return me, no hearts will be broken." I nodded, knowing I was lying through my teeth. If Lucy dumped me, I'd be broken.

She bit her bottom lip for a second before taking a deep breath and giving a quick nod.

"Deal."

I smiled and moved my thumb along her cheek. "Deal."

Chapter Fourteen

Dirty Talk

Lucy

Who was I? Where did these words come from? I wasn't just flirting. I was knocking it out of the park.

And what had I agreed to with Shep? There was no way hearts wouldn't get broken with this man. He was everything and more, writhing around in a blanket of red flags.

Besides his humor, his intelligence shook me to my core. I could bring up anything with him, and he punted it right back to me, full of facts and opinions.

Now, he was standing at my stove, cooking me an amazing dinner while I stood nearly shaking in my socks that I'd just committed myself to a night full of sex.

What was it I'd said?

Mad, passionate love was going to be made tonight?

Gaaah!

It was like I'd put my courtroom hat on and the snarky, sexy remarks just flowed. I always treated the courtroom like my stage, and somehow, I'd carried that over to Shep.

And the weird thing was that the person in the courtroom was more me than ever, and I was actually showing that side to, of all people, Shep.

The cocky, playful stud of a man who owned a gaming company and kept nipping at my heart with each encounter.

"Halibut should be done in a minute," Shep said, spinning around in one of my frilly aprons and holding a wooden spoon in the air from the risotto he had just stirred.

"Do your friends know how dynamite you look in ruffles?" I ran my fingers over the pink apron he was wearing.

"No, and if you tell them . . ." He grinned and bent over to open the oven and pull the halibut out.

"First, I'd have to meet one."

Shep turned off the oven, put the glass dish with the halibut on the stovetop, and turned off the pot of risotto while flipping the asparagus in the pan on the back burner.

"Saturday. My place. My sister is coming over with her family, and my buddy who just got married will be there too."

"I'll think about it." My stomach turned into a maze of knots, tightening with every second. Meet people? As in his people?

I cleared my throat. "You really know your way around a kitchen."

I opened a couple of beers and put them on the dining table while he plated our dinner.

If I tripped over the chair now, I could spend my night at the emergency room instead of putting myself in a hot mess of a situation, showing Shep just how inexperienced I was at the whole intimate relationship thing.

Okay, sex. I suck at sex.

And I was pretty certain he was the king of copulation.

"You okay over there?" He turned to me, holding two plates.

I chuckled. "Yeah. I was just wondering how bad of a self-injury I could produce to get a ride to the ER tonight."

His eyes widened. "You mean in bed?"

I shook my head, laughing. "No. To avoid sleeping with you."

Shep walked over with our dinner and put the plates down on the table. "You have an uncanny ability to confuse the shit out of me."

I grinned and sat down before sipping on my beer. "Thank you."

He took a seat and studied me for a brief second. I could feel my cheeks warming, and I hoped they didn't rosy up on me.

"Listen, I won't hold you to what you said earlier if that's what you're worried about," he said with a smile.

"I want to." I stopped myself. "But . . . I'm not very good at it."

"At what?" he asked, picking up his fork.

"Sex."

He smiled and shook his head. "It's okay if you don't want to do the dirty with me."

"No. It's true. I'm awful."

Shep took a deep breath. "I highly doubt that."

"No, it's true. I have no imagination for it."

"I can fix that." His blue eyes locked on mine, and my body heated up instantly with a pool of warmth between my thighs.

All from a smoldering look in my direction.

I chuckled. "I think you might be right."

Which scared the crap out of me.

Grabbing my fork, I stabbed a piece of fish and took

a bite. "This is delicious. Amazing."

"Glad you like it." He watched me closely. "Swift change of topic."

"Love it. And the risotto. Yum to the tenth degree." I ignored his comment.

Shep's smile only widened. "Imagine if I were to trail my fingers along your thighs while my mouth slowly opened, pressing my lips just above your belly button. Your body shudders slightly as my warm breath spreads across your bare skin."

I stared at him, feeling every cell in my body hopping around like jumping beans. My chest became heavy with desire, but the weight of what I wanted to do with him lifted every wall I'd magically put up in the last ten minutes.

My mouth parted as I slowly licked my lips to gain my bearings. The heavy pounding of my pulse shuffled through me.

"And then what?" I asked, unable to rip my gaze from him.

His eyes darkened, and he was silent for a few seconds.

"I'd push your legs apart, look into your eyes, and—"

"Wow." I caught myself breathing heavily.

"And all I have to do is look at you to have those kinds of thoughts tear through my mind, Lucy." His eyes remained stormy as he smiled. "So, if you don't think you're any good at sex, you're wrong. The men you were with just didn't understand a woman's body. You make sex good by showing up. Any man would be lucky to be with you."

The entirety of my being was swirling in a wicked rage of emotions. I wanted to push all logic aside, slide the plates off the table, and have him take me right here in the dining room.

It made no sense, except that Shep was good at flirting. At making women feel good about themselves. I thought back to his sister's and her best friends' dare about dating their Mr. Wrong. Shep was absolutely my Mr. Wrong. Even how we met was filled with big warning signs. But somehow, he made me feel like me.

Shep dabbed his mouth with a napkin and smiled at me.

"But I think we should wait on all that until you're ready," he said softly. "Enjoy dinner."

I laughed and shook my head. "Enjoy dinner? How am I supposed to think about halibut when you've flooded my mind with crazy thoughts?"

"Because I can cook as well as I . . ."

I waved my hand in surrender. "Okay, I get it. I don't think I can stand any more of your bedtime stories."

I was like a puddle of confusion sitting in front of Shep. Never in a million years had I, Miss Divorce Attorney, thought that a man could spin me in such knots.

"So, back to Saturday." He took a bite of halibut. "You ready to meet my sister and best friend Mike?"

"As what?"

A thoughtful expression flickered through his features. "As whatever you're most comfortable with."

I let out a deep breath and thought about how easy things were for Mae. If she liked a guy, she dated him, slept with him, and then let it play out.

My mind didn't do that.

Instead, I was busy eating an incredible dinner with an extremely interesting man who looked like he'd stepped out of the pages of *Seattle-Men-R-Us*, all the while trying to logically parse out the odds of our lasting five, seven, or eleven months or years before the relationship imploded. With questions bombarding me, like, would his friends no longer be my friends, and would my friends want to stay friends with him?

And kids? What about kids?

Who gets them, and for how long? Would we be good

at co-parenting?

Would the prenup hold up?

Those were not the thoughts of a normal human being about to hop into bed with someone.

I was doomed. My mind was a servant to the law. I couldn't shake the unromantic nuances of living life with the opposite sex.

"How about friends?" I asked. "That seems simple enough."

"Not your Mr. Wrong?" he teased, but I felt my cheeks blush.

It was as if he could read every single secret thought I had while sitting in front of him.

"I have to confess that you don't feel like my Mr. Wrong." I chuckled and took a bite of halibut. "Apart from that moment when you lied to me and said your name was Terry. No red flags there at all."

"Perry," he corrected, smiling.

"Right. Something to tell our grandkids," I teased.

"If only I could be that lucky." He sat back in his chair and watched me while I played with my food for a brief second.

"Do you really mean the words you say?" I asked, genuinely curious.

In a courtroom, I did a dance. It was my job to believe what I said so I could convince jurors or a judge of my convictions. But in the dating world? There was no dance.

"I do." He sat up and pushed his empty plate away. "You intrigue me, Lucy. You're this scintillating woman who goes to work every single day with the intention of helping people untangle themselves from nasty situations. And because of that, you won't let yourself open up to love."

"I wouldn't say I can't be open to love."

His brows arched in surprise while I groaned.

"Okay. You know me well in a very short period of time." I shrugged and laughed. "Now, how are you going to help me?"

Shep's head cocked slightly. "You want help?"

"I don't want to be loveless forever, and we've already established that lying to me from the moment we first met is going to be an issue for me, but I like spending time with you. Maybe you can be my teacher and send me out into the world when you're all done with me. Maybe you really are my Mr. Wrong, and if we go into it knowing that, I can at least learn what I need to before getting my heart shattered by some jerk out there."

Shep looked intrigued but didn't say a word. Instead, he stood and nodded as a smile slowly crept onto his face. He grabbed his empty plate and mine and walked to the sink to wash them before spinning around to face me.

"You really are full of surprises." His gaze flicked to mine.

"Is that good or bad?"

"I'll pick you up at three o'clock on Saturday, *friend*," he told me, and I realized he was no longer staying.

"Or student. You could call me your student," I offered.

"That would make for some interesting dinner conversation on Saturday." He laughed and slowly walked out the door while I sat glued to my chair, wondering how I kept getting in deeper and deeper with Shep.

It probably would have been easier just to sleep with the man.

Chapter Fifteen

Just Call Me Mr. Professor

Shep

I didn't know what the hell had happened. My plan the other night had been to cook dinner for Lucy, sweep her off her feet, and have the best night of my life with her.

Now, we were standing in my living room with my sister, her husband, their child, and a baby-on-the-way all fawning over Lucy while my best friend and his wife, Skylar, snickered in the corner. He'd recognized Lucy instantly from the woman who'd ignored me at the bar and won him five hundred bucks.

Meanwhile, I'd somehow been duped into helping to sexually train Lucy so I could send her off into the world for another man.

What the hell did my life turn into?

Were all divorce lawyers this complicated, or was it just Lucy?

Was she even capable of finding her Mr. Right since I was her Mr. Wrong?

And did she really want to be my student? Did she really expect me to teach her the Shep ways before she ditched me?

The thought got me all riled up.

"What do you think, Shep?" she asked, giggling.

I turned my attention back to Lucy and felt my knees nearly give out and the breath rush out of my lungs. She was gorgeous, but I couldn't let myself go down that path. Not with her latest offer. So, I took a sip of beer. "About what? Sorry."

Mike walked over and patted my shoulder. "Looks like your mind is elsewhere, buddy."

I grimaced. "You could say that."

"I told them what I do for a living and how you're my complete Mr. Wrong." Her smile grew, and she reached over to squeeze my hand. "Which is why we're destined to be friends."

My sister stomped her foot. "No. That sounds like a match made in heaven." Winter's brows wiggled up and down while her husband laughed.

"Oh, no." I shook my head. "There is no match here. Lucy has made that wildly clear."

"And why is that?" Lucy teased. "Would you like to inform them of our first meeting?"

I waved my hand in the air, noticing a playful smirk on Lucy's lips that drove me insane. I just wanted to kiss those lips. "A little prank gone wrong."

She tapped her foot playfully while my sister looked intrigued, as did Mike's wife.

Mike already knew the backstory, obviously.

"I wouldn't call it little." She tipped her chin and let out a laugh. "He met me at a matchmaking event. Only he said his name was Terry."

"Perry," I corrected, wishing I hadn't bothered.

Lucy's right brow went up. "Right. Perry, and he had the sudden urge to confess right there."

I let out a groan. "But it was too late. I'd screwed up my chances."

"Wow. That's low," Winter chided. "Even for you."

But my sister already knew a lot of this from the brunch at her house, so why she wanted to kick me while I was down told me she liked Lucy.

"Blame Mike. He's the one who placed the bet with me." I gave him a wicked grin. "Who's snickering now?"

Mike shook his head and chuckled. "We've really been trying to work on our gambling issue."

"Not hard enough," Skylar prompted, giving Lucy a sympathetic look.

Mike nodded. "Right. Because there was that second—"

I coughed, interrupting him and Mike laughed, not realizing I never told Lucy about the bet in the bar about whether she'd give me the time of day.

Lucy shrugged. "That event was a good reminder that I'm not programmed to date. Maybe just experiment with meaningless encounters."

Mike chuckled while my sister's husband almost choked on his drink.

"That sounds like Shep's motto," Skylar said, eyeing me.

"Ah, my brother will settle down one day." Winter let out a wistful sigh and touched her belly. "One day, there will be a woman who knocks the air right out of his lungs and makes his knees buckle, and before he knows it, he'll want lots of little Sheps running around."

"Is the world ready for lots of little Sheps?" Skylar joked, and Mike clanked his beer bottle with mine.

"So, I decided to make the best of this odd situation,"

Lucy continued, and my expression fell.

She wouldn't.

Would she?

"He's obviously a master at his craft." Her full lips formed a perfect pout. "And I've come to realize that I need some lessons."

"Don't say it," I muttered. "Don't say it."

Mike gave me some side-eye as Lucy's smile widened.

"Shep agreed to teach me how to—" She stopped herself when she saw the horror in my eyes. "To flirt."

I let out a deep breath when I realized that was all she was going to say.

Of course, it was all she would relay to them. She was a professional with a career that relied on integrity and truth and loyalty.

"Well, he's a master at that." Mike smiled and nodded. "No doubt about it."

"As much as I love getting roasted here by my student and ex-family and friends, the oven dinged."

"I didn't hear it." Lucy eyed me.

"Trust me. It dinged." I reached for her hand, and our fingers curled into one another's as I nearly pulled her to the kitchen.

"Seriously?" I studied her expression, which was completely void of any emotion.

"Seriously, what?" She played around with a towel hanging from the fridge. "These are the closest people in your life. Why would you hide our little experiment?"

"Maybe I don't like our experiment." My voice lowered. "Or that you seem to think you can just use me like that."

Lucy's eyes widened. "Excuse me? Use *you*?"

I nodded and tore my eyes from hers and opened the oven to pull out the two trays of hot wings. The heat and spice coated my eyes in misery as I placed them on the counter and looked up at Lucy.

"Now you're crying about it?" Her hand flew to her hip.

I used the potholder to wipe my eyes as I felt a hand on my back, rubbing me gently as the stray cayenne pepper from the potholder somehow embedded into my eye.

"Shit. This sucks." I dashed to the sink and tried splashing water into my eyes.

"You're not the first grown man I've made cry."

"I'm not crying over you. I'm bawling my eyes out because I got hot sauce in them."

"My gosh." Lucy grabbed some paper towels and

handed them to me with my face under the sink faucet. "I feel so bad."

"You should," I mumbled, trying to take the sting out of my eyeballs.

But I secretly loved that Lucy thought I'd cry over something she'd said.

"For the record, it would take a lot more than you just telling my sister and best friend that I'm training you to flirt, which by the way, I think you already do a great job at. Maybe if you'd mentioned the sex part, that might have stopped me in my tracks, but I still wouldn't cry over it. I'm not a pansy."

"Yeah?" she asked, taking the wet paper towels away. "Should we pour milk in your eyes? I've always heard that helps with the heat."

I chuckled as the water ran down my cheeks, and I stood up. "I'm glad you went to law school instead of medical school."

Mark cleared his throat across the kitchen. "I swear I never heard a word, and I'm just going to back out of the room now." I pried my eyelids open to see Lucy spin around and laugh.

"Whatever you think you heard, I'm sure it is far crazier in real life." She swatted my back and grinned. "Right, Shep?"

"I haven't the foggiest." I glanced at Mike and pointed at the food before he made his way out of the room. "Just take a tray of wings and put them on the dining room table."

When Mike left the kitchen with food in hand, I stared at Lucy. "You don't care if he thinks I'm teaching you all about doing the dirty-*dirty*?"

"I'm a grown woman." She rolled her eyes. "I'm allowed to have sexual relations with a master of coitus. And who the hell calls sex the dirty-*dirty*?"

I flinched. "Dear gawd, woman. Is that how you see me? You make it sound so clinical."

"Really? Is coitus too technical of a term? I thought it sounded kind of hot."

I studied Lucy, trying to figure out whether she was serious.

I had no idea.

"What? Am I wrong?" she whispered, bowing her head closer toward me. "Just hearing you talk about what you'd do to me at my dinner table made my mind go to places it's never been before."

Surprise thrummed through me. I had no idea Lucy was into my little bedtime story.

Maybe the Master of Coitus really did turn her on.

"Really?" I leaned in, waiting for Mike to hop back into the kitchen and scream, *Gotcha!*

"If I didn't have two stellar paralegals, I would have filed the wrong pleading with my best friend's case yesterday. I've been absolutely a mess since you came to my house and made me halibut." She shuddered. "I can only imagine what the chicken wings will do to me."

I laughed and shook my head. "And I made homemade potato chips and ranch dip, in case you're keeping score."

"Anything I can help with?" Winter asked, walking into the kitchen toward the fridge. "I feel like something bubbly. Do you have any sparkling water?"

"Yeah. Top shelf," I told her as Lucy kept her eyes on mine.

"I grabbed the men some beers," Winter called out, leaving the kitchen with her arms full of drinks.

Lucy tightened her gaze at me and leaned against the counter as my sister left the kitchen.

"I haven't agreed to your offer," I told her.

She looked surprised. "It wasn't an offer. It was a deal we made."

I smiled and shook my head. "I never agreed to it. I don't know if it's something I want to do."

"You most certainly did agree to it." She pursed her lips into a deep frown. "You can't go back on the deal. I'm counting on you. A verbal agreement counts in this state as much as a written one."

Heat flamed through her gaze, which only made me smile wider.

"I walked out of your house without giving you an answer."

"You told me you'd pick me up for today's dinner."

"Which is not agreeing to your offer," I muttered, feeling an ache in my chest.

There was nothing I wanted more than to show her the ropes she wanted to explore and taste her lips and feel her body under mine and on top of mine and next to mine. The thought made me hard, and the idea of losing her made my chest ache and my stomach burn.

The whole thing was horrible and completely uncharted territory.

It wasn't that I didn't want to be with her. I'd been thinking about her nonstop since she reached over the table to throttle my neck. It was that I couldn't bear the thought of any other man having her after me.

She looked pained and shrugged. "Fine. I'm not going to force you to sleep with me."

She was always so confident, but I caught a waver in her voice.

And before I knew what came over me, I closed the gap between us and slid my hands along the back of her head, her hair coiling around my fingers. With every flick of her eyelids and pouty expression staring up at me, the pressure building in me was more than I could handle. I needed this woman, and I certainly didn't want to hurt her in the process.

Her cheeks flushed when I dropped my eyes to her mouth.

"Damn it, Lucy. Fine. If it's the only way I can have you, I'll do it."

The need running between us was thrumming through the air, and without a wasted second, my mouth found hers, and a tender moan escaped her lips. I hardened instantly as she moved up against me and kissed me. I wanted her so badly, I physically hurt, and there wasn't a goddamn thing I could do about it with a house full of friends and family.

But I knew at the end of this game, one of us was going to get hurt, and it wouldn't be her.

Chapter Sixteen

Third Base

Lucy

My lips wouldn't stop tingling, and I couldn't tell whether it was from the hot wings or the kiss with Shep in the kitchen. No one saw it, and I prayed no one heard it.

Out of nowhere, I'd moaned.

Moaned from a kiss!

What was wrong with me around this man?

I felt my cheeks warm again as I thought about the heat of his kiss, the sweet taste of peppermint, and the woodsy and lemony smell that just made me want to fall into his arms.

All from a smart selection of body wash?

I was a mess.

Would I survive this?

Would my career survive this?

I glanced up and caught Shep watching me, which only made me blush more, and the weird thing was that I practiced law for a living and never, ever blushed. Nothing made these cheeks flame red except for Mr. Flirt sitting across from me.

"I think these are the best potato chips in the world, Sheppy," Winter said, completely oblivious as she munched on the fried goodness.

I nodded. "I second that."

Shep's gaze remained on me, and he smiled. "Is this dinner as good as the halibut I made the other night?"

"Might be even better," I confessed, feeling a swirl of happiness tickle my senses. To feel this light and airy around a guy confused me and enticed me all at the same time.

"You know, I think this could be a really good fit for Shep," Mike said, glancing at Shep. "He needs someone to keep him in line."

Shep frowned. "It's not like I'm a wild zoo animal that needs taming."

Winter chuckled. "Well . . ."

My belly tensed as I watched Shep's comfort level change. He glanced over at me and pressed his lips together.

"He's not that bad," I assured them. "He's funny and always up for a challenge."

"That's for sure."

"And he's smart," I added.

Winter nodded in agreement, happily eyeing her brother. "He is. Now, Colton might argue that he's smarter, but I think it's a tossup."

Shep laughed and shook his head. "No. There's no contest between Colton and me. He's the smarter one by a longshot. I've just been lucky."

Mike shook his head. "It's not luck, Shep. We joke with you a lot, but you're an amazing entrepreneur."

"Thanks, but I still say Colton is smarter."

"I love how much you care about your siblings," I said softly, thinking back to Mae. I'd do anything for her. In fact, I sometimes think I went to law school just to ensure I could provide for her whenever she needed me in life.

But I also knew I liked to kick butt in the courtroom, even if it came with plenty of work hazards for my own love life.

Shep's gaze caught mine, and he nodded. "We'll always be here for one another."

"Absolutely." Winter held up her glass of water. "Always."

I turned my attention to Winter. "Shep said that you and your husband resulted from some crazy pact or something?"

Winter groaned. "Oh, yes. The high school vows gone wrong."

Her husband scowled. "Hey."

"I mean, they eventually went right." She laughed. "It was kind of a crazy thing. My besties and I all scribbled a set of vows describing the men we'd never date. Mind you, this was coming from a teenager's perspective. We made a pact, which was if we were single by the age of thirty, we'd have to revisit our vows and date the exact type we swore off when we were teenagers."

"And it worked?" I asked in shock, glancing at her attractive husband.

"Who knew a professor could be someone's Mr. Wrong?" Her husband rolled his eyes playfully.

"Mine was a little more complicated than that, thanks to our father, but yeah. This guy right here is my Mr. Accident turned Mr. Right. My little Brad."

"That's so sweet."

"So, the moral of the story is to never count out love in not-so-obvious places." Winter grinned.

"Good advice." I snuck a look at Shep and realized he was watching me, which made my entire body warm with desire. It had been so long since I'd had someone look at me like that, and it was exciting.

And scary.

Winter let out a little burp, and her cheeks turned red. "I can't believe that happened. I'm so sorry."

Skylar laughed and shook her head. "It's only because you're pregnant. All sorts of sounds escape my sisters whenever they're carrying around human cargo."

I chuckle, thinking back to Danni and how whenever she bent over, she tooted. Ah, things to look forward to someday. I glanced at Shep and wondered if he'd ever thought about having kids.

Enough!

What was I doing?

I was falling right into the trap that all my clients fell into.

Love.

Lust.

Imaginary friends.

I shook myself out of it as Winter stood with her husband and rubbed her belly. "Dinner was amazing, but I think I need to go to bed."

"You okay?" Shep asked, standing from the table.

"Totally fine, but I tend to hit the sheets by eight now."

Shep laughed, looking completely surprised. Mike and Skylar stood, too, and followed their lead.

"Us too. We should head out."

"Oh, okay." Shep glanced at me, and the realization that we'd be alone hit me fast.

I said my goodbyes to everyone, and as Shep closed the door behind them, he chuckled.

"My friends aren't known for leaving quite so early."

"Was it something I said?"

He shook his head. "No. I think it was because I couldn't stop staring at you. You're stunning, Lucy."

I swallowed my surprise as he took a few steps toward me.

"Thank you," I managed to squeak out, grateful that none of my adversaries were around to see that I had a weakness and he was standing in front of me.

"Did you want me to take you back to your place or . . . ?"

Without realizing it, I shook my head and smiled at him.

A blaze of fire ran through his blue eyes, and I felt my entire body light up. He touched my cheek and ran his fingers down my jaw, leaving a trail of sparks in its wake.

Shep closed the space between us, and my breath

hitched the moment his eyes landed on my lips.

Nothing had happened yet, and I was already a hot mess.

His fingers grasped my chin firmly as he tipped my head up slightly. Nerves jingled through me at an unstoppable pace. I couldn't fall for him. I couldn't let myself take that next step, even though every cell in my body wanted to be consumed by him.

"I—"

Shep stopped me with his mouth, pressing it against mine in a passionate kiss. I parted my lips as his tongue slid past in a frenzied rush of desire. He tasted so good, and his body felt so firm as he pulled me into him.

My knees trembled as his hands slid along my back, and his touch made my knees weak with desire. We were two fully-clothed humans, and I suddenly felt completely vulnerable and at his mercy. I wanted so much more.

A little hum escaped my lips as our kisses ignited, and he lifted me up.

I felt like I was on cloud nine. No man had ever carried me, and Shep was still kissing me. It was like right out of a movie.

I wrapped my legs around his waist as he moved us swiftly down the hall in a blur of ecstasy. My lips tingled as we consumed each other, tasting, pecking, nipping. It was crazy and intense and nothing like I'd ever had the pleasure of experiencing.

Shep put me on the bed, reluctantly slowing our kisses as he helped me out of my clothes. With only my bra and underwear on, he tore his clothes off and threw them on the floor before climbing back on the bed, caging me in and bringing his lips to my neck.

A shudder of desire rippled through me as he teased me and let his hands roam along my body. I moved my hands along his abs and into his underwear. His body shook as I curled my hands around him, and he moved his fingers along my belly.

"Shep, I only want to go so far tonight," I whispered as his touch made me tremble and his fingertips left my body in need.

"You just tell me how far, Lucy," he whispered, kissing me deeper as my body relaxed against his and his hands explored parts of me I'd long since forgotten about, and I knew I'd never be the same.

Chapter Seventeen

Back to the Office

Shep

My head lolled on the pillow, and I smelled the familiar sweet scent from yesterday and quickly remembered that last night wasn't a dream. I blinked my eyes open to see Lucy cradled in the crook of my arm with her messy hair sprawled against my shoulder and the white pillowcase.

She was gorgeous.

And seeing her in one of my flannel shirts I'd tossed her last night made my chest pull in all kinds of directions it wasn't used to. We hadn't even fully slept together, but it was everything and more. It also told me I was right. The thought of letting her go when all this was over with would hurt more than I could bear.

Lucy let out a little groan and pushed into me as her

green eyes fluttered open. Once I came into focus, shock registered over her features, but she quickly nestled in tighter.

"How'd I do?" she asked, looking into my eyes.

"Good morning to you, too," I said, pushing away some strands of hair that fell into her eye.

She giggled, and it was like a veil had been pulled back. I didn't see the sometimes snarky, determined attorney in front of me. I saw the sweet and vulnerable woman who made my knees buckle. My heart ached with worry that she'd leave me worse off than when she'd found me.

"You don't need me to teach you anything, Lucy." I pulled her in closer.

She laughed and propped herself up on an elbow as she looked at me, tracing my cheek with the back of her index finger.

"Very nice of you to say, but you have to admit, I'm completely vanilla and as basic as they come."

I laughed and propped myself up on an elbow to match her stance. "First of all, there is nothing about you that is vanilla, and you're certainly not basic. If it makes you feel better, I had to pop some Ibuprofen before I fell asleep last night."

Lucy's brows rose. "Really?"

"Yup."

"And we didn't even have sex." Her body relaxed next to mine, and she let out a deep breath. "I have to go into the office."

"On a Sunday?"

She rolled over, and this time her bare breasts fell out of the gaping flannel I'd lent her and onto my chest. The softness of her skin made me instantly want her again.

"I eat, breathe, and sleep my job," she confessed.

"What if you don't go in?" I prompted.

"Well, I cut my day short yesterday to be here," she said wistfully, curling her hands into fists as she moved on top of me. "And I have so much to do this week."

"But I could maybe spare an hour more?" she said softly, dragging her lips against my neck as she ground her hips on top of me.

I sucked in a breath and closed my eyes, wrapping my arms around her waist as I kissed her.

Right when she straddled me and I didn't think my morning could get any better, her phone chimed, and she shot off me so fast to grab it, I thought I'd gotten a rug burn from the flannel.

"Oh, crap," she muttered, glancing at her phone.

I sat up in bed and pulled up the sheet to my waist. "Everything okay?"

"That dirtbag of an ex—" She stopped herself. "I mean my BFF's ex."

I couldn't help but smile as she'd apparently remembered our chat about his still being the father of her BFF's child.

"Sent her a letter to vacate the premises."

I frowned. "He can do that?"

She shook her head. "No, but he did it anyway. It's like you've already cheated on her, abandoned her and your baby, and now you just want to rub it in a bit more?"

Lucy fumed over the series of texts that ran over her screen. "He feels that he and his new girlfriend need the space more because it's closer to his office."

I shook my head. "What does that have anything to do with things?"

"Exactly. It doesn't. But now, I have to run interference with a judge and . . ." She let out an aggravated grunt. "This sucks. I mean, it's hard enough right after giving birth, and if I could get that man in an alley . . ."

I laughed and shook my head. "Is there anything I can do to help besides bring the shovel?"

She glanced at her pile of clothes on the floor and smiled. "I'm just sorry I have to leave."

"I totally understand."

And I did, but I also realized that Lucy's life was work, and work was Lucy's life.

She let out a sigh. "It's probably better to go into the office before you have your way with me again."

I choked a laugh and shook my head. "My way with you? You mean Mr. Coitus to the rescue?"

Lucy rolled her eyes and started to unbutton the flannel shirt. "The phrase was 'Master of Coitus'."

"Ah, right. I'll have to remember that."

She slid off my shirt, her full breasts lifting slightly as she put her hair back in a quick braid before she bent over and picked up her clothes.

"Do you promise me a raincheck?" she asked, pulling on her jeans.

"I would be the luckiest guy in Seattle."

"You know, I was thinking."

I laughed and shook my head. "I don't know why that worries me."

"Since this is more my experiment, I don't want you to feel like you have to be monogamous. I don't want you to miss out on *the one* if she just so happens to rotate into your orbit during our little sessions."

Her words crushed my soul into a million pieces. It all but confirmed that she would never be able to go down that road with me—I would never be *the one* for her.

"Okay. Good to know." I nodded. "But I'm not really looking."

She shrugged. "Okay. I'm just saying."

Lucy pulled her sweater over her head and looked completely oblivious to how her words hit me, but I wasn't going to let Lucy run this show.

She'd spent her entire education and career making decisions that steered her away from the possibility of finding someone. I wasn't going to go down without a fight, especially after last night.

"How long do you think you'll be today?" I asked.

Lucy scowled as her mind drifted to the workload waiting for her. "At least seven or eight hours."

I nodded and smiled. "So, not too bad then."

She scoffed. "Not too bad?"

"Sounds like you'll be done right about dinner time."

Lucy stared at me. "Yeah?"

"And you need to eat."

She smiled. "I do."

"And I need to eat."

"You do." She nodded in agreement.

"So, what if we eat together?"

Lucy thought hard about my offer, and at about the

sixty-second mark, I got nervous until she finally cracked a smile.

"Sounds good. I've been craving Italian and had already planned on stopping to get some takeout."

"Perfect. Then I'll meet you at your place at five o'clock with dinner, but it won't be Italian."

Lucy frowned and shook her head with a laugh. "Why's that? Are you allergic?"

I laughed and stood with the sheet draped over me. "You're just way too into making all the decisions, and I count too. Aside from this breathtaking physique, I have brains and ambitions too. I need to be heard, so if I feel like a burger, then we should have a burger."

She walked over and leaned against my bare chest as I clung to the sheet. "Do you just like seeing me get aggravated?" Lucy's eyes stayed on mine. "Because I felt like Italian."

"It's me or the spaghetti, Lucy," I said calmly. "Let me treat you to something that will blow your mind."

"Again?" she asked, tapping my chest.

"You're saying I blew your mind last night?" I wrapped my arms around her waist.

"That's an understatement," she said, smoothing her palms over my chest and looking into my eyes.

And for a brief second, I even caught that she truly wanted to stay in bed with me today.

Not go to the office.

But she was built of determination and discipline and everything that I'd managed to skip over since adulthood.

I wouldn't say I didn't put energy toward my company, but I also recognized fairly early on how my weaknesses were others' strengths, and I didn't want to get in the way of building my own company. I learned when to step away.

Lucy, however, was just perfection. She knew where to spend her time, and her knowledge was what made her successful, and I certainly didn't want to get in her way.

But maybe what she needed to learn had absolutely nothing to do with sex and everything to do with time.

"I'll take *you* over spaghetti anytime. But your timing only gives me seven hours, which means I'd have to leave the office in six hours to make sure I'm home in time."

I nodded and laughed. "I'll make it worth your while."

She rolled her eyes as a smile replaced her annoyance. "Fine. But only because you've given me early access to my favorite video game of all time."

I laughed and shook my head. "That's the only

reason?"

She winked at me. "Only reason."

"Tell me one thing." I let my arms fall from her waist as she reached over to grab her purse. "Do you plan on seeing other people? You know, you told me I could. Do you expect the same courtesy?"

Lucy cracked a smile but didn't say anything. Instead, she slid the ride share app up on her phone and winked at me, leaving me completely naked in my bedroom to wonder how I was going to handle falling in love with a woman I couldn't have.

When I heard the front door click, I sat on the edge of my bed with nothing more than a sheet draped over me.

And that's when I realized that she already knew the rules better than I did.

Staying here with me would make things complicated and real. She wasn't ready for real.

I probably wasn't, either. But there was this irritating feeling ramping up inside me whenever I thought about her being with someone else.

All because I met her at the wrong time, doing the wrong thing to the wrong person while pretending to be the wrong person.

I placed my head in my hands and let out a groan of

frustration that, for the first time in my life, I'd found my person. The one woman who would tell me like it was and put me in my place while turning me on with every glance in her direction.

Every part of Lucy's being made me want to unwrap all of her. I didn't believe that her being a divorce lawyer was the only reason she was against relationships. I wanted to know the real reason. I wanted to be the person to change her mind. I wanted to convince her that love wasn't a disease, but first, I had to convince myself.

Chapter Eighteen

The Spread of Shep

Lucy

Danni had specific instructions and a very important piece of paper to hold up if her ex tried to intimidate her or call the police on her for living in her own house. I also had a few connections at the police department and filled an officer in on what was going on and that there was a newborn at the house.

The last thought made my stomach knot.

How could another human being do that to their own flesh and blood and the mother who birthed the tiny and helpless little baby?

The pain from my palms made me gasp, and I quickly unclenched my fists, not even realizing I'd been digging my nails into my skin at the thought of everything happening to my best friend.

No one deserved this.

And this was one of the many things I was afraid of.

Being hurt and bullied and torn apart.

I wasn't like Danni. I wasn't sure I could put myself back together again.

Watching my mom struggle while I grew up and having to step in and raise Mae made me rethink a lot about what I wanted in life. The resounding answers always seemed to center around stability.

I wanted emotional stability and financial stability.

Judging by my chosen line of work, the easiest way to obtain those things was to remain single.

I sat back in my office chair and stared at the glass wall overlooking my two paralegals' workstations. It was Sunday, and they obviously didn't need to be here.

And did I?

The thought of spending the day with Shep ate at every thought I had. I'd never been good at relationships. They weren't a priority. They couldn't be one for so long that I forgot that some people actually liked having a second half.

But then I hopped right into a profession that demonstrated the ugly side of getting emotionally and financially entangled with another human being.

I shivered and hugged myself, running my hands up and down my upper arms to make the chill go away.

Yet, it was nice having someone to laugh with over the weekend and trade glances over the dinner table while sharing inside jokes that his friends and family weren't privy to, and just being held . . .

I let out a sigh and chuckled, shaking my head.

"Don't let Cupid fool ya," I muttered to myself, pushing away from my desk. "He's fun now, but he's also the man who showed up to a dating event impersonating someone else."

One of my coworkers, Karlie, popped her head into my office and smiled. "I thought I heard the elevator earlier."

"You know how it goes."

She smiled and let out a sigh. "Especially when you're a woman hoping to break through the barriers and nab partner at the firm."

I chuckled and nodded, knowing I'd been an associate for far too long with the money I brought into the firm. It was an unspoken truth that no matter how hard we worked, how many hours we billed, and how many cases we won, we still had to work ten times harder than many of our male counterparts to gain the same promotions and recognition. Sometimes, it felt like stepping back into a time warp with the good ol' boys club. When I was in law school, I'd roll my eyes at such notions, and then I stepped into the real world. There were days when I dreamed of leaving it all behind and opening up my own firm, but that came with many pitfalls too.

"Did I hear you say something about a dating event and an impersonation?" Karlie stepped into my office. "Please tell me I did so I don't feel so bad about my own dating life."

I chuckled and nodded. "I'm glad to help in that area. If you're ever feeling low about things, just knock on my door."

"So, you tried one of those dating events?"

I nodded slowly. "I did, and it was a disaster. I could have been disbarred had I gotten my hands on the guy."

Karlie chuckled. "Ah, good times. Always a good day in Seattle when you feel like strangling a potential suitor."

"Right?" I grinned. "And would you like to hear the best part? Or maybe it's the worst part."

She nodded eagerly. "Let me have it."

"I ran into him again thanks to my sister, and the next thing I know, I'm agreeing to coffee." I shook my head. "It's like I should already be setting aside a retainer for your services."

Karlie chuckled. "Don't be too hard on yourself. You could represent yourself in the divorce."

I laughed and stood, reaching for my purse. "Are we doomed? Did this profession doom us to a fate worse than divorce?"

"Have you already had coffee with the guy?" she asked.

"Yes, and I've even met his sister." I sounded absolutely defeated. "He's a great guy apart from all the red flags waving around in front of me."

She leaned against the door as I strapped my purse over my shoulder. "So what? He pretended to be someone else at a matchmaking event? I wish I had enough guts to do that."

I snickered. "I like your way of thinking."

"Calling it an early Sunday night?" she teased.

"I'm headed to my house for dinner with him."

"Oh, wow. This is very unusual for you."

"It is, and I'm sure this time next month, I'll be regretting everything, but we're keeping it casual."

She nodded and waved something in her hand.

"Well, you probably don't need to see this, then, since you might be taken."

"What?" I asked, walking toward her.

"Since you're addicted to that game on your phone, I just had to show you this, and he's as hot as sin." She unrolled a magazine and slid it in front of me. "Now, maybe you can

161

figure out how to hook up with this guy and get all the free game play you can have. And FYI, the article about him was actually pretty good." She chuckled as I stared down at the glossy magazine to see Shep's face blown up for the cover shot.

I looked up at Karlie and had this sudden urge to laugh, cry, and get sick all at once.

"You look like you just saw a ghost."

"Long story." I snatched the magazine from her hands. "Mind if I read it?"

"You can keep it."

"Thanks. Have a nice Sunday night. Try not to stay too long." I clutched the magazine as I headed toward the elevator, unable to hide my fascination with what was inside these pages.

What I'd learned so far about Shep was that he was kind, intelligent, funny, liked a challenge, and didn't like to stay a long time in any one relationship. I also knew he loved his family more than anything.

But we were in the beginning stages of all this, and I had so much more I wanted to know about him. Even though I'd merely tapped his shoulder to teach me a few things, I wanted to learn about the real Shep. Not the side his friends used to place a bet or joke about his relationship status. I wanted to know the whys of it all.

And I had a start right at my fingertips.

It almost felt like cheating to get this type of information. I could get some real insight into what made Shep tick. He was adamantly against cheating, from everything I could garner from his reaction to my poor friend's situation, but I didn't know the dirty details about his life.

Yet, I hopped into bed with him. Granted, we didn't fully sleep together, but just as I almost begged him, I saw a glint of something in his eyes that scared me.

The sweetness in his gaze as he looked at me hit me hard. It was like his soul could read mine, and that freaked me out.

Because I promised myself it wouldn't mean a thing with him.

Not a thing.

It couldn't with his track record. He'd just end up finding the next shiny and new object of his affection, which was why I told him it was okay to see other people. If he had done it in front of me, I could have come to grips easier than creating a fantasy that didn't exist.

The elevator chimed, and I walked inside, pushing the button to the lobby as I stood refusing to look inside the magazine.

While the carriage whisked me down, I guilted myself into refusing to look at the article about the man, the mystery, and the legend Shep appeared to be. I wanted to hear it from his lips before I read all about the guy I was about to sleep with.

As I crossed the lobby from the bank of elevators to the parking garage, I was a confused mess of emotions. And by the time I slid into my car, I'd decided to take one little peek inside. I'd read the first paragraph and then slam it shut.

After all, he did agree to the interview, and it's public information. It wasn't like he didn't know what was in the magazine.

Shoot. He might even think I'd already read it.

Exactly.

I buckled my seatbelt and turned on the overhead light before flipping to the page where the most eligible bachelor beckoned me.

Interviewer: You've earned your title well, Shep. You're a successful businessman who owns several homes, has a great bond with your sister, and has generously donated to several charities, including your best friend's animal shelter, yet you haven't found that special someone to share all this goodness with.

> *Shep: My title?*
>
> *Interviewer: Most Eligible Bachelor.*
>
> *Shep laughs uncomfortably.*
>
> *Shep: That's where the magazine and I differ. I don't really see myself as eligible.*
>
> *Interviewer: Really? Do we have our facts wrong? Are you in a relationship?*
>
> *Shep: No. I'm not in a relationship, but I'm not looking. I'm not eligible. I'm too . . . jaded."*
>
> *Interviewer: Jaded?*

My heart pounded wildly. What was I doing playing with fire?

> *Shep: Everything in life breaks. Cars break. Love breaks. Hearts break. I'm in the business of building and surviving. I don't have time to break.*
>
> *Interviewer: That's pessimistic.*
>
> *Shep: Realistic.*
>
> *Interviewer: So, you're basically breaking hearts across Seattle by declaring you're not looking for love.*
>
> *Shep laughs.*
>
> *Shep: I can promise you that love isn't looking for me, either.*

I gulped so much air it hurt. I slammed the article shut. For some crazy reason, it felt like I was invading his space, his mind.

Sliding the magazine to the passenger seat, I leaned my head back and groaned.

It was like Shep and I were the same people.

This was doomed.

Even my bright idea of keeping it casual so I could learn a few tricks was a twisted testament to the messed-up way we viewed love.

No matter how badly I wanted to pry those pages open to keep reading, I wanted to hear it from his lips, and that was what I intended to do tonight.

Maybe.

Chapter Nineteen

Who's the Boss?

Shep

Even though I was determined to prove my point and not get her the one type of food she craved, I stopped by her favorite Italian restaurant and ordered enough for an army.

It was a few minutes after five, and I stood at her door with four silver trays of food. I'd gotten spaghetti, manicotti, chicken parm, and lemon chicken Piccata.

The moment she swung the door open, I took a breath and couldn't wipe the smile from my lips.

She was fascinating. I could never get tired of seeing her standing in front of me.

I could never get tired of her.

There was just this sense of comfort in being with Lucy, and I didn't understand it at all.

"It smells like you hijacked a garlic plant." Her eyes

widened. "I thought you didn't want Italian. Didn't you need to show me who the boss was?"

I chuckled as I walked into her house. "I think we've established that."

"Oh, yeah?" She ushered me into her kitchen. "Who is it?"

I smiled, putting the trays of food down on her counter. "Me."

She winked at me and gently tapped my chest to placate me. "Whatever you say, big boy."

"How was your day?" I asked, grabbing some plates from the cupboard.

It wasn't until I started serving us both that I realized how familiar and reassuring things felt around her. Like we'd done this a million times before. I pushed the thoughts aside.

She'd made it clear that this wasn't a love story set for the ages.

This was just going to be a few fun bang sessions sprinkled with happy thoughts and no commitments.

"Superb. I made sure Danni had all the weaponry she needed if her ex tried to take any actionable steps toward his threats." She shook her head. "And I'm going to stop by tomorrow night to have dinner with her and her sweet angel. Did I tell you what my little goddaughter's middle name is?"

Seeing the joy in Lucy's gaze made my chest tighten. The emotion was so pure and wholesome.

"Shep?" I asked, smiling.

"Ha." She giggled and shook her head. "Try Lucy."

I nodded and took the tinfoil off the first tray. "That makes more sense for a goddaughter."

"It has a nice ring to it, don't you think?"

"I do. I love the name Lucy."

And I could imagine saying it for the rest of my life in complete bliss.

"I'm glad you were able to help."

She nodded, and a funny look came over her.

"What? Did I order the wrong things?"

Lucy laughed and shook her head, glancing at all four trays as I recited what was in each.

"No. This is pretty incredible. It'll be enough to feed me for a month."

I glanced at her, and she scowled. "Oh, who am I kidding? This would probably last me a day or two."

But I noticed the same look fall over her features. "Did anything else happen at work today? You seem kind of . . ." I let out a breath and scooped some of the manicotti onto my plate. "Reserved might be the word."

"Really? Do I?" She let out an exasperated grunt.

I nodded, walking over to the dining table.

She sat down across from me with a plate filled higher than mine and smiled. "You know what is so weird?"

"Many things, but enlighten me."

"In a courtroom, I can control my expressions, my thoughts, my words, my movements. Everything is managed according to the situation, but when I'm around you, it's like I lose control. My thoughts go all over the place. You manage to read my expressions with a quick look in my direction." She squished her lips together in a delicious pout, and I had to laugh.

"I'm guessing that isn't exactly a courtroom expression either?"

She let out a sigh and shook her head. "Not at all. But back to your earlier observation . . ."

Lucy stood from the table and wandered to the living room, where she bent over and grabbed a magazine.

My heart froze.

Damn it.

I'd completely forgotten about that article, not to mention the photoshoot. It was something Winter had convinced me to take part in. I never read it once it came out. But my staff was more than willing to plaster the images from the photoshoot all over my office as a prank, and I'd kept them up as a good reminder not to fall prey to my sister's incessant obsession with love. The photo with the towel hanging off my hips wasn't one I was particularly proud of.

Lucy sat down and slid my mugshot over to me. "You look really sexy on that cover, but I'm sure you know that."

I smirked and shook my head. "So, did you just read it for the article then, or did you peek at some of the photos?"

Her eyes widened. "There are more photos?"

I scowled. "You haven't looked at it?"

She pulled the magazine back. "No. I didn't. Well, I saw the first paragraph, and then I closed it."

Her green eyes locked on mine, and I saw a wave of caution roll through her. Maybe I should have read what they wrote about me.

Lucy cracked a smile. "Had I known there were more photos, I might have kept thumbing through."

I laughed and took a bite of spaghetti. "I never know what to expect from you."

"I could say the same," she said, taking a sip of water. "But I have to confess that the first few sentences of your interview pretty much gutted me."

I scratched my head and tried to think back to what I'd even said to the journalist. The interview had been like six or seven months ago.

"Not to sound like an ass here, but I don't actually remember what I said."

"You haven't read it?"

I shook my head.

"It must not have been that great if you didn't want to go past the first paragraph," I joked, but she looked horrified at the insinuation.

"Actually, I felt like I learned more from those four sentences than I had the whole time we've been together."

"Oh. Wow. Really?" I took another bite.

"Yeah, which made me feel like a peeping Tom reading it." She let out a deep breath and picked up her fork. "I decided not to read it until I know more about you from you."

I leaned back in the chair. "Interesting. You want to know more about me, even though we're keeping things casual?"

"Absolutely casual, but I still want to know the man behind the swagger." She took a bite of the chicken Piccata and let out a happy moan and wiggled in her chair. "Nobody does this better."

I nodded in agreement, but I was still stuck on her previous words. Was there maybe a crack in her façade? A hole in her plan to just use me as a test case? Could there be more?

"I mean, you're my first attempt at the love 'em and leave 'em type of fling, but I would like to know a little more about the man who's willing to teach me a thing or two in the artform."

"The artform, huh?"

Apparently, my hopes were meant to be instantly dashed. There was no hope of something more with this woman.

Lucy continued while I glanced at a photo of her sister, Lucy, and another woman who I guessed to be her mom.

"It is something of an art. It's not easy to be able to check emotions at the door and sleep with a person. It takes talent and practice. I need to master it if I'm going to be a somewhat decent human being."

I couldn't hide my surprise. "You think I check my emotions at the door?"

"Don't you?"

Not with you.

"Well, I . . ." I cleared my throat. "I am always upfront with a woman about my intentions. I don't ever want to lead someone astray."

"That message was loud and clear in the first bit of

the article."

"Really?"

Maybe I should read it.

"You said something about things always breaking."

"What kind of things?"

She was silent for a few seconds and bit her bottom lip. "Cars. Hearts. You made it clear that you didn't want to break hearts or have yours broken."

I nodded, steepling my hands. "True."

It felt like my insides were being squeezed and stretched like an accordion. I was sitting across from a woman who I had the distinct feeling I could fall in love with. Yet, I'd already shown her the side of me I'd worked so hard to preserve. The guy who never settled down and thought life was a joke, and if it wasn't, it could be made into one.

And now *I* felt like the joke.

I'd screwed myself hard with this turn of events.

She was quiet for a few minutes while she ate. I'd lost my appetite.

When she looked up at me, my heart pinched with the hand I'd been dealt.

Loneliness dug deep at the thought of losing her before I'd even had her.

"Why are you so afraid of things breaking?" she

asked, swirling a piece of pasta around her fork and spoon.

Shocked silence bit my tongue, and then out of nowhere, anger spun its evil web. I crinkled the napkin in between my fingers and gritted my teeth as I looked away at the photograph again.

"Is that your mom?" I asked, ignoring her question.

She followed my gaze to the picture and nodded. "Yup. That's her."

I brought my eyes back to Lucy. "She looks sad."

"She is. She always has been." Lucy drew a breath that made her chest rise and fall with great quickness.

"Are you close?"

"In a way." She kept her eyes steadied on mine, and a ripple of guilt ran through me.

How could I get angry at Lucy? She didn't do anything other than point out a grave I'd already dug for myself in the world of relationships.

"Tell me about them," I said softly.

Lucy shrugged. "My father ran out on us when we were young, and my mom had to do what she thought she had to do in order to take care of us. But she was miserable every step of the way."

I nodded, realizing how much more we probably had in common than either of us knew. "I remember you mentioning that our first night together."

"You do?" Her eyes widened in surprise. "When?"

"The night you wanted to choke me to death. You opened up a bit, and I felt like an even worse jerk."

She laughed, sitting back in her chair. "That's right. So, like I told you that night, I basically wound up raising my sister, Mae. My life was full of chaos and uncertainty growing up, and the moment I had a say in things, I tried to make life stable for Mae." A sardonic smile ran across Lucy's features. "I saw how my mom's world imploded from going after my dad for financial support. Between legal fees and emotional trauma, I knew I wanted to help people like her. I also knew the people who helped folks like my mom had stable lives, and we didn't."

She shrugged and glanced at the family photo.

"I vowed that I would never be dependent on someone else. I crave stability in all its forms." She flashed a wry smile. "And divorce attorneys don't run out of clients."

"Wow. That's a lot to unpack."

"Now you know why I have a heart built as thick and cold as an iceberg." Her eyes pointed on mine.

"But ice melts."

"It can, but if it's thick enough, it can survive in very hot temps and reshape when it hardens again to withstand the heat even more." She studied me closely to see my response like I was on a witness stand.

So, I gave none.

"I'm good with a chisel. When was the last time you saw your mom?"

"Last Christmas. She found someone and is living in Arizona. He's a good guy. I think. I hope. I have no idea, actually." Lucy laughed and glanced at the picture. "Anyway, how did I wind up telling you all about me when I asked *you* the question?"

I propped my elbows on the table and studied Lucy. She was just so damn attractive and so . . . broken. Yet, you'd never know. She never let anyone know.

But she let me in.

A little.

"My father cheated on my mother and basically decimated our family. My mom raised us knowing my father was an asshole, but she didn't want to screw up our idyllic idea of family. So, she let herself be emotionally tortured by a man who had another woman who he supported and took to our own lake house and spoiled her like she was our mom. Not to mention, he had others as well. My mom waited until Winter was out of high school to file for divorce, but we knew earlier. He'd come home smelling of another woman's perfume. He'd miss dinners with us so he could wine and dine the other women." My teeth ground together as I thought about my father. "At times, I can separate my father from being a husband. I can tell myself that he showed up to my baseball games and was there to play catch with me, but then I'd be lying to myself. I'd be blocking out the times I'd hear my mom crying in her bedroom with the door closed or the times he couldn't make it to my games or my sister's dance recitals because of the other women. As I got older, but I wouldn't say wiser, I saw a side of him I despised."

"I'm so sorry, Shep." She reached over and held my hand. "That's awful."

"It is, and I don't ever want to be in a situation where I hurt someone or someone else hurts me. That's why women know there can't be more. I'm incapable."

Until I met Lucy.

I nodded, letting go of her hand.

"Then it sounds like the arrangement we have is the best for the both of us," Lucy added.

My heart shattered as I nodded my head and stood to leave because I couldn't do this with her.

I couldn't play games.

"Don't go," she said softly, "or I'll read the rest of the article."

And I realized there was something this woman could do better than anyone.

She could make me a fool for believing in something that was never meant to last.

Chapter Twenty

I'm Not Your Therapist

Lucy

"Great." Danni laughed, nestling her little bundle against her chest. "You've found someone else just as screwed up as you. How much are you charging me again?"

I chuckled and winked at her. "I'm your lawyer, not your therapist. And this is pro-bono."

I sat on Danni's couch across from her as she rocked her little one asleep, and my chest tightened. I'd always thought I'd be a good mom, and I had a great practice run with my sister, but I also doubted it was in the cards for me.

"I have some big news about *my* Blair Lucy," Danni said, eyeing me cautiously.

"What's that?" I asked, relieved the topic of Shep was getting dropped. "She's been voted most beautiful baby of the century?"

Danni's eyes turned dopey.

"No. Not yet. However, I know I asked if I could name her Lucy for her middle name, but I feel like she's more a Lucy Blair, not a Blair Lucy."

My jaw dropped. "What are you saying?"

"I want to name her Lucy."

"Can you do that?" My heart skipped a beat.

She tilted her head. "Do what?"

"Change her name?"

"I'm her mom. Of course, I can change her name. In fact, I already did it."

I muffled my squeal of joy to not wake little Lucy as Dani grinned at me.

I had my own little Lucy. I mean, she wasn't *my* Lucy, but she was kind of like my Lucy.

"I will babysit for you anytime you need it."

Dani smiled. "And all I had to do was name her after you?"

I touched my chest with my palms and closed my eyes, willing the tears away. "You're actually naming her after me? It's not just because you like the name?"

My eyes blinked open to see Dani smiling wider than I'd seen in a long time.

"See, you do have emotions other than anger." She chuckled and repositioned her baby. "I knew they were in there somewhere."

I laughed softly, throwing my head back. "I'm not that bad, am I?"

"Truth or sugar-coated?"

"Truth. Always truth."

"You've gotten a bit hard over the years, and I'm sure my recent situation hasn't exactly mellowed your heart."

"But I win cases," I reminded her. "And I'll win yours."

She shook her head and looked at little Lucy. "But is there really any winning in a case like this?"

Her words shook me to my core, and I found myself glaring at her wedding pictures still hanging on the wall.

Danni was right. There was absolutely never a win in the case of families breaking apart.

"I'm sorry." I let out a sigh. "I'm just so used to combat mode. I see the courtroom as a battlefield, and I block out everything else."

"And that's great for trials," Danni added, smiling. "It's why I know little Lucy and I will be okay."

I nodded in silence.

She was right.

What had happened to me?

Was I even capable of feeling other emotions besides annoyance, bitterness, anger, and betrayal? The worst part was that these things hadn't even happened to me, but I'd been bottling up all my clients' rage for so long that I lived, ate, and breathed it too.

Damn philanderers, cheats, conmen, and psychopaths.

They were seriously messing with my perception of the beautiful world I lived in.

The world where little Lucys made their moms forget what a crappy sperm donor did to them. Or how magical playing Jingle Berry Balls on my phone could be after a grueling day in court while I'm curled up on my couch with a glass of wine and a mammoth bowl of potato chips.

Danni raised her finger. "But I have noticed that in recent weeks, you've softened slightly."

I perked up and brought my gaze back to hers.

She smirked at me. "Any particular reason?"

"I have a confession."

"Lay it on me. Is it that guy?"

"You mean the one I shouldn't still be seeing but can't seem to stay away from?"

"Yeah. Him. You know, you've never told me his

name."

My heart started pounding erratically, and I clenched my fists as nausea rolled through me. Why did I get so weird when I had to face facts?

And the facts, in this case, were that I really liked a man I should never have let myself get to know.

He, for some crazy reason, made me feel a little less bitter and angry about the unfair hand so many people faced when it came to love.

I bit my bottom lip a little too hard and then sucked on it to make sure it wasn't bleeding and that I was still alive because I suddenly felt numb and confused and . . .

"Remember when that guy at that matchmaking event made up a name and went there on a bet pretending to be someone else?"

She frowned and patted little Lucy's back.

"Yeah. Why?"

"Well, my sister's birthday party was at a bar where he happened to be hanging out."

"The fates have aligned." Danni smiled. "That's really weird. Seattle's not exactly a small city."

"He lives across the street from the bar in one of those swanky condos."

"You've been to his place?"

I clenched my eyes shut and nodded. "I've met his sister and best friend too."

"What? How've you been keeping this all from me?"

I stared at Danni and grinned. "I didn't think anything would come of it, and you've got so much going on."

"Never too much for this kind of development." She eyed me suspiciously. "Are you falling for him?"

"No. It's crazier than that."

She rolled her eyes with a nervous giggle. "Of course it is."

"I asked him to help me learn the art of flirting and everything that comes with it."

She sharpened her gaze on me. "What do you mean, *everything that comes with it*?"

I shifted nervously on the couch, unsure how Danni would take it. She always pointed out the truth, and the truth didn't look good. He'd shown his true colors right off the bat.

"We, umm . . ."

Her eyes nearly tumbled out of her head. "You've slept together?"

I shook my head and glanced at her baby. "Should we be talking about this now?"

"I can assure you, little Lucy is dreaming of milk and lullabies right now. Spill it."

"Fine. No, we haven't slept together, but we've come close."

"Why are you smiling like you've just won the lottery?" Her right brow arched.

"Am I?" I dropped my smile, but it snuck back on. "I don't know, Danni. I know it sounds crazy, but I like the guy. Like a lot. And I know he's absolutely not a man who's going to settle down anytime soon."

"How do you know?"

I debated how much to reveal. "He's said as much, privately and publicly."

She scowled. "Publicly?"

"He was voted Most Eligible Bachelor in Seattle, and they did a whole spread on him, and he confessed to not looking for anyone."

She sat back on the couch with little Lucy still snug to her chest. "I'm dying over here. How could you keep this from me? Yeah. He didn't strike me as the settling-down type."

"Huh? How do you know?"

"I read the article. I saw the pics. My gawd, Lucy. If you can be taught by him, let him be your instructor all night long."

My cheeks flared red, and I giggled. "Seriously? The

photos are that good?"

She nodded. "They left little to the imagination. You're telling me you haven't seen them?"

I shook my head. "No. I have the magazine. Karlie just gave it to me the other day, but I didn't want to read it and come up with conclusions based on some interview."

"That's interesting."

"Why's that?"

She shrugged as she slowly walked Lucy over to a small bassinet and put her inside.

"If you're just trying to get some pointers from a cute guy, what do you care what's said about him or what he says in an interview?"

"It's my profession. I like to go to the source."

"Keep telling yourself that, Lucy."

I chuckled. "It's true."

She wandered to the kitchen and poured us some sparkling water. "Then why are your cheeks still as red as Cupid's butt?"

A few seconds of silence hovered in the air as she wandered over with a glass for me.

"Because he makes me feel incredible."

Danni smiled lovingly as I took my water from her and shoved my feet underneath me.

"It's okay to like how a man makes you feel. It's not a crime to let someone into your heart."

I took a sip and nodded. "It's not a crime, but it's dangerous."

"Only if you think it is."

"Did I tell you he made homemade potato chips that were worth dying for?"

"No. There are a lot of things you haven't mentioned. But I want you to know one thing more than anything. I would never take back a second of my relationship with Bill. I'd let him pour gasoline on my heart a million times if it meant I could be with my daughter." Danni shook her head and looked toward the bassinet, and I knew in that moment that there truly wasn't a single moment of Danni's life that she regretted. Even though her heart was being shredded into a million pieces, she knew she had the best gift ever from a very trying set of circumstances.

Yet, I wasn't sure I could see life like that. I'd trained myself to be on the lookout for doom and gloom.

The thing with Shep was that he had this superpower over me. He made me spill my guts. He made me sweat. He'd get me all tangled up inside, and that wasn't a position I was used to being in. Ultimately, he made me feel vulnerable, and I wasn't accustomed to that sensation.

In the courtroom, it was my job to be anything but vulnerable. I had to have a glacial heart and bones made of steel so that nothing slung my client's way or mine would make me quiver.

But everything about Shep made me quiver, and I liked it. His kind of vulnerability made me feel like jiggly Jell-O inside that needed to be scooped up and smooshed back together again.

"I told him he could see other people during this little experiment."

"Yeah? Was he happy about that?"

"Technically, he didn't seem to think he'd agreed to help me figure out the dating thing in the first place."

She looked surprised. "Really?"

"But I assured him that he had agreed to it." I thought about his reaction and how he'd almost seemed offended when I mentioned he could see other people. "And he didn't seem really interested in seeing anyone else."

She nodded without a word.

"I suppose that's because he's a sweet guy and didn't want to look like he'd won the Lotto."

A funny look crossed Danni's features. "Could be."

I nodded. "Yup."

"Or he might actually like you."

I laughed and let out a sigh. "I wouldn't be surprised if Shep liked me, but that's only because I'm the shiny new object in his periphery. He's not a relationship type of person."

Tension coiled in my belly at the thought.

Danni stared at me. "And neither are you."

"Exactly. A match made in heaven," I said flatly, but I didn't feel like that at all.

"I suggest reading the article," she added. "Now, are you going to order us that pizza or what?"

I smiled, thinking back to our college days of pizza and cheap wine. I had so much history with Danni. She knew my secrets and fears. She loved me unconditionally, just like I did for her. She was absolutely my best friend.

But what I was feeling toward Shep was my scary secret.

I liked the way he made me feel, and I didn't want to lose that.

Chapter Twenty-One

Meatloaf is Done

Shep

Let's be honest. My dating history was treacherous. I wasn't exactly the guy women wanted to bring home to their parents and best friends. More to the point, I didn't want to be the guy anyone would ever think of placing me in front of accusing stares as I got grilled by an angry mother and father because I oozed the opposite of monogamous. They did like to show me off when we went out or to their friends', but that was as deep as it went.

It had happened to me once. I was young, it was awful, and I'd vowed never to be in that position again.

And that had all led me to become a . . .

Gigolo trainer?

No.

Because thankfully, she hadn't offered money.

Sex trainer?

I shook my head, shoving my fingers through my short hair.

It had led me to a mess of a situation.

How was this even supposed to work?

Did Lucy expect me to come up with some sort of working schedule? Was I supposed to figure out a syllabus of sexual moves for this woman by the day of the week? Did she want flirting tips?

I walked over to my living room window that stretched floor to ceiling with crystal clear glass as I glared down at the bar across the street where I'd been ignored by Lucy and offered a hand by her sister.

I owed a lot to Mae, even if she didn't realize it.

Because the moment Lucy said yes to me, my world changed. My axis shifted just enough to make me wonder.

Wonder what?

That wasn't the point.

I never wondered before.

I never wondered what would happen after I slept with a woman.

I never wondered who I'd spend Christmas with.

I never wondered whether I could love someone for

the rest of my life.

Lucy changed that, which freaked the shit out of me.

And now I was left with nothing because I'd managed to screw up my chances with a woman who rocked my world and managed to throw me off my game by becoming the Game Master.

I let out a sigh, realizing I couldn't swipe the grin off my face when I thought about her. Lucy was supposed to be at my place any minute.

I'd made the least romantic kind of dinner I could think of and had it in the oven . . .

Meatloaf.

It had been all fun and games with Lucy, but if she seriously wanted me to teach her something when she clearly didn't need to be taught a thing, I needed to get to the bottom of things with her.

So, I doused the potatoes in onion and garlic butter, layered the French bread with even more ooey, gooey garlic cheese spread, and managed to make a fresh blue cheese and bacon salad.

Kisses wouldn't be on the menu tonight, so we could talk shop.

Get the details out of the way.

Set expectations.

A faint knock sounded at my door, and I spun on my heels as if a fire alarm had just sounded.

Just the thought of seeing Lucy made me feel like I had a shot.

By the time I reached the door, my heart hammered in my chest, and Lucy stood in the hallway, looking as beautiful as ever.

She smiled, and I nearly tripped over my two feet to kiss her adorable lips, but I gained control of myself and slid a soft kiss on her cheek instead. I had to stick to business.

"Something smells amazing." She walked inside and slid off her coat to reveal the sexiest suit known to man.

The light pink tweed skirt and jacket hugged all of her curves, and she'd swept her hair back.

I hung her coat in the closet and caught my breath. She smelled intoxicating.

"Meatloaf. The meatloaf smells amazing."

She chuckled. "You're kidding. I haven't had meatloaf since my grandma made it."

"Seriously?"

Lucy nodded and walked down the hallway toward the kitchen. "It smells more delicious than I remember."

I moved past her toward the oven and opened the oven door.

She strained her eyes and chuckled. "You even put the ketchup on top. Wait a second. Is that a heart?"

I closed the oven door.

"You're telling me that Mr. Flirt squirted the shape of a heart onto his meatloaf? Rather apropos, I suppose. The potatoes look incredible too."

"Tonight's theme is garlic, and since when have I been Mr. Flirt?"

"The moment I met you, and why garlic?"

I nodded, slapping a kitchen towel over my shoulder. "I realized after Sunday that I need to set some boundaries."

Surprise washed over her. "Mr. Flirt needs to set some boundaries?"

Why does she think I was born emotionless?

I nodded. "Yeah. I need questions answered. And garlic tonight would be a clear divider while we talk shop."

She twirled her finger in her dark hair. "How so?"

"I don't know if you're really serious about this whole deal."

She was quiet for a second or two as I poured her a glass of wine, and she took a sip.

"You mean showing me the ropes?"

I nodded. "I don't believe you need me to show you anything. Saturday night was incredible. It was the best night of my life, and we didn't even fully sleep together."

She raised her glass. "We came pretty close."

I laughed softly, remembering fondly. "Yeah, we did."

"Fine. I'll tell you this. I freeze. I choke under pressure. I clam up. I close my legs. I tense. Physically, my body becomes rigid, and I am scared spitless of the deed. I just need someone to show me how to relax and let things flow naturally."

"Lucy, I'm not sure if we're talking about the same person because you were completely relaxed and limber and full of—"

"Because I was with *you*," she cut me off. "I don't know what it is about you, but all I have to do is look in your direction, and I feel safe and comfortable. I need that before I go trying things with strangers."

"Maybe you shouldn't try those things with strangers," I suggested.

"Have you ever had a one-night stand?" she asked abruptly.

I nodded. "Yeah."

Her eyes flashed me a knowing smile as I took a sip of wine.

"Maybe I want that. I'd love to be sexually free like

you and just stop off at a bar after a long, hard day at the office and just pick a dude and make him a plaything."

I choked on the wine I'd just swallowed, and she ran over and smacked me on the back while I recovered, using my wrist to wipe away the residue on my lips.

"That sounds horrible, Lucy. Why would you want that?"

"So, it's okay if a man wants to have a one-night stand but not a woman?"

I shook my head, setting the wine glass down. "I didn't say that, but it's just . . . It's not you."

Lucy frowned and set her glass down. "How would you know?"

"I know enough to recognize that you want a connection."

"And what I'm telling you is that I want a physical connection. If I want to relieve some stress, I want to be able to do it with no strings attached." She picked her wine back up. "And that's where you come in."

My chest tightened in a panic at the thought of Lucy spending nights with any man but me.

"Why are you looking at me like that?" She studied me as I fought for an easy answer.

"Meatloaf is done." I pulled out the dish and slid the

French bread onto the rack.

"Did I offend you?" she asked, getting in front of me.

"It would take a lot more than that to offend me, Lucy." I smiled, watching the spark ignite in her gaze. "We can discuss particulars over dinner."

I put the oven to broil for the bread.

Lucy laughed. "I didn't think it was that difficult."

"Did you ever show up and find your law professors ill-prepared?"

She grinned. "No."

"There you go."

Lucy's mouth parted, and her tongue slowly slid along her bottom lip, driving me instantly crazy for her.

"You don't have any effing clue how sexy you are," I muttered, glancing at the bread in the oven.

She patted my chest and laughed. "I think you're just in a dry spell."

I shook my head and cupped her hands in mine. "Don't do that."

"What?"

"Put yourself down like that."

She was thoughtful for a second and nodded. "Okay."

"Lesson number one, Lucy. Know your worth."

Her green eyes caught mine, and my heart ached. I

wanted to taste every square inch of this woman right here and now.

"I can do that."

"You're an insanely sexy, intelligent woman who could strike down most men with one look."

Lucy's eyes stayed on mine, and she nodded as I moved toward her.

"Thank you."

"It's the truth, Lucy. You have nothing to thank me for. I haven't done anything." My eyes moved to her lips as I fought the urge to kiss her.

Suddenly, the smell of burnt bread permeated the air as I jumped from Lucy and reached for the potholders as smoke billowed from the oven.

She coughed a few times as she held a towel to her nose and turned on the kitchen fan while I tossed the tray on the stove and swatted the air to rid it of smoke.

Lucy walked over to me and glanced at the burnt cheese bread. "I'd still eat it."

I laughed, looping my arms over her shoulders as I pulled her into me.

The curves of her body fit perfectly against me.

"You make it extremely difficult for me to remember what it was I set out to do tonight."

"I thought we were going to have dinner."

Feeling her fit into me so perfectly made me question everything.

I cleared my throat and glanced at the bread as I took a step back. "Tonight is about setting up boundaries."

A slight curl to her lips drove me insane.

"Ah, boundaries." She reached for some plates out of the cabinet and set them next to the meatloaf I was cutting.

"Perfect. The meatloaf firmed up while I was busy burning the bread, so it won't crumble all over." I sliced the meatloaf and placed it on our plates while she scooped potatoes and attempted to salvage the bread.

"Good to know. Looks delicious."

This was crazy. I needed to toughen up. Who cared that she dropped me to my knees? She asked me to do something so she could broaden her horizons, and I should man up and quit worrying about the future.

Besides, she'd made it clear that there wouldn't be one with me, and at least with her arrangement, I could spend some time with her.

We sat down at the table, and she looked up at me and smiled.

"Okay, let me have it." She picked up her fork and waited for my response.

"It's not just about me. I want to know your expectations. As I've told you, I don't think you need my help."

Her smile widened. "And as I've told you, that's only because I'm with you."

Then why won't you give us a chance?

"Fine. How many lessons a week do you want?"

She took a bite of the potatoes and closed her eyes. "These are delicious."

"Thanks."

"I think I could fit three evening sessions in with my schedule. Is that too many for you?"

God, no.

"That should work." I took a bite of food.

"Would Thursday, Friday, and Saturdays work for you?" she asked.

I nodded.

"Do you want to practice dating? Going out to dinners? Practicing picking me up in a bar? What are we truly talking about here? And how long do you want this to last?"

Her laugh filled the dining room, and I wanted to hear it for the rest of my life. "I don't know. I hadn't really thought about any of the details that much."

"I see."

"Maybe just until I'm ready?"

I nodded as a gnawing sensation threaded through me. "I think we need an actual finish line."

Lucy nodded, shoving a piece of stray hair behind her ear. "Oh, right."

"What do you think? A month?" I asked.

"That seems about right to get me ready for the world." Her cheeks flushed, and she laughed. "I can't believe that I even asked you to do this for me."

I smiled. "I don't mind."

"You're such a guy."

I shook my head. "I'm a guy who wishes I could start this whole thing over."

"Yeah?"

I nodded. "But anyway, it sounds like you want to practice the entire ritual of dating or meeting someone, not just the deed."

"Yeah. Let's work on the whole process, but I firmly believe I do need to practice the deed." A glint of something unrecognizable flashed through her eyes. "Surprise me. If we go out to dinner, I'll pay for the food and drinks. You're already giving me your time."

My stomach knotted, and I shook my head as her lawyer mind turned this into strictly transactional.

"No. I'm buying our meals. Sorry to disappoint." I stared at her, and her cheeks flushed. "I don't need to be paid for my services, as grand as they may be. This whole experiment is already out of my comfort level. And I do have one rule. If you find someone else you're attracted to during this experiment, tell me immediately."

Lucy chuckled nervously and took a bite of the meatloaf. "This is really good. You might actually need to add cooking lessons to the lesson plan."

"Family recipe. Can't do it."

Lucy's eyes flashed to mine. "Are you serious?"

I nodded, loving to toy with her.

"I bet I could get it out of you." A smoldering look rested behind her gaze as she took another bite of meatloaf.

How in the world could she make meatloaf look sexy?

She pulled the meat off her fork, and I laughed, shaking my head.

Lucy playfully scowled. "What?"

"I'm pretty much doomed."

"Says who?"

My heart.

My mind.

My body.

Skipping her question, I shook my head. "So, I've got

Thursday through Saturday nights inked in for you. I'll vary things a bit and try to keep you on your toes."

"Good plan."

She finished her meal, and I'd barely touched mine.

"Since today is Wednesday, should we skip tomorrow?" I asked.

Lucy looked horrified. "No. Why would we do that?" She stopped herself for a second. "Oh, wait. Do you have plans with someone tomorrow?"

"No, Lucy. I don't have plans with anyone else."

Relief fluttered through her, and she stood to get more food while I pushed mine around on the plate and wondered why I'd ever agreed to do this with her.

"Do me one favor before tomorrow," I told Lucy.

"What's that?"

"Read the article."

Chapter Twenty-Two

I Can Keep You Warm at Night

Lucy

I drew a breath and stared at the page laid out in front of me. I was sitting at the bar across the street from Shep's condo. I'd been swamped at work and hadn't had the time to read his article yet, and I had a few minutes before he was set to show up.

My pulse zinged with uncertainty as I focused my eyes on the next section I hadn't read yet. Did he think this would be a good companion piece to what he was teaching me?

I didn't know.

But I felt like something had shifted between us.

Last night after dinner, we just had a quick hug at the door after he handed me my coat, and that was it.

He closed the door, and I went home.

I guess there was some part of me that kind of fantasized about spending the night with him and doing the walk of shame in the morning, but it didn't happen.

In fact, I wasn't sure what last night was all about. It was good that we got a lot of the parameters set, I suppose. But what was that about me finding someone else? When would I do that? I'd already planned to spend a good chunk of my nonexistent free time with Shep.

I closed the magazine and decided to read it later. I'd already snuck a look at the photos, and my heart could barely handle it. The man knew how to make panties melt all across Seattle. I was sure of that. It was like he instinctively knew how low to let the towel hang or exactly where to raise a shirt and lower his jeans. It was eye candy for the soul.

However, tonight, I needed my mind to be freed up and ready for whatever Shep had going on tonight.

The bartender walked over to me with a drink. "Miss, the man over there wanted me to bring this to you."

My cheeks blushed as I scanned the bar, but I didn't see anyone.

"Oh. Well, okay. Thanks."

He winked at me and dropped the drink order off at my table while I continued to look for Shep.

Finally, a guy I didn't recognize sauntered over and smiled at me, stopping at my table.

"Are you waiting for someone?" he asked. His dark hair framed his features well, and he was cute.

But not Shep cute.

He didn't have that familiar sparkle in his eyes and the cheekbones and jawline that made me drool.

"I am, actually."

He looked briefly disappointed. "Mind if I slide in for a second?"

"Uh, no? I don't mind." I looked around the bar, thinking this had to be a setup by Shep.

"You're so beautiful."

I laughed and shook my head. "It's the lighting. They keep it dark enough to confuse everyone."

The man laughed. "I don't believe that for one second."

"It's true." I chuckled, scanning the bar and waiting for Shep to hop out of his hiding place.

"Are you dating anyone?" the man pressed.

I tried to figure out whether I was supposed to play along and say no or what Shep might have in mind.

"No. I'm not seeing anyone seriously. You?"

He shook his head, and his eyes lit up, which made

my stomach churn into an uneasy mosh pit of nerves.

"I'm Julien."

I nodded. "Nice to meet you. I'm Terry Bartholomew."

Oh. Shoot. Or was it Perry that Shep used that first night? Either way, I'd have some fun with this.

Maybe Shep was listening in. He could be in the booth behind me and I didn't know. Maybe it was time to heat up my flirting skills. Maybe this was a test.

"Ah, Terry is a nice name. It's one of those that can go either way."

I laughed. "I suppose it could. So, what brings you here this frosty night?"

He waved the bartender over and ordered the same drink he'd had delivered, which I had no plan of drinking.

"Just unwinding after work a bit, trying to get out of the cold."

"I know how that goes." I let out a sigh and asked myself what Shep would do. "Maybe you could use someone to keep you warm tonight?"

The man's eyes nearly bugged out of his head, and he immediately straightened up. "Well, yeah. I wouldn't mind that one bit."

"Really?"

"Of course, really. It sounds incredible."

"Doesn't it? We could get into fuzzy jammies and sit by a roiling fire all night."

"Terry, you're the most incredible woman I think I've ever met." He looked like he wanted to lean over the table and lick my face right when Shep appeared from nowhere.

"Am I interrupting something?"

I laughed and glanced up at the man who literally made my heart skip a beat. "I don't know. You tell me."

He cocked his head slightly and eyed me. "I wouldn't know."

A gasp of horror slid from my lips as I looked at Julien and back at Shep before looking at Julien.

"Is this the person you were waiting for?" Julien asked, glancing at Shep.

Horror settled deep into my bones at the sudden realization that this man had not been sent by Shep.

Julien looked up at Shep and smiled. "Hey, bro. She and I have something going here right now."

Shep looked amused as I squirmed in the booth. "Oh, yeah? I wouldn't want to intrude."

"You're not intruding," I muttered quickly.

Julien scowled at Shep. "Seriously, man. We're headed out soon."

I shook my head. "No. No, we're not. There's been a huge misunderstanding."

Shep chuckled. "Misunderstanding?"

Julien drew a deep breath. "What are you talking about? You were going to keep me warm tonight. Those very words rolled off your tongue."

My entire head felt like a volcano was erupting as both men looked at me.

"I meant like . . . I mean . . ." I shifted in the seat.

Shep smirked and kept his eyes on me, which made my pulse soar.

"I thought . . ." I bit my bottom lip and let out a grunt. "I didn't mean what I said."

The bartender showed up with a drink for Julien, who shot up from the booth. "So, you're one of those broads. Figures. All talk and no action."

I grimaced. "Afraid so."

Julien not only grabbed his drink, but he also grabbed the one he'd ordered for me, too, before sulking off to an empty table by the bar.

I refused to look at Shep, so I stared straight ahead and hummed a little song as I played with my napkin. I'd managed to turn the fabric into a swan and then into a cube before crumpling it into a mess of fabric.

"Keeping him warm?" Shep finally prodded, sliding into the seat across from me. "He doesn't strike me as your type."

I finally forced myself to look at the sexiest man alive, who looked far too amused with this entire debacle.

"I thought he was a test. I thought you sent him and were listening or something. I wanted to do my best at flirting for a one-night stand." I smiled.

"I'm not that clever."

I laughed, feeling the immediate chemistry I kept trying hard to shake. "Says the man who crashed a matchmaking event."

"And how did that go for me?"

"Well, you're here."

Shep let out a deep breath but didn't take the bait. "So, you offered to keep him warm tonight?"

I nodded, fidgeting with my napkin.

This was worse than interrogating my own client.

"But not for real," I added.

Shep's smile widened. "I don't think he knew that."

"Apparently not. Maybe lessons were a bad idea."

Shep reached for my hands the moment they'd released the napkin and clasped them in his. "Lucy, I would never send another man to do my job. In fact, I'm not exactly thrilled that when you're done with me, it's all for another guy to enjoy."

His words carved a chunk out of my heart.

"It's not exactly like that." I shook my head and drew a breath.

"It is, actually, but that's for another day." He winked at me and let go of my hands. "Sorry I'm late. We had a mini-crisis at the office that involved two developers nearly fighting one another over a new feature."

"Sounds lovely."

"I always thought computer guys were laidback, but they're really passionate when it comes to certain topics, particularly gaming."

I laughed, seeing the light behind his gaze before it slid to the magazine I hadn't read yet.

"That was a pretty smooth line you gave to Juliette."

"Julien," I corrected. "And I told him my name was Terry Bartholomew."

Shep laughed. "You mean Perry Bartholomew? The man who handed me a fate worse than death?"

I chuckled and shook my head. "Why would you say that?"

"Because I don't get to have you, Lucy. This is all pretend to you."

His words dug deep into my soul.

Again.

Shep gave a nod with his chin. "Did you read the article yet?"

"Full confession," I said with a smile. "I did not read the article. I only stared at the photos of you."

Shep laughed. "And did it sway your opinion of me?"

"You mean that you have an insane body and a way with the camera? No. I knew that already."

The bar was getting more crowded. Julien found another woman to buy a drink for, so I felt a little less guilty about that situation. As more drinks were served, the volume of the place went up, and I wondered what was next.

"I just want to go on record with you, Lucy."

"About what?"

"I don't think you need my help at all. Not with the way you handled that guy, and never with the way you've handled me. I think you're amazing and could land any guy in this bar. If I hadn't already learned my lesson about placing bets, I'd offer a wager."

My stomach clenched at the thought as I looked around the crowded room with men holding drinks, flirting with women, and chatting with each other. As I brought my eyes back to Shep, a sinking feeling shoved its way through me.

The man I wanted was sitting across from me and was completely averse to the idea of monogamy.

"I only had that confidence because I thought you'd sent that guy over to me. I'm usually a wreck."

"Okay. Prove it. I want you to bring me a drink with your best pickup line. The bartender has two waiting for us."

"He does?" I glanced over at him.

"Yeah. I ordered them before I came over to the table."

"Okay." I wasn't sure I could do this. "I think I already gave up my best line to Julien."

"We'll see." He motioned for me to leave, so I reluctantly got up from the table and made my way over to the two lonely drinks at the end of the bar.

Just as I reached for the drinks, a man came up to me and brushed his fingers along the counter. "Please tell me you're just really thirsty and not here with someone."

I looked up to see a rather attractive man starting at me. I chuckled and shook my head.

"Sorry. I'm here with someone."

He shook his head and groaned. "That's what I was afraid of. Have a great night."

"You too." I clutched both glasses and spun around to

see Shep's eyes right on me.

No doubt he saw what just happened, and I couldn't help but love the feeling. I never went out, but I certainly hadn't expected to have two men try to pick me up. That was usually how it worked for Mae, but not for me.

As I walked over to Shep, he didn't take his eyes off me.

I set the drinks down, and Shep smiled.

"I thought you might be extra thirsty, so I brought two drinks." I scowled as the words came out.

Shep's smile widened. "Um. Thank you?"

I grunted and collapsed into the booth. "Sorry. Can I have a do-over? I was trying to recreate what that guy just said to me."

"You mean the one who still can't keep his eyes off you?"

My cheeks warmed. "Seriously?"

Shep nodded, taking a sip from the drink I brought over. "He's a doctor. His name is Cliff."

"How do you know?" I asked, glancing in the stranger's direction.

Shep was right. He was looking over here.

"He's a regular. When you live across the street like I do, you kind of get familiar with the lay of the land." Shep smiled and swirled his drink around. "Is he your type?"

I shrugged. "I don't have a type."

"If I weren't here, would you have gone for him?" Shep watched me intently, and his attention felt good.

It shouldn't have, but it did.

"I don't know. Maybe. Probably not." I let out an exhausted sigh. "That's the problem. I don't go for anyone."

Shep's eyes fell to my lips, and I wanted nothing more than to be kissed by him again. I knew I shouldn't want it. He'd always been clear about his intentions with dating.

And we all knew I was an absolute mess with no hope of settling down, thanks to the daily reminders of where relationships end up.

So why was I making it so complicated?

"Okay." I smacked the table, and Shep jumped. "I got one."

"One what?"

"A pickup line."

He motioned with his two fingers and smiled. "Lemme have it."

"I hear nothing lasts forever," I started, and Shep cocked his head. "So, will you be my nothing?"

Shep winced as his lips puckered. "Boy, that really gets right to the point."

I giggled, nodding and extremely proud of myself.

"How about this?" I tried another.

"I'm afraid to hear."

"Do you have some rubbing alcohol?"

Shep's smile grew. "Why?"

"I scraped my knee falling for you."

I was totally getting the hang of this.

Shep hung his head in his hands and laughed.

"I can tell you now." Shep shook his head and looked at me. "You could use those lines on any guy in this bar, and they'd be eating out of your hand like a puppy dog. And that's regardless of the fact that your pickup lines sound like knock-knock jokes."

I rolled my eyes. "I'm glad you think so highly of my ability to persuade the opposite sex, but I can assure you it's not like that. Do you want to know what men have told me?"

"Like what?"

I twisted my lips into a scowl. "Let's see, I've heard I look angry. I'm distracted. I'm not soft. I'm rigid."

"If men told you those things, it's because they don't know you."

He polished off his drink and looked around the bar. "The night's young. Do you want to head back to my place?"

"Yes, please." I smiled as my pulse raced, and I shot

out of the booth while Shep still sat there. "I thought you said we were going back to your place?"

Shep chuckled. "That was just an example of a solid line that works, but if you want to get out of here, we can."

My hands rested on the table. "I don't know how you do this to me. I really don't."

"Do what?"

I swallowed down the tightness I felt as I looked at the one man I really wanted.

Chapter Twenty-Three

Who has the Upper Hand?

Shep

Everything about Lucy drove me mad. She didn't have a clue what a catch she was and how many men would be willing to run over each other to have a chance with her. But the worst part was that she didn't want to be caught.

"Today was nuts at work," she confessed. "It's nice to have a night out with you, even if it's working on a subject that I despise."

I opened the door to my condo. "And what is that?"

"Love."

This woman was really tough as nails. Even when I thought I was thawing out her heart a smidge, she'd come at with me a line like that one.

I touched her back softly as I helped take her coat off,

and I felt her stiffen.

"Do you really hate love?" I asked, putting her coat in the closet.

She was quiet for a few minutes as she looked around my condo. I was sure it didn't look that much different from yesterday, but I felt like she was buying herself time.

I'd always liked this condo. It was close to my office and restaurants and was much larger than most in the areas. But for the days that I couldn't handle being in the city, I had a place toward the mountains. I looked at Lucy and realized how little we actually knew about one another. She didn't even know I had more than one home. But I also kind of liked that. She wasn't getting to know me for any reason other than me. Not what I could give her.

"I don't hate the idea of love. I hate what it does to people," she said flatly before walking into the great room.

I followed, going into the kitchen instead. "Did you want something to drink? Water? Beer? Wine?"

She shook her head and took a seat on the couch while I poured myself some sparkling water.

Lucy sat up straight and bobbed her knee up and down.

"What do you want to get out of this tonight?" I asked, taking a seat next to her. "We already saw that two men wanted to get with you tonight. I don't know what more you want in terms of a lesson."

She still sat rigid, but she turned to me and smiled. "What would you normally be doing on a night like tonight?"

The question took me by surprise.

"Probably exactly what I'm doing now. Minus the session on dating."

She nodded and turned her attention out the window, which overlooked a portion of Lake Union in between office buildings.

Lucy drew a breath and looked back at me. "So, you'd have a lady here, and you'd be making the moves for another successful night."

I laughed and shook my head. "No. I'd probably be here on the couch by myself, drinking some sparkling water while contemplating what to cook for dinner."

Lucy smiled. "Without a lady here?"

"It's not like I'm with a woman every single night of my life."

She stretched her legs out and finally started to relax. "Maybe just every other night."

"Not even close."

Lucy quirked her brows as I took a sip, but I couldn't take my eyes off her. "I don't believe it for a second."

"I'm not pretending to be celibate, but it's not like I'm on the prowl every single night of my life."

"Do you ever get lonely?" she asked, leaning back into the cushions. She didn't look at me as she asked the question.

"I suppose I do. That's probably why I do spend a fair amount of time with someone."

"Ah. So, we did get a confession that it's been upgraded to a *fair* amount of time." She kicked off her heels and tucked her feet under her. Her tiny toes had pink polish on them, and I bit back a smile.

Why did I even notice the small things about her?

"You really love law, don't you?" I teased. "I didn't confess to anything. Just like I didn't truly agree to help you with your crazy plan at first."

She laughed and filled my condo with something it had been missing.

Her.

She shook her index finger at me. "Devil is in the details."

"And an angel can come from chaos," I added.

"Ooh. That's a good one."

"It's true."

"Which one of us is that angel?" she joked.

"I haven't figured that out yet."

But that wasn't true. Everything about Lucy was like she'd been sent from heaven to mess with my emotions and make me feel again.

Something I hadn't let myself do for a really long time. It was crazy to me how much Lucy and I had in common. After being burned when I was young, I stripped away the emotion from sex and focused on growing my business. It freed me to have company now and again without the heartache and hassle. The only difference was that Lucy chose to abstain from enjoying someone's company.

"What are you thinking about?" she asked.

"You probably don't want to know."

"I wouldn't have asked if I didn't want to know." She studied me while I took a sip of water.

"How much we have in common."

She rolled her eyes and grinned. "Just because we both love Jingle Berry Balls does not mean we have a lot in common."

But she dropped her expression when she saw I was serious. "Okay. Let me have it."

"It's going to blow your mind."

Lucy laughed and shook her head. "We'll see."

"You love focusing on your career, and so do I."

"But you know how to shut it off," she pointed out.

I nodded in agreement. "True, but it wasn't always like that."

"Fair enough. What else?" She scooted a little closer.

"Neither of us knows how to open our heart up."

She moved even closer and scowled at me as she lifted her hand to my chest. "Not fair."

"What's not fair about that?"

"I could open my heart up if I wanted to."

I softly touched her cheek. "Are you sure about that?"

"Absolutely. But I know it wouldn't be productive."

"Don't you think that's more of an excuse than a reality?"

"Would you have gotten to where you are today if you'd been bothered with breakups and heartache and all that kind of tedious relationship stuff?" She rested her head on my shoulder, which I wasn't expecting.

"Who knows? Maybe I could have built something even better," I offered, wrapping my arm around her shoulders. How in God's name was I suddenly the romantic, and the woman I fantasized about was the cynic?

The irony wasn't lost on me.

She shook her head. "It's not like that for me. I need complete concentration. I need time to devote to billable hours. I just don't have room for a relationship."

I let out a deep sigh. "Lucy, then why are you really here? We both know you don't need lessons. You've made it explicitly clear that I offered up too many red flags to ever be a potential fit for you. What's really going on?"

Lucy slowly straightened from me and let out a deep breath before turning around, balancing on the couch on her knees.

She didn't answer me as her eyes locked on mine, and every part of me raged for her. I needed to feel this woman in my arms and take as much as she was willing to give me. Because I knew it wouldn't be long before she was out of my life.

Before I had a chance to react, Lucy straddled me and rested her hands on my shoulders as she drew a deep breath.

"The truth is that I didn't want any other man in that bar, Shep. It was you who I wanted, and we both know that's not possible."

My hands ran up her spine, tangling in her hair as I brought her mouth to mine.

The kiss scorched my lips, turning my mouth nearly numb with desire as my tongue tasted her lips and then her tongue. Sweetness filled me as a little moan escaped through our kiss as she pressed her body against mine.

When she felt the hardness between us, I felt her mouth lift into a smile between kisses, which only made me want her more. The warmth of her body on mine made my body ignite into a flurry of need so raw that I ached.

I pulled my mouth away ever so slightly, and she shook her head, combing her fingers through my short hair. "Please don't stop."

I smiled, reaching for the remote to shut the blinds, and she giggled.

"I didn't even think of that. They could get an eyeful." She pressed her forehead against mine before running her fingers under my shirt, over my stomach, and to my chest.

"If I'm lucky," I whispered, feeling her body melt into mine.

Her fingers sliding along my chest made me shiver as our eyes remained connected to one another. I'd never experienced that before with a woman.

Part of me wanted to shove her clothes off and devour her, and the other part of me was afraid that once we fully went there, she'd find an excuse not to see me again.

Lucy nuzzled her nose against mine, and any reluctance she'd had earlier seemed to have vanished as she ground her hips against me.

I shook my head with a smile and kissed her again in

between her tugging my shirt off with one hand while caressing my chest with the other.

She pulled her mouth away slowly, softly nipping at my bottom lip before she sank her mouth to my chest, softly kissing each area as if it were new to her.

I opened my eyes to see Lucy's arms running over my bare chest and her mess of hair sprawled over it, making the fire burn hotter.

Lucy had me in a complete stupor as her hands slid to my pants and began to unbutton them. I hissed as her hair slid across my stomach.

She looked up at me, licking her lips, and I pulled her on top of me, yanking her top away and slipping her bra off.

It was as if I needed to consume this woman, feel every part of her skin against mine. The way her breasts squished into my chest. Her nipples were hard and enticing as we kissed again.

This time, it was me who let out the moan when her hands went into my boxers. She tightened her grip around me, easing me into unexpected ecstasy as I cupped one of her breasts in my hand while the other was in my mouth.

Her body writhed against me, and we weren't even completely naked as she brought me so close to the edge, but I shifted away without breaking our kiss. The throbbing only built as I moved my hand down the front of her slacks, lifting the edge of her panties as my fingers slid into her.

Lucy let out a little whimper of pleasure as my thumb found her perfect rhythm.

And before I knew what was happening, her fingers clenched back around me, and we both fell over the edge of pleasure, her breathing ragged as her voice freed something inside me.

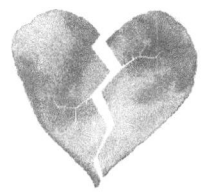

Chapter Twenty-Four

Stuck at Third

Lucy

"A swing and a miss, Danni. I feel like I'm back in high school, but I never got this far back then." I laughed, changing my phone to speaker mode as I sat curled up on my couch in the family room. "We get so close to sex, and then somehow, we just do all sorts of other things. I'm scared to let him take me to that next step."

Danni snorted. "I wish I had your problems. God forbid. You're playing footsie with Seattle's Most Eligible Bachelor."

I groaned. "I can't believe I just did that. And it's more than footsie, just for the record."

"How much more?" Danni teased.

"Think of all the things you can do without going all

the way. That's what we've done."

"Wow, Lucy. This is definitely uncharted territory for you."

I sat back on the couch, pulling two chenille pillows over me. "I know, and I can't help myself. It's like a drug."

Dannie was quiet for a couple of seconds. "*It's* like a drug, or *he's* like a drug?"

I pulled one of the pillows over my head and groaned into it. "Fine. He's like a drug."

"Lucy, you have to admit that you're falling for Shep."

"Don't say that," I mumbled into the pillow.

"Is that really a bad thing?" Danni asked as little Lucy fussed over the phone.

"Don't you need to take care of mini-me?"

Danni laughed. "Nice try. She's just hungry and about to latch. You can't get out of this discussion with me tonight."

"Fine. The problem is that he came signed, sealed, and delivered to me with a box full of red flags." I removed the pillows and sat upright on the couch, muting my television. "He's adorable. He's super smart. He makes me feel like the most important woman in the world."

"Okay, so what's the problem?" Danni asked.

"He's so adorable that he gets any woman he wants.

He's so smart that he knows how to play them." I let out a sigh. "And finally, he makes all women feel like they're the most important in the world. It's not like I'm special. I've seen what happens to women who fall for his type."

"Lucy. That's not fair to you or to him. How in the world do you know that's how he makes other women feel?"

"He's good at what he does. I just know. He seems to think he's always been straightforward with women, but I'm sure he's left broken hearts all over the city."

"If you say so."

"What's that supposed to mean?"

"You know, it is true that some people are able to just go have fun and not put all kinds of emotions to the deed. There are even apps for hooking up, but what if that's not what this is about?"

"We both agreed that this wouldn't become serious."

"Then what is any of this?"

"Shep vowed to teach me the ways. I need a lesson in having sex without emotions getting in the way and without the promise of more in front of me."

"How romantic," she said dryly.

"He's the perfect guy to help me. He knows where he stands with me, and I know I can't let myself get tangled up in his messy web of pranks and bachelor ways."

Danni didn't say anything, and I always knew from studying the law that loose lips sank ships, so I stayed quiet too.

I didn't want to tell my best friend how I thought about Shep most minutes of the day. That I imagined him changing his ways and settling down. That I even imagined myself as the woman who changed the man who pranked his way through life.

Nope. I wasn't going to say any of that.

"Anyway, do you know what my nickname for him is?"

"Tell me."

"Mr. Flirt."

Danni laughed. "Well, if the shoe fits."

"Oh, it fits. He can make a person feel like they are on top of the world with just one look. I swear, Danni . . . all I have to do is see him waiting for me, and I feel like the luckiest woman in the world to be in his presence. That takes talent to do that."

"Or you're falling for him."

I swatted the air as if a gnat just flew by. "Psh. I'm definitely not falling for a man who told me his name was Perry and crashed a matchmaking event impersonating someone else. I don't have time for that kind of a jokester."

"It seems like you're making time . . ."

"It may seem like that, but I'm in control here. I'm getting what I need out of him before anything gets messy."

"Lucy, messy can be okay. Emotions aren't like hives. They don't spread to every area of your life. You can be in love and still be a good divorce lawyer."

I froze.

Was that what I was worried about? That I'd soften too much to be good at destroying the enemy?

I shoved the idea aside.

"I . . . no. I'm just not exactly surrounded by happy endings."

"Don't let my situation tip you over the edge."

I didn't have the heart to tell Danni that her ex hadn't just tipped me over the edge. He shoved me over in a fiery wreck of rage.

But I'd used that to Danni's advantage, and I knew I was making her ex's legal team worried over whether we had to go to trial. There was absolutely no way that hooking up with another woman as your wife was giving birth would go over well. The most ideal situation was to scare his entire legal team into convincing him to settle before a date was set.

"I promise you that my heart was solid stone before any of this happened to you and our little Lucy."

Danni laughed and let out a sigh. "I have a confession."

"Hit me with it."

"I'm already dreaming of someone who will treat my daughter and me right, where I don't have to wonder where he is at night. Where he doesn't say I look terrible before a shower or that I ruined his career."

I thought about my best friend's words. She'd just gotten her heart trampled on, and yet she hadn't given up on love.

"Wow. You give me hope, Danni."

She laughed. "What? You think I would have been ruined by love? Absolutely not. I know it's out there for me."

"I do too. You deserve the world, Danni."

"And so do you," she said quietly, but it was as if the words wouldn't quite lodge into my heart.

"On that note, Shep is on his way over."

"Ah, Friday night is date night, huh?"

"He sees me three nights a week for the next few to get me situated with the opposite sex before sending me off."

"You really confuse the crap out of me, but like you said, you're my lawyer, not my therapist, and for that, I'm very grateful. Have you read that article about him yet?"

"Nope. I know I should. I just haven't had the time."

"I'd seriously make the time."

I laughed. "Alright, Alright."

"Have a fun night full of everything but emotions." Danni scoffed. "Love ya."

"Love ya too."

I slid off the phone and collapsed on the couch as I thought about Danni.

Maybe I really wasn't the relationship type. The idea of being used and abused by someone wasn't my idea of fun, and I certainly couldn't imagine pulling myself up by the bootstraps and signing up for more.

But Danni always left me in awe. She had a heart of gold and believed in something I just couldn't bring myself to believe in.

Regardless, I walked over to the kitchen and put in a tray of enchiladas that I'd picked up from the deli on the way home. I tossed some lettuce, cherry tomatoes, and sliced cucumber together and shoved it in my fridge and went to sit at the dining table where my laptop was open.

Before I left the office, I'd sent a scathing email to the legal team for Danni's ex. I could feel it in my bones that they were concerned about their client's behavior and what more he'd pull out of his hat as a trial neared.

My team had combed through the financials that the

forensic account handed over, and I felt really good about the fact that Danni would be handed two rentals free and clear, along with the house she was currently in.

I think his side knew those concessions were more than fair, considering what else I could throw on the table if we chose to do so, which could make things far more painful for him, but Danni wanted this done quickly. I scanned my inbox and had no new emails from them, which led my mind to worrisome places.

The infamous magazine with Shep's smiling mug stared at me from the table. I tapped my finger and debated whether or not to dabble before he showed up.

My stomach tightened, and I glanced around the room like I was doing something I shouldn't. But he even said I should read the article.

As I slid my fingers along the glossy pages, I landed where I'd last left off, and my heart sped up a little.

I stared at the last sentence I'd read and started again.

Shep: I can promise you that love isn't looking for me, either.

Interviewer: Indulge me. Let's pretend your heart was ready, and you wanted to find that forever person.

Shep moved uncomfortably in his seat and flashed his

boyish grin. (Editorial insert: If this interviewer wasn't already taken, I'd probably bat my lashes and wish for a hotel key.)

Shep: Fine. She'd beat me at my own game. I want a partner who's ready to tell me when I'm out of line. Knock me down a few notches when I'm getting ahead of myself. I don't mind a little friendly and not-so-friendly banter thrown at me. I want someone intellectually stimulating, but she doesn't mind if I take control once in a while. Someone who asks me where I've been all night or what I did in my day. I want someone who asks questions and delves deep for answers. In a perfect world, I want someone who hates love as much as I do while miserably loving every part of me, flaws included.

Interviewer: Sounds like you should find yourself a divorce attorney.

Shep laughs.

Shep: Is that so?

Interviewer: You perfectly described my own.

Shep smiles.

Shep: Yeah? What's her number?

Interviewer: I would never have guessed that you wanted someone so challenging.

Shep: You forget one key piece of information. You asked me about a hypothetical woman, and I've already pointed out that I'm not interested.

Interviewer: Right. Yet, you had an answer.

Shep: Indeed, I did.

My pulse pounded wildly as I reread the repartee. Was that what he saw in me?

The doorbell chimed, and I sprang off the chair to answer the door. A shiver of delight ran through me at the thought of getting to see Shep again.

Last night was incredible and steamy and filled me with something I still couldn't put my finger on.

And now this article, which I still hadn't finished, got me all wound up like a Jack-in-the-Box.

Everything that happened at his condo last night was unexpected and completely unlike me, but Shep always managed to pull out that side of me. The only thing I could attribute it to was that I knew neither of us wanted much of anything.

Right?

The article said as much.

Multiple times.

Until you got to the hypothetical part.

When I nearly threw open the door, Shep stood at the threshold with a huge bouquet of pink roses. His eyes locked on mine, but he wasn't smiling. He stepped inside and shut the door behind us.

"Everything okay?" I asked breathlessly as my mind spun to the interview.

Shep nodded, still holding the flowers.

"The rules of the game are changing," Shep said flatly, handing over the roses. "It's my turn now."

Chapter Twenty-Five

Who's the Player?

Shep

She looked as shocked as I felt. But I'd had it. I sat in my office all day, listening to software developers and salesmen clash while all I could think about was Lucy.

And that was when I realized I'd been played.

Lucy wanted parts of me while checking others at the door, and I wasn't all about that. There was something about her that very first day that made me want to confess who I truly was because I wanted her to see me for Shep.

There was no taking back my foolish pranks, but she was the one stringing me along now. Until when?

No more.

Lucy frowned but took the time to inhale the roses. "They even smell marvelous."

I shook my head and smiled. "Don't do it. Don't try to distract me."

She smirked and looked at me over the roses. "Okay. Fine. Tell me what's on your mind."

"You," I said flatly.

Lucy looked surprised. "Me? What's that supposed to mean?"

"Lucy, I'm not buying it. You don't need my help."

She stomped her foot. "I'm completely inexperienced. I trust you. What more do you want?"

I laughed and shook my head, falling for her even more. "Isn't it obvious?"

Lucy turned and started toward the kitchen. I quickened my pace to keep up with her.

She was reaching for a vase above the stove hood when I came to help.

"I don't know what it is you think you want, Shep Jensen. But my professional opinion is that it's only because you know I can't give it to you."

I smiled, focusing on Lucy. "Not true."

Lucy shrugged and filled the vase with water before arranging the roses.

"These are the new rules." I smiled at her, refusing to back down. "There are no more scenarios where we pretend

I'm teaching you anything because the fact of the matter is that you're plenty skilled. Instead, I will treat you how you deserve to be treated. I'll wine you and dine you as if you were mine. If I decide to take you on a weekend trip, you're coming. I don't want to pretend with you. I want to believe I have a shot. I also want you to know that I have an equal say in all things between us."

Her brows rose. "Says who?"

"Me." I took a step forward. "And you can't keep saying that this thing between us is nothing."

She squinted, and I had to catch myself from chuckling. I think it was her best attempt at an evil eye. "Then what is it?"

"You know as well as I do that we have a connection. We had it that first night we met, Lucy. It's what made me want to tell you everything in that lousy ballroom of the hotel."

"I'm only interesting because you can't have me."

"Don't do that, Lucy. You know you feel it too."

Silence weaved between us.

"You said it yourself in the article. You're not looking for love, and love certainly isn't looking for you." She licked her bottom lip, and my body instantly responded.

"That was before I met you, Lucy."

"You're falling in love with me?" Her eyes stayed cool. "Try lust. I've seen it with my clients time and again."

"I'm not your client, Lucy. Life isn't always stitched into black-and-white litigation." I shook my head. "I'm falling for you, Lucy. I don't know what that means for our future, but I know if you refuse my offer tonight, we'll never know."

"Why's that?"

"Because I can't keep seeing you if it's just to prep you for other guys, and I can guarantee you that no other man would treat you as well as I would."

"You're sure about that," she said dryly.

"Surer than anything, Lucy. Let me have a real chance with you."

Lucy let out a thoughtful sigh. "And if I say no?"

"I'm canceling my end of the agreement. I can't see you any longer. It's not fair to me, and it's not fair to you."

Her jaw clenched. "Was it something I did last night?"

I laughed. "It's probably more what we didn't do."

She frowned. "How so?"

"We're managing to do everything under the sun except sleep with one another." I pressed my lips together and drew a breath, knowing this next statement could go either way. "And I believe it's because you're scared."

"Ha. Scared?" Lucy coiled her fingers at the bottom of my shirt and tugged me over. "I'll take you right here to prove you wrong."

I smiled, shaking my head. "You are such a lawyer. Always have to have the last word. Always have to be right."

"Thank you," she hummed, letting go of my shirt. "But that's quite a stereotype."

"Like you haven't done the same to me?" I prodded. "I'm the eternal party boy, right? It's impossible to fall for a single woman? Have feelings? Stop messing around?"

"You said it yourself," Lucy said, pointing at the table where I spotted the magazine.

Damn it, Winter. Why did I take your advice and do that spread?

"That's not what I said at all." I shook my head. "Listen, it sounds like this is all too much for you. I came here and said what I had to say. Take it or leave it."

I knew I had to stand my ground with Lucy. I didn't want any more meaningless romps with her because every single one of them meant something to me, and I realized that last night when she left.

I also figured out that there was a reason we weren't going to that next step.

It meant something to her too.

"Fine." She kept her eyes focused on the roses.

"Fine, what?"

I needed to hear the words.

Lucy kept her eyes averted and drew a deep breath while I glanced around her bright and cheery kitchen.

I leaned against the granite counter and smiled, taking in everything about Lucy. Her hair had been swept back into a messy bun. She'd changed out of her work clothes and sported a pair of joggers and an oversized red sweatshirt. Everything about her pushed a future into my world that needed her in it. As I lay in bed last night, I fantasized about her coming home late from a trial while I had dinner laid out for us to eat, movies lined up to watch, and a new bed for us to cuddle in.

Cuddle!

I wasn't a cuddler until I met Lucy, and now all I wanted to do was cuddle with her, and she would never give me the opportunity. Instead, she was busy orchestrating some crazy idea to keep me at a distance while also keeping me near enough to toy with my heart.

And I refused to believe this wasn't toying with hers.

Lucy turned to me, sucking on her bottom lip and concentrating on something very hard before she finally said something.

"Since we're at the point in this endeavor where we're up for renegotiations, I have a request," she said.

I nodded. "Let's hear it."

"I don't want you to be with anyone else while we're seeing one another."

Her words felt like the biggest gift in the world. Maybe my hunch was right. Maybe I could be the one to break down her walls, to melt her icy heart.

I smiled. "I think that's more than fair, but I have a request. I ask for the same."

Her eyes lit up, and she nodded. "Okay, so it's set. You're no longer my teacher. You're my . . ."

"Well, we can't say lover because we've never gotten there."

Lucy laughed. "True, and we may never."

"I think you enjoy torturing me."

She smiled even wider. "I think I enjoy it too. Are we starting over? Dating as if we'd just met? No more high-speed challenges to get me to the next level?"

"You're already at the next level," I teased. "I'm pretty sure you could teach me some things."

"I'm nervous," she confessed, and I could see it in her eyes. This was asking a lot of her.

"How about this?" I slid my arms around her waist

and gently pulled her into me. "How about you let me take you out for Valentine's Day? It falls on a weekend, so clear both days for me."

"I don't think I can . . ."

I saw the panic rise in her eyes and let out a deep breath. "Clear both days and keep your laptop with you. I'll let you bill as many hours as you want as long as you're sitting in front of me."

Lucy slid her hands up my chest and rested them there as she looked into my eyes.

"Why are you being so nice?" she asked.

"This is being nice? It's wanting to spend time with you. If you're working away and need a glass of water, I want to be the one to run to the kitchen and get it for you. Hungry? I'll make nachos for you. I just ask for one thing in return."

"What's that?" she asked softly.

"Don't ice me out. Don't put me in the same bin as your clients' exes that you've gone after in court. Let me be Shep and make my own ridiculous mistakes. Don't make me the enemy."

She let out a deep breath and rested her cheek on my chest. "That's going to be hard, but I'll do everything in my power to stop letting the negative in."

"And I will do everything in my power to grow up a

little."

"But not too much," she teased. "I like the playful Shep."

I grumbled a laugh and felt my chest fill with sweetness.

"That's good because I'm sure I can't do too much to tame him."

"Third person speak now?"

I laughed some more and held her close. "I do that sometimes. Mike has mentioned it's not a good look a few times."

"He's probably right."

And then I thought of that night she walked away in the bar and remembered something important. Mike and I had placed a bet, and he'd videoed my complete rejection. It wasn't a big deal, but I needed to tell her. I wanted to clear the air before we moved forward.

"This feels good," she said, propping her chin on my chest.

Lucy wasn't letting go, and I wasn't letting her go.

"I've never been out on a date for Valentine's Day."

"Really?" I asked, surprised.

"True confession."

"It will be fun, but first things first. What are we

having for dinner tonight?"

She tapped my chest and took a step back. "Funny you should ask. I made my enchiladas."

I cocked my head in surprise. "You got off late from work and made dinner for us?"

"Okay, maybe not. More like I stopped by the deli, and they made a delicious heat-and-eat dinner that I'm cooking up for us."

I snuck behind her as she reached for a potholder and kissed the back of her neck. She stopped and let out a little gasp as my breath skated across her skin, and I inhaled her familiar scent.

She chuckled as I stood back so she could get into the oven. "There's no denying our chemistry is on point."

"Couldn't agree more." I watched her lift the tray of enchiladas out and had to bite my bottom lip to control myself because if I had my way, I'd be ripping her clothes off and devouring her.

But we were kind of starting from scratch. She said so herself, and if that was what made her most comfortable, I'd follow whatever rules and boundaries she set for us.

Lucy turned around with a spatula in her hand. "And no more secrets, right? We're all caught up, I gather."

I laughed and nodded. "And I promise to take it easy

on placing bets with my buddies."

She pointed the spatula at me and winked. "Good call."

Her eyes locked on mine, and she smiled. "To our first date tonight."

"Our first date."

Chapter Twenty-Six

I'd been Played

Lucy

Shep was sneaky. No doubt about it. Under normal circumstances, I would have declined his offer and refused his demand.

But I was under pressure.

And I didn't want to lose him.

The last thought nudged a little worry of something under the surface.

I was starting to like him.

Things were about to get complicated.

I let out a sigh and opened my eyes as the door to my office swung open, and my assistant popped in to tell me my four o'clock was here.

"Thanks, Ann," I said, standing and smoothing my

skirt.

I followed Ann out of my office and went to the lobby of the spacious law firm, where a frail woman sat with a red nose and puffy eyes.

A perfect reminder of why I couldn't let myself get wrapped up in Shep's good looks, splendid personality, and body of an ancient warrior.

This was the aftermath of such good fortune.

"Leslie, it's nice to meet you," I said gently, reaching my hand out to shake hers. "I'm Lucy."

She smiled as best she could and stood with her purse falling off her shoulder and a tissue falling to the floor.

"Sorry. I'm a mess." Leslie bent down to pick up the used tissue before stuffing it back into her purse.

"You've been through a lot, and I hope to make things easier for you."

We walked past the receptionist, who smiled kindly to my client and me as we made our way back to my office, where she walked in and sat on the chaise near the window rather than a seat across from my desk, which told me it was going to be a long session.

I gently shut the door and took a seat behind my desk.

"Thank you for seeing me on such short notice."

I nodded, smiling. "I'm glad we had a cancellation."

And I truly was. The husband I was representing in what was tipping into a nasty divorce decided to give his wife another chance in spite of her recent fling with a co-worker. I wasn't sure how it would work out in the end, but if that was what his heart said to do, he had to follow it.

"My husband's been lying to me. I should have known from the beginning." She sniffled and dug her dirty tissue out of her purse. "He was always getting into it with the boys. It's like he never grew up."

I stood quickly and put a trash can next to her and a brand-new box of tissues in front of her.

"I'm not the first, huh?" Leslie's eyes looked painful. They were so puffy.

Shaking my head, I frowned. "Unfortunately, no."

She wagged her finger in the air as if she were talking to her guardian angel and not me. "There were red flags the very first time I met him." She brought her eyes back to me. "And what did I do? I ignored them."

My stomach knotted before turning queasy as my mind drifted to Shep. He lied about who he was without a second thought for people's hearts, all in the name of a prank.

"Let's start with what brought you in here today, and then we will start from the beginning."

She nodded. "My husband drained our bank account,

quit his job, and moved to Colorado."

"Is he with someone else?"

"Besides our dog? No. Not that I know of, but the whole thing is beyond me."

"Were you aware of problems in the marriage?" I asked.

She shook her head. "Nothing more than any other couple. We'd get in little arguments about his spending money at the casino or not coming home on time."

I nodded, taking notes. "How much did he take from your bank accounts?"

"I was a good saver," she said, twisting her tissue. "He took about seventy-five thousand from our joint savings account and ten from our checking."

I nodded. "Did he tell you he was going to do that?"

She let out a distorted sob and shook her head. "I came home one day and noticed that all of his clothes were missing from his side of the closet, and he took everything of his from the dresser too. I froze when I realized what I was actually seeing. I ran into the kitchen, and everything looked normal. I looked over at the family room and saw he'd taken the flat-screen television, gaming consoles, and his favorite chair."

"Was there a note?" I asked.

"Nothing." She let out a deep breath. "As I stood in the kitchen, completely dumbfounded, a thought occurred to me that I should check our bank accounts, so I logged in on the phone and saw that he'd left like a buck in the savings account and about three hundred dollars in the checking."

"When did this event happen?"

"Last Thursday."

"And you're sure there wasn't someone else?"

"I don't know anymore."

"How'd you find out he went to Colorado?"

"His plane ticket automatically populated into our shared calendar, and I was able to see a cashier's check cut to a moving company. I called them, and they confirmed where they were moving the items to."

I smiled and nodded. "Nice work."

"So, there wasn't a big event that led to this or an out-of-the-ordinary fight?"

She shook her head. "No, but I noticed he was getting antsy. He'd come home from work and barely talk to me. He spent a lot of time on his phone."

There is someone else, and I'd be willing to bet she's in Colorado.

"Well, I have good news and bad news, but let's start with the good news."

Leslie dabbed tears away and nodded as I went into explaining her options, how we would get the money back, and what to expect in the future. Relief slowly crept over her features by the end of our appointment, but I felt worse.

A lot worse.

By the time I'd said goodbye to Leslie, I had closed the door and collapsed on the chaise.

Not because her case was any more difficult than any others.

But because it struck a nerve.

This was exactly the problem with trying to date while I handled the breakup of everyone else's marriages. The parallels were uncanny. I had a giant red flag waving right in front of me on our first date. He'd lied to me. Sure, he confessed, but why would he think that was okay in the first place? And he never hid the fact that he wasn't into relationships.

And yet here I was, about to play into his hands.

What if it were all a game?

Why was I willing to suddenly put common sense aside and fall into his trap?

I hung my head in my hands and let out a low groan of annoyance.

Having parameters where we both knew what we

were getting into was perfectly settling. I knew I couldn't allow myself to fall for Mr. Flirt. I'd just use him for his expertise and move on with my idea of one-and-dones all over town. What he came up with on Friday night was completely unsettling, and worse yet, we hadn't seen one another since. It was now Monday, and on Friday night, we'd decided to scrap the three nights a week and let things naturally fall where they may.

Except nothing fell into place.

Did he just want to see if I'd agree to his plan and that was enough of a win for him?

I shook my head and let out an exasperated sigh just as Ann knocked on my door again.

"Special delivery."

"Yeah?" I stood from the chaise and tried to make myself look less rattled than I felt.

Ann brought in an orchid plant, larger than the top half of her. In fact, I think it had to be several orchids together.

"Should I put them on your desk?" she asked, spitting out a pink stalk from her mouth.

"That would be perfect." I eyed the arrangement and shook my head as I pulled out a card.

"I never thought I'd see the day," she said, chuckling.

"What's that supposed to mean?"

Ann's brows raised, and she leaned toward me. "Was it supposed to be a secret?"

"Was what supposed to be a secret?"

"That you hate men," she whispered.

"I don't hate men."

Surprise washed over her features as she backed up. "You don't?"

I frowned and nodded. "No."

"Are you sure?"

I laughed and smiled, taking in the beautiful arrangement but refusing to open the card while Ann stood in my office.

"I'm positive. They're necessary for the survival of the planet," I teased.

"Well . . . that's debatable." She winked at me and looked at the card in my hand. "I'm going to head out and meet my husband for drinks. Do you need anything else before I leave?"

"No. Go have fun with your man." I smiled as she grinned and shut the door after her.

I yanked out the card, excited to see what Shep had to say for himself since the silent treatment.

I hope these get there before I do. Surprise! I'm

bringing my favorite Greek takeout to eat with you while you work tonight.

My heart swelled up twice the size it should as I tucked the card back into the envelope and let out a happy sigh. He knew I had to work late most nights, and instead of making me give up my own dreams, he was willing to work with them when he could.

Wow.

Just wow.

I sniffed the fresh smell of the orchids and closed my eyes, willing away all the bad thoughts from earlier when I was with my client.

I couldn't keep painting all relationships with the same brush. Some did work out.

Then why did I have a gnawing feeling chipping away at me with every passing second?

I glanced around my office and the stacks of paper I needed to review before tomorrow morning, not to mention getting the ball rolling for Leslie from this afternoon.

Never mind always worrying that I'm going to wind up with a broken heart after I date someone. How would I ever be able to carve time out for a relationship?

I was the one who'd agreed to see where this could

go.

Shaking my head, I kicked off my heels and unzipped my skirt, quickly changing into a pair of jeans and a sweater. It was after six, and I'd decided long ago that once I stopped seeing clients and it was after hours, the least I could do for myself was to be comfortable.

My work phone beeped, and I wandered over to answer.

It was security.

"There is a visitor to see you. His name is Chip."

I chuckled, knowing it was Shep and he probably didn't even care that the guard mispronounced his name.

"I'll be right out." I quickly pulled my earrings off and dashed to the empty reception area, where a security guard had replaced our receptionist.

Shep was standing by the couch with three full plastic bags of food.

"Smells incredible," I said happily, waving at the security guard.

Shep nodded and glanced at the guard. "Thanks for getting ahold of her."

"No problem, man."

I ushered Shep to follow me down the hall to my office, where the giant orchids overtook my desk.

"Was it too much?" he asked, glancing at the arrangement.

"Not even a little bit." I smiled, taking one of the bags from him. "I have to confess. It made me feel really good after a really shitty day."

"Tougher than usual?" he asked, taking a seat in front of my desk as we unloaded all the food cartons. I shifted the stack of papers to the credenza behind me.

"New client. Those appointments are always grueling."

Shep nodded sympathetically. "It can't be spiritually uplifting to always hear what tore down another relationship."

"Exactly. Speaking of tearing things, I'm starving," I told him, ripping one of the takeout bags open rather than trying to untie it. "This has to be one of the sweetest things anyone has ever done for me."

"You mean like feed you?"

I laughed, nodding. The spread was magnificent.

We had dolmas, chicken skewers, pita, hummus, stuffed eggplant, and souvlaki.

Shep reached for a dolma and chowed on the stuffed grape leaf, and I wondered if this actually had a shot.

Chapter Twenty-Seven

Risky Business

Shep

Lucy's eyes lit up last night when I brought dinner over to her office. It was the craziest thing with her. The women I'd dated before always cared about where I took them out for dinner, what gifts I bought them, and who would see them on my arm.

Not Lucy.

She didn't seem to care about any of that stuff. I doubted she even finished the article that ran about me in the magazine. It was refreshing to find someone who didn't give a thought to any of that superficial crap.

But it was unsettling. This entire relationship type was new to me. She didn't even want a relationship with me to begin with.

For obvious reasons.

And I wasn't sure she even did now, but I was convenient and familiar. I think those two things were more important to Lucy than she even realized.

I let out a deep sigh and kicked my feet up on my desk. My assistant just left with an armful of folders and a determined look on her face. Tara didn't like having to always dig through all my receipts at the end of the month for expenses, so she was going to create a new filing system.

Shaking my head, I smiled, knowing I didn't have the heart to tell her that my previous assistant had tried the very same thing a year before.

It just didn't work for me. Filings, folders, and notebooks were all too tedious and rigid. My system worked plenty fine. I'd write on the back of the receipt who attended and for what if it were for a meal or what the item was needed for if it were something else. Then at the end of the month, I'd hand them all over to reconcile the expenses or deduct anything personal that interfered.

I scratched my chin and thought back to last night when I left Lucy at the office. She had slight shadows under each eye, but she looked just as beautiful as any other day. But I wondered if she was doing too much and if she'd ever let herself rest.

There was one thing I'd done well in life after starting my own business, and that was carving out enough *me* time, which might be one of the reasons I got into so much trouble at times. I shouldn't be dreaming up silly bets all the time, or I'd wind up like my father.

The thought chilled me to my core.

It wasn't that I didn't like my dad. I just knew that I had to keep him at arm's length, or all the bad memories from when my parents split would bum me out.

Really hard.

And then I'd usually try to console myself by finding a beautiful woman.

It was a vicious cycle and made absolutely no sense.

But the weird thing was that since I'd screwed up my chances with Lucy on the first night at the matchmaking event, I hadn't actually slept with anyone. I didn't even know why. It was like things just became meaningless, and I felt like a complete ass, which I'd always managed not to do when dating women. I was always upfront with them. They knew before climbing in the sack with me that there was nowhere for the fling to go but down.

Until Lucy.

Then the thought of other women just started

feeling . . . gross. Like why did I need quantity? What was I really searching for, or more to the point, avoiding?

And last night, I wanted so badly to rip Lucy's clothes off and taste her skin, rub her back to make the tension go away, slide inside her and . . . just be.

But I knew better.

It didn't matter that we'd already been teetering on that line of having sex. She'd made it a point to get us very close before putting a stop to it, and I respected that. I always would.

Just like last night.

If we were really starting over, I needed to pace things with her.

The thought made my pants tight, and I brought my legs off my desk to hide the surprise that had suddenly erupted from merely thinking about Lucy.

She sighed so heavily last night over and over again as she'd stared at her pleadings, took endless notes, and looked up things online that I couldn't imagine how she found what she did pleasurable. Instead, it seemed to drain her.

When I'd left, she still thought she had another hour or so before she could go home. I offered to stay, but I could see that she needed some time.

But the moment I left her office, I missed being near

her.

It was funny how the little things turned me on about her, like when she'd scan documents, she dug her teeth into her bottom lip and sucked a little, making a clicking sound. Or when she needed to look at something online, she'd always rub her eyes and tilt her head before scrolling on her screen. Or the way she'd take notes with her knee bobbing and her hand angled so the pen wrote fluidly. But my favorite was when a piece of hair would get in her way. She'd do a couple of poofs of air from her rounded lips to blow the strays away.

Tara came back in with a stack of colorful folders and set them down on my desk. I was grateful for the shield between us so she didn't spot anything unusual from my daydreaming about a woman who was most definitely out of my league.

"Okay. It shouldn't be hard to train yourself. Red folders are for office items. The green folder is food and beverages. Yellow is travel." She looked up at me.

"Oh, a little different from when Lila did this for me."

She scowled. "What do you mean?"

"Last year, we gave this a go, but it didn't last long."

"Well, I'm not a quitter."

I chuckled and slid the folders toward me and read the rest of the categories.

"I'm headed out early today to pick up my parents from the airport."

I nodded. News to me. "Yup."

"You didn't remember, did you?"

I laughed, shaking my head. "Nope."

She tilted her head slowly. "You've been kind of out of it lately."

"What do you mean?"

She shrugged.

"You can't tell your boss that and not explain."

"I don't know. You've always been pretty laidback, but recently, I've noticed you kind of drifting off."

"Like falling asleep?" I was sure that hadn't happened, even when the developers droned on about something that I didn't need to know the details about.

Tara laughed. "No, like staring at a wall. Forgetting when I have time off. Not remembering the receptionist's birthday."

My jaw dropped, and she winked at me. "Don't worry. I remembered and got her a great gift card to the spa down the road."

"Thank you."

"Is everything okay?"

Tara and I always had a pretty open dialogue since

she'd been promoted from reception. She was down to earth and loved to set me straight. When my other assistant moved to a different department, I had to nearly beg Tara to apply. She didn't think she had the qualifications, but I knew she'd do great. And I was right.

"Yeah. Just trying to sort life stuff out."

"Is it the fallout from the magazine spread?"

I laughed and shook my head. "Fallout?"

She grinned, flashing a wicked grin. "You know, declaring that you're impossible to love or whatever it was you said had to set hearts a-blazing in Scattlc."

I rolled my eyes. "I doubt that. But thanks, and no. It's not about the article. I'm just kind of wondering if I'd made the right choices over the years."

She glanced around my spacious office and smiled. "I'd say you're doing just fine, by the looks of it. Whatever's going on in your life, just trust your gut. It's done good things for you so far."

I smiled and gave a quick nod. "Thanks, Tara."

"You're welcome. Now, use those folders." She left my office and closed the door behind her while I thought about what she'd said.

She was right on many levels. When it came to taking risks professionally, I'd been right ninety-nine percent of the time, and the other one percent was because I didn't see the obvious. I didn't listen to my heart.

But the same couldn't be said about my personal life.

It had been a complete failure from the moment my dad and mom divorced. It didn't help that it paralleled my own breakup. My high school girlfriend cheated on me the moment we stepped foot in college. From that moment on, I stopped thinking there was a future with women. It was more of a short-term preoccupation.

That way of thinking, doing, acting, behaving, and living worked just fine for me.

Up until Lucy.

The walls I'd built around my heart for every meaningless encounter felt as strong as steel.

Up until Lucy.

Now, I wasn't sure I wanted something without meaning. But I also didn't have a clue how to do the other kind of relationship.

The one where you actually had to work at things and work through things if issues arose.

But that was the thing.

With Lucy, it didn't feel like there would ever be any issues.

We were so in synch. She knew how to flip it right

back to me, and she didn't care if I did the same. I liked our banter.

I reached for my phone and texted her.

You free for lunch?

I saw the little dots as she typed back.

I have a client lunch scheduled at 12:30, but I never eat during those. You free at 2:00?

Surprise dashed through me. I'd totally expected her to tell me she couldn't. Maybe this thing could work.

Absolutely. How about the café at the bottom of your building?

She wrote back.

The Pakistan spot or the sandwich spot?

Ah. I didn't know there were two.

The Pakistani place, for sure. I love their Chana

Curry.

Her texts nearly trampled mine.

I've been thinking about you.

Me too!

My chest squeezed into a new sensation. It was like I was nervous and excited while feeling like I was completely doomed with where this was headed. But I couldn't let that text go without replying.

I've been fantasizing about you every second since I left last night.

Her text slid right over.

Fantasizing? Like what?

I smiled.

Like I'd tell you. Then it won't come true.

She quickly replied.

That's a wish, not a fantasy.

I chuckled and typed a few words.

Either way, I'm not risking it.

After a couple of minutes, a new text popped up.

Since when have you stopped being a risk-taker?

Since I started to fall for you. I stared at my screen and decided not to text.

Chapter Twenty-Eight

All Valentined Up

Lucy

The smells coming from the café were intoxicating. There was something about the rice and spicy chickpea combo that just made my mouth water. I spotted Shep in the corner by the window, and he stood and waved before coming over to me. He looked really good. His broad shoulders filled out his button-down, and he looked like he didn't shave this morning, which gave him a more rugged look. He was impossible to ignore in a room full of suits.

The café was set up like a cafeteria, so he left his jacket at the table and met me over where we grabbed a tray and pointed at which curries we wanted the chef to pour over our rice.

Shep glanced around the place and noticed most of the suits sitting down and smiled.

"If it didn't look like half your office was down here, I'd lean over and kiss you."

The mere mention of kissing made me rattled and hot at the same time. It also made me feel slightly vulnerable since a kiss was something that I wanted, and he knew it.

I cleared my throat. "It's nice to see you too."

Gawd. Why did I sound so prim when what I really wanted to do was kiss him back?

We slid our tray to the cashier, and Shep paid for our lunches. By the time we sat down, I'd said hi to several coworkers and realized Shep was right.

As he took a seat, I studied him, wondering how he could be so considerate like this yet also take up a bet with someone to sabotage a dating event.

He was an enigma wrapped in a Greek god's persona with the humor of a rehabilitated frat guy.

I took a bite of curry and happily sighed.

"Were you in a frat house?"

He looked up at me. "Why do you ask?"

I shrugged and took another bite. "Just trying to put the pieces together."

He frowned and shook his head. "About what?"

I pushed around my rice and twisted my lips into a pout. "Well, how you can be so considerate. You brought me dinner when you knew I would be working late. You volunteered to have a late lunch just to fit my schedule today. Yet, you'd do something kind of dumb for a bet. You're smarter than most men I've met. But . . ."

A fleck of guilt darted through his gaze while his jaw tightened. He swallowed hard as his throat constricted and nodded, wiping his mouth with a napkin.

"Briefly. But it wasn't for me. Being around that much testosterone didn't seem like my idea of a good time."

"Even though they have great parties?" I teased.

"You went to some frat parties?" He laughed his deep rumble of a laugh, which made my insides beat for him. There was just something so mischievous about the sound.

I held up my index finger and smiled. "One, but only because my friend at the time begged me to go." She shivered. "Way too much testosterone."

"Unfortunately, my bad habits can only be blamed on me. And Mike."

I chuckled. "No shame in taking him down?"

He smoothed his fingers over a rough patch of stubble along his jaw. "None at all."

"Good to know."

"You know Valentine's Day weekend starts tomorrow, right? You haven't forgotten our deal."

"You mean the romantic part about me being able to bring my laptop? No. I haven't forgotten. But tomorrow isn't the fourteenth."

"Right. It's the thirteenth, but our weekend getaway starts tomorrow."

Shep's phone buzzed, and he glanced at it. "Just my sister." He didn't bother to look at it when my phone buzzed as well. "She didn't text you too, did she?" He grinned, and I glanced at my phone when another message slid over.

"Nope. Mae and Dani." It was odd that they both messaged at the same time, but I didn't want to be rude to Shep. He didn't read his message, and I would do the same courtesy.

He leaned a little closer. "I have a secret."

"Only one?"

He smiled wider and shook his head. "I can't stop thinking about you."

My cheeks warmed, and I took a deep breath to get ahold of myself. The truth was that when I wasn't zoned into my clients' cases, my mind always drifted to Shep.

"I'm kind of in the same predicament," I confessed.

Shep looked relieved and somewhat amused, which

276

worried me on some deeper level, probably all relating back to my chosen profession and upbringing . . .

But was this thing turning real between us, or was I just another conquest, someone who played a little harder to get who intrigued him? I just didn't know.

Mae texted again, so I silenced my phone. But I got a little worried. Mae rarely texted back-to-back unless she needed something.

Shep spotted my worry and nodded toward my phone.

"If you need to do something or read your messages, I'm totally fine."

"Thanks. Sorry." I slid my phone on and saw the beginning of Mae's text, and realized I didn't have to worry.

Did you see what just went viral?

I didn't bother to continue reading the message since all limbs were accounted for, and there didn't seem to be an emergency. Leave it to my sister to be on top of whatever was floating around social media.

I looked up at Shep, and I saw genuine concern in his eyes, which tugged at me. That couldn't be faked, right? Why would a guy put that much effort into something that was just a number or another notch in the belt? He couldn't.

"Everything okay?" he asked.

I chuckled and nodded. "Thankfully, just some fashion or gossip emergency from today's social media blitz that my sister forwarded me. I'll catch up later."

Shep winked and nodded. "My sister keeps me informed of all that too."

I rolled my eyes. "Lucky us."

His eyes stayed on mine, and my blood filled with heat that I couldn't blame on the curry. This man could excite me midday in a café full of lawyers.

It was infuriating and delightful all at once.

I bit my lip and drew a breath. "You know, I'd love to have you over for dinner tonight. I can't promise anything fancier than a pizza."

Shep pushed away his empty plate. "Count me in."

A tingle of excitement ran down my spine at the thought of seeing him somewhere other than a public place. Maybe I'd finally get enough courage tonight to dive into the next level.

"I have a meeting at six tonight, but I bet I can be at my house by eight. Is that too late?"

"Not in the slightest." His smile only widened as he took a look around the café before bringing his face back to mine. "Now, if only I could figure out what to do for the next several hours to occupy myself rather than fantasizing about tonight."

I crossed my legs, feeling heat pool in my belly as my mind went to the night as well. It would take every ounce of restraint I had not to sleep with Shep.

My phone dinged, but this time it was for a meeting, and I knew I had to get back

"That one sounded different." Shep glanced at my phone.

"Yeah. I've got to get back upstairs. I have a client arriving in ten minutes."

"Totally get it." He nodded but reached for my hand across the table. All it took was his touch to send my mind spinning and my body swelling with warmth again. "But I appreciate you carving time out for this."

"A girl's got to eat," I joked.

Shep's eyes swept to my mouth before meeting my gaze. "I'll remember that."

My heart stalled for a brief second when he looked at me, and I couldn't believe how he made me feel like the most beautiful woman in the world.

"Thank you."

He gathered our paper plates and napkins to take to the trash but stopped.

"I'm the lucky one here, Lucy. I appreciate you making time. I know I have a lot of work to do to earn your respect."

His words sank into me as my heart and mind collided with one another, praying there was a future with him.

But with every day spent with him, I realized I was becoming more and more fearful that I would end up irrevocably broken when this was all done.

"Keep feeding me, and I'm sure all will be forgotten."

"But how about forgiven?"

I smiled, realizing how perceptive Shep was, and I refused to believe a man who merely collected women would care. Shep cared.

He closed the space between us and moved his mouth next to my ear. "If there weren't so many of your coworkers here, I'd pull you into my arms so you could feel how much I'm craving you."

My breath hitched as his words swam around my mind, and he took a step back.

His words left me dizzy with something I'd never felt for another man. But I couldn't show him all my cards.

Eyeing him coolly, I let barely a smile touch my lips. "I look forward to that, Shep."

He laughed as I turned and walked out of the café,

wishing with every ounce of resolve I had that I didn't need to be kissed.

Chapter Twenty-Nine

Strangely Sexy

Shep

Last night with Lucy was incredible, and all we did was stay up all night talking. I learned so much about her family, and I confessed things to her that I probably should have kept to myself.

But there was something just so easy about being with her that I couldn't help myself.

If we'd met under different circumstances where I wasn't a dumbass, and she'd met Shep, the CEO of Pesh Gaming, I was certain things would be different.

She'd be able to trust me with her entire heart. There wouldn't be any reservations like there were at the moment.

Deservedly so.

And that question yesterday at lunch about me belonging to a fraternity was a punch to the gut. I'd obviously behaved like I'd been the president of partying, gambling, and womanizing with the best of Alphabet Row.

I slipped a receipt into one of the colorful folders my assistant set up for me and shook my head. Maybe I could learn a new system.

I used to think if it wasn't broken, don't fix it. But the definition of broken was a little subjective, and obviously, growth was good.

I closed my laptop and glanced out the window. A thick blanket of grey clouds hovered over a quilt of varying shades while the sky furiously shook droplets upon us.

It wasn't exactly the perfect weather for a drive to the mountains, but it was a typical Seattle day in February.

All morning, I'd tentatively waited for a message from Lucy to come over, canceling the whole weekend.

By lunch, I felt pretty good about it.

My assistant peeked her head into my office. She had a funny look on her face.

"Everything okay?" she asked.

I nodded. "Absolutely. Do you have any plans for Valentine's Day?"

Tara lit up. "My hubby is treating me to a weekend of

nothing but books, candles, baths, and comfort food."

"Nice. I could take some lessons from him."

She beamed and nodded. "He's a great guy."

I nodded in agreement.

"Okay, then. I'll just get back at it. I just wanted to make sure you were doing okay."

She spun around, and I scowled, wondering why she thought I wasn't okay. Had I been talking to myself? I scratched my head and let out a sigh just as the clock struck two.

I grabbed my jacket and walked over to Tara.

"I think I'm going to head out early."

She nodded sympathetically. "I totally get it. You need to decompress and figure things out."

"Thanks." I scratched my head, unsure of what she meant. Did I seem that confused today?

I certainly felt conflicted, but I thought I did a better job of hiding what was truly running through my mind this morning while sitting in on a developer meeting.

As I made my way to the elevator, a text came over.

Oh, no. This was it.

The big cancellation from Lucy.

I slid on my phone, stepped on the elevator to the parking garage, and looked down at the screen.

I'm counting the minutes. I can't wait to see you. I worked doubly hard so I wouldn't have many distractions this weekend. Can't wait.

All of my worries washed away as I reread her text and replied with a heart. But then I thought maybe that wasn't enough. So, I sat in the car and typed a quick message.

Is it bad that I can't get enough of you?

She wrote back quickly.

Not bad. Amazing.

I couldn't wipe the ridiculous grin off my face. I needed to see Lucy again. I wanted to hear about her day, what she worked on, how many clients she saw, and what cases gave her the most grief. I wanted it all from her.

It took everything I had not to wind myself up into a blithering idiot by the time I pulled up in front of her building.

I texted that I was out front, and within seconds, she wheeled out an expensive piece of luggage and made her way toward my car while trying not to laugh at the vehicle I'd pulled up in. I'd chosen this car just to make her smile.

Lucy looked even more beautiful than I remembered, and my car trick worked. It was like every day was a freaking surprise with her, and I loved it. The softness of her smile and the way her green eyes sparkled as they met mine made me ache for her. It didn't hurt that her pink blouse tugged slightly at her breasts when she took off her jacket. I hopped out and put her bag into the car as the passenger door magically rose.

"You don't have a bag?" she asked, glancing into the car.

"Don't need one."

"Really? I thought we were going somewhere." She stood in front of the passenger door that I'd opened.

"We are, and I'll give you details on the way there."

She eyed me and then looked at the car and laughed. "Fine, but I don't usually get into cars with strange men without knowing the destination."

I clutched my heart as she climbed into the car.

"Sexy. Addicting. Provocative . . ." I smiled. "I've heard them all. But not strange."

She laughed as the overhead door closed before I walked around and climbed into the driver's seat.

After all, it wasn't every day that I drove my DeLorean. It was a goofy car for goofy occasions.

Lucy turned in her seat. "Why does this car look like it belongs in *Back to the Future*?"

"Because it does. You're riding in a DeLorean. I just try to find things to make me happy. Life is too short as it is." I glanced at her, wondering what she thought. "Plus, I hoped it would make you smile."

Her eyes widened in surprise. "These things are real? Does it come with a flux capacitor too?"

"Ah, so you know eighties movies well?"

She smiled and nodded. "I had a whole list I'd watch with Mae on the weekends back when DVDs were a thing." She glanced around as I pulled into traffic. "And we even had some VHS tapes floating around."

"No way," I deadpanned.

She rested her head on the seat and looked out the window.

"I can't even tell you how long it's been since I took an early afternoon from work."

"Don't you have PTO?"

She laughed as if I'd said something ridiculous before realizing I was serious.

"It's frowned upon. They even have a plan where you can donate your PTO to a charity of your choice in pay."

I shook my head. "Wow. I always make sure my

employees take advantage of their time off. I guess it's different when every minute is billable."

She nodded. "Every second is something they are considering. The software is out there."

"Doesn't it exhaust you, Lucy?"

I pulled onto the freeway heading east toward the mountains.

"It does, but I paid a lot of money to make a lot of money. I can't let the system beat me down, especially before I make partner."

I let out a deep breath, nodding. "You are an incredible gift to the world."

She chuckled. "I don't think most people in the world would view a divorce attorney as a gift."

"Do you know what's crazy?" I asked.

Lucy shook her head and hummed no.

"Even though we were literally just talking about your profession, I wasn't thinking about you as a divorce attorney. I just see you as Lucy."

She smirked and glanced at me. "You don't see a tough-as-nails, blood-dripping invoice waiting to happen?"

I laughed. "Well, when you put it that way . . . still no."

"Then what do you see?"

"I see a woman who is kind, family-oriented, smarter than any human I've met, compassionate, and beautiful."

"Humph." She stretched her legs. "I'll have to remember that."

"Please do."

"Do you want to know what I think about when I look at you?" she asked softly.

"You mean the sexy stranger?"

She nodded. "Yeah. Him."

"Just let me down easy, okay?"

"I see a grown man who still has boyish good looks and a mischievousness that reminds me how good it is to be alive. I see a guy who is extremely intelligent and loving. And someone who is as broken as me when it comes to love. And you pulling up in a ride like this after the crappy day I had made me happier than you could imagine."

Hearing her voice describe me in a way very few saw me made my chest tighten. It was almost hard to breathe.

Maybe because I was worried no one but Lucy would see me like that.

I slid my hand over to her knee, and she placed her hand on top of mine.

She giggled and glanced at the ceiling of the car. "And thank you for thinking of picking me up in this beast. It made my day."

I squeezed her hand and smiled as we continued the drive to my second home.

"Okay. We aren't headed to any airports, so where are we going?"

I glanced at her as I turned onto the highway, taking us up the mountain to my home.

"You really want to know?"

"Obviously."

"I have a home up in the mountains."

She looked shocked. "You do?"

I nodded as I slid my hand off her knee.

"For a guy who proclaims he doesn't do the relationship thing, you do a really good job at it."

I shrugged. "Maybe I just never found the right person."

"That's smooth, Shep."

"It's true." I let out a deep breath. "In fact, you're the first woman I've ever brought up to my place."

She narrowed her eyes on me. "How long have you owned it?"

I laughed, shaking my head. "You are such a lawyer."

She groaned and slid down in her seat a little. "Sorry. I can't help myself."

"And I think it's adorable."

"Adorable? That's not one I've heard before. Annoying . . . know-it-all . . . boring." She grinned at me. "But not adorable."

"The one thing you aren't is boring. You keep me on my toes at all times."

She tucked a piece of hair behind her ear, and I wished we were closer to my place so I could kiss her right behind her ear and smell her intoxicatingly sweet scent of soap and perfume and whatever else that was uniquely Lucy.

She was heaven.

"Well, I don't know if that's a good thing, but I'll take it."

Lucy rested her head on the seat, and I noticed that within a few minutes, she fell asleep, and I knew she needed this escape more than most. I only hoped she wasn't disappointed.

Chapter Thirty

Cozy Cabin of Dreams

Lucy

I didn't know how long I'd slept, but when I woke up, it was nearly dark, and Shep had just turned onto an exit.

Piled snow lined the edges of the road, and I sat up straighter.

"Is this really the car we should have taken up here?"

He laughed. "Probably not, but it was worth the smile I got earlier."

Even though the snow was deep, the road was bare, and within minutes, he made a left down a country road with nothing but trees bowing from the weight of the latest snowfall.

"This is absolutely perfect," I said, looking out the window.

He slid his hand to my knee, and I felt a thrill from the unknown. Heat pooled deep within my belly, and I couldn't believe I was actually in such a beautiful place with such a great guy.

I snuck a look at Shep, and I couldn't help but feel a little squeeze of hope in my chest.

What if I'd accidentally found the one? That guy who thought my quirks were adorable and my annoyances were worth embracing?

I cleared my throat and looked out the window as I tried to push down the excitement for the weekend ahead. This was how people got caught up in relationships that never should have happened.

Hormones.

I needed to take one step at a time and not jump over the entire getting-to-know-a-person thing.

What I hadn't told Shep yet was that I'd gone into the office super early this morning so that I could get most everything done before our getaway.

Judging by the happiness on his face, he'd be thrilled to find that out.

"Here we are." Shep pulled down a long driveway with Douglas firs towering over the small, freshly plowed road with snow piled taller than our car. "I have to confess that I'm relieved that my snowplow guy is reliable. Otherwise, I really would have regretted my vehicle selection."

I chuckled and nodded as my cell buzzed in my pocket. "This car sets the tone for the weekend, but it wouldn't have been completely awesome having to hike in from the road."

Shep nodded. "So, I owe the entire success of the holiday weekend to the plow guy, or this car's insufficiencies would have been on full display."

"You do." I let out a happy sigh as Shep slowed the car even more. "But the car really did tell me a lot about what to expect this weekend."

I glanced at my phone and saw it was another gossip text from my sister and shoved it back into my pocket.

He looked at me. "What did the DeLorean tell you?"

"Let's see . . . happy, fun, and light. No real boundaries or responsibilities. The possibilities are endless." I grinned at him, feeling like I was a teenager experiencing my first crush. "Perfect for Valentine's Day."

"Wow. That is a lot of pressure." Shep laughed, keeping his eyes ahead. "But I hope you have an amazing weekend. You more than deserve a little break."

His voice was so tender, and when I snuck a peek at him, it looked like he meant it. As if he wanted to swoop in and make our getaway absolutely perfect.

The rush of emotion that coated every part of me was impossible to shake.

Shep was a good guy.

Even though he was probably exactly the opposite of any guy I thought I needed, he was the one who'd somehow managed to make me feel fun again.

"It's been a long time since I've been on a getaway."

"Yeah? How long?" Shep asked.

"Uh, forever."

Shep chuckled as the car slowed, and I turned my head to see his house come into view.

This wasn't a little cabin or A-frame. This home was sprawling, with a large garage jetting off from the L-shape of the main house. The style was cozy and farmhouse with a mix of rustic touches to fit into the mountains.

"This is completely opposite from your place in the city." I glanced at him as he pulled us into the garage, where several cars were parked in tandem.

"Wow. You like cars, I see."

He shrugged. "When you're young and get a lot of money pretty quickly, it seemed like the logical next step. Buy useless cars and let them sit in a garage."

I chuckled. "This car is not useless. It made me forget

about my work this morning."

"Good. Mission completed."

The garage was spotless. The area seemed fit for a museum with spotless, shiny epoxy floors and bright white walls with several old gas station signs pinned up.

"I just had no idea about any of this." And I wasn't even sure what part I didn't expect. The fact that he was a really decent guy or that he had a mountain home with a garage bigger than my own place.

"Yeah?" He looked at me with a smirk. "Impressed?"

"Would I sound completely shallow if I said yes?"

"Not completely . . ." He winked at me and climbed out of the car and raised my car door to help me out.

"Those car doors are really Space Age."

Shep grinned. "Nothing like the eighties to remind us how far we've come in the world."

He brushed a piece of hair that had been stuck to my cheek. I had a bad feeling that I might have drooled during my nap.

"I hope I didn't slobber on your seats."

He chuckled, pulling out my bag. "You feel better after the nap?"

"Immensely. I'm so sorry for falling asleep."

"No. I totally get it, and now you'll have plenty of

energy for the rest of the weekend."

My brows lifted. "Is that so? What kind of activities do you have planned? What kind of energy are we talking about?"

Shep didn't answer. He didn't need to. The twinkle in his gaze told me there might be a lot of surprises for the weekend, and I couldn't help but feel dizzy with excitement. I honestly couldn't remember the last time I didn't let work hang on every thought, where I felt human again.

I followed him to the door to the interior of the home and felt my nerves go on edge with each step. Just being alone with him for an entire weekend created a frisson of electricity within me.

He opened the door and rolled my suitcase inside. "After you."

"Thank you."

I stepped inside an enormous mudroom where skis and snowboards hung on the wall, along with snowshoes, tennis rackets, and a purple sled.

"You go sledding often?"

He grinned. "It's for Hunter. My nephew."

"Ah, right." I spun around, taking everything in and trying to reconcile it with the condo he kept in Seattle.

"Okay. Fine. I sled too."

I chuckled as his fingers grazed along my back, sending a thrill of the unknown through me. It was as if Shep was a magnet of unexpected trouble for me.

Maybe that was why I'd become so drawn to him and downright enamored with everything about him.

Shep was obviously smart. He had a way with words. He was cute. He didn't expect things from me.

"I can't thank you enough for bringing me here," I told him as his gaze locked on mine. His smile grew as he took in my reaction to his home. "It feels like a true vacation, and I'm still in the mudroom."

But I knew I didn't need to see any more to know what I sensed. This place felt so homey and cozy. I wouldn't be surprised if there was a reading nook screaming my name in one of these rooms. It wasn't like his condo wasn't warm, but it felt very modern and sleek. Here, the bright white trim contrasted the rustic wooden furnishings nicely.

"This is really homey."

He shut the door behind us. "You think so?"

"I do. I'm shocked."

"What? You think I don't have it in me?"

"Have what in you?"

Shep's brows quirked. "The ability to be a family guy."

"I don't know. I never really thought about it before."

Okay, that was a lie. I might have wondered if he'd ever want kids with the woman he settled down with, but that was after convincing myself he would actually settle down with someone.

"It's nice to see another side of you," I confessed.

Shep smiled and rolled my bag into the hallway leading out of the mudroom. "Then I'm glad I brought you up here. Maybe someday, I can dig myself out of the relationship grave I put myself in with you."

My heart tugged. Did he really want more, or did he just know how to make me feel wanted?

I shoved the thoughts away. It didn't matter. This weekend was all about fun.

I stepped into the hallway, which was filled with paintings of old cabins and snow scenes.

As I followed him down the hallway, he stopped and turned to face me.

He put his hands on my shoulders and braced himself. "So, big question."

"Let me have it."

"I have a King bed in my room, or you can choose a guest room you'd rather stay in."

"You mean by myself?"

He nodded with a glint in his eyes.

"I didn't come all this way to stay in a bed by myself."

Shep lit up and nodded. "I'm really good at keeping the bed warm. It's like I was born to be a radiator."

I nodded, remembering the first and only night we'd spent together. We hadn't had sex, but we'd had an amazing time, and I did remember he was warm.

And naked.

"Do you sleep in pajamas?" I asked, wondering if that was a one-time deal.

"Sometimes. I certainly can, if you want."

My cheeks warmed at the thought of him sleeping next to me in the nude, and I couldn't wipe the smile off my mouth that had taken over.

"I take that as a . . ." His voice trailed off.

"Well, I don't want to put you out. You know. Whatever you feel most comfortable with," I explained. "I mean, if you need to be in the buff, by all means . . ."

The way Shep looked at me made my world spin into a completely chaotic one where everything was tilted slightly, and I couldn't count on myself to make smart and sound choices.

But being in front of him made that all okay. It suddenly didn't matter if things were wonky in my world with

Shep at the helm.

Because he somehow also made me feel like he'd protect me and shelter me from the chaos.

Basically, I was completely confused.

"Okay, so on to the rest of the house. The entrance to the house is actually here." He pointed over to the right as I snuck next to him to see a vaulted ceiling with light pine timbers spanning the space and a rustic chandelier larger than his DeLorean dangling in the middle of the room.

"Beautiful," I said softly, truly in awe.

It wasn't that I hadn't seen nice things before, and I certainly brought in a large income, but this type of elegance wasn't something I'd ever been exposed to growing up. The moment my dad walked out on my mom, things went from tight to impossible. It was one of the driving forces behind wanting to provide a good living for myself and ensure that I could send Mae to college, which I'd managed to do.

But this felt . . . incredible.

Surreal.

"I'll show you around the rest of the house later, but I had a chef come and prepare some dinner for us. There's a steak salad in the fridge, along with some dessert. And there is a quiche waiting for us to pop into the oven in the morning."

My jaw dropped. "Really? This feels like it's straight

out of a movie."

Shep looked confused, and that's when I realized that his parents' divorce was very different from mine. We were in different leagues.

I suddenly felt self-conscious about being in awe.

Kind of foolish to think that my degree and profession could prepare me for this kind of world.

"Are you okay?" he asked. "We don't have to eat if you're not hungry."

I bit my lip and let out a slow breath, feeling absolutely insecure for the first time in a very long time.

"This is all so . . ." I waved my hands around. "This is a lot."

Shep glanced around the house and brought his eyes back to mine.

"I didn't grow up with this kind of normal. The townhome I bought myself was the nicest home I've lived in."

"And it's gorgeous," he added. "It's amazing. You're amazing."

"I just . . ." I closed my eyes and shook my head. "I can't believe I'm admitting this, but I feel out of my league."

Surprise splashed across Shep's face. "Over this house?"

I nodded slowly.

"Lucy, you are out of my league. You could stomp my guts in court, and I pray you never will. You eat men like me for breakfast. You're smarter than any woman I've met, and I've met a lot of them." He closed his mouth when he realized what that sounded like.

I chuckled. "I know I've got brains. It's not like that. It's just these are things I've dreamed of providing for myself and my family, and here you have it all. I mean, you had a chef come out to prepare meals? I mean, I'm excited when I go to the swanky grocery store on the way home and pick up some prepared meals."

"All I did was get lucky in life, and I do that most of the time myself."

"I don't believe that for a second," I assured him. "You created a highly addictive platform akin to crack that makes me giddy just thinking about it. That takes talent, dedication, and hard work."

"Well, then, thank you for buying the chandelier indirectly." He winked at me and grimaced at the same time. "I know my upbringing put me in a solid place before any of this happened. I mean, I'm fully aware that while my dad was busy entertaining ladies other than my mom at our lake house, we kind of had a lot."

"And we had very little." I couldn't believe this was

hitting me so hard. "But you seem so down to earth."

"Realizing what my father did to my mom all those years ago and what she sacrificed for us made me strive to do better. I wanted to show my dad that I could be just as successful. I could have more than one house. I could have lots of cars. But I could treat people well while doing so. Sometimes, I think my parents' divorce didn't screw with me, and other times, I know it completely skewed how I view things. But this." Shep twirled his finger around the room. "It's just stuff."

My chest started to loosen as Shep's words sank into me. He might always seem fun and carefree, but his father's actions messed him up more than he cared to admit. Just like mine had.

"You're right. I don't know why I let this big house and your fancy cars get to me." I chuckled, feeling kind of silly about it. Life wasn't a competition, and even if it were, we all had to begin at our own starting line.

"I have a confession."

"Oh, no," I muttered, shaking my head.

"I don't want to turn out like my dad. I don't see myself living in a condo in the middle of Seattle for the rest of my life. This is what I want. A house. A family to fill the house. I'm tired of the chase, Lucy. I don't want to be single forever."

I nodded, feeling a lump in my throat. Was this where we would start over? Really start over and peel back the layers?

So what that he'd made a mockery of a matchmaking event? He'd confessed and felt bad about it and swore to leave bets and pranks behind.

Shep was letting me see a side of him that was rare to the outside world. I could feel it deep within me. I wanted to believe in the idea of love.

He looped his fingers through mine and pulled me toward a great room down a hall overlooking the snowy woods. A stone fireplace took up the corner, reaching toward the second story.

"This is beautiful," I said, seeing an ivory bouclé sectional that looked cozy enough that I wanted to dive onto it and never leave.

I couldn't even imagine what it was like to spend the holidays up in the mountains in a lodge like this. The idea had become a definite family goal for Mae and me.

Shep squeezed my hand and let out a deep breath.

"I hope you like it here," Shep said softly.

I turned and looked into his beautiful blue eyes, feeling a flutter of something I couldn't decipher. "This place is really special, Shep. I hope your dream comes true someday."

His eyes locked on mine, and he nodded. "Me too."

Chapter Thirty-One

Without Another Thought

Shep

I wanted to kiss Lucy so badly my lips ached. I reached for her other hand and pulled her into me.

"I hope so too, Lucy."

Her brilliant green eyes stayed on mine as she nodded, but I couldn't help but shake at her words. *I hope your dream comes true someday.*

She didn't include herself in there. She was distancing herself from me once again. It was so hard to know where to go with her, what to say sometimes.

There were moments when I felt so close and connected to Lucy and like we could actually start this thing and make it forever, and then other times it felt like no matter what, I'd sealed my fate the night of the matchmaking event.

I just didn't know.

Maybe it was all too much. Maybe I'd just been pushing my hopes and dreams on her whether or not she wanted to really try something between us.

But I couldn't handle not knowing.

"Lucy, I'm going to come clean with you."

"Your name isn't really Shep?" she teased while her eyes still stayed on mine.

I chuckled and shook my head. "I'm definitely Shep. I deserve that." I let out a deep breath, realizing I really might have screwed up any chances with Lucy since she first knew me as Perry.

"I'm falling really hard, Lucy. I can't get you out of my mind. The thought of going along with your little experiment where I primed you for other men nearly killed me. I couldn't do it. I don't want to think about you with anyone else. You make every day brighter in my life just knowing you're wandering around Seattle somewhere, and maybe I'll bump into you. Or better yet, convince you to have lunch or dinner with me." My pulse pounded as I confessed something I didn't think possible.

She tipped her chin toward me and nodded slowly. "I'm scared, Shep. I don't want to wind up like the crying men and women in my office. I don't want to end up a shell of myself because I let my heart fall too hard for something that is unattainable while my mind kept screaming no." Lucy sucked her bottom lip for a second and let out a sigh. "But this feels so right. I feel safe with you, and that's what worries me."

"Why does that frighten you?"

"Because isn't that how women fall hard? They finally let their guard down because they feel safe?" She groaned. "What if this is the beginning of the end?"

Lucy's eyes landed on my lips, and she uncoiled her fingers from mine as her chest rose with a deep breath.

Without another thought, my lips crashed down to hers. I couldn't take it any longer. I had to have her. I needed to prove to her that I wasn't going anywhere. That I loved her. That we would be okay. We would be one of those couples who'd last forever.

The taste of her lips reminded me of a candy store, and I couldn't help myself from smiling between kisses. She giggled and hesitantly pulled back.

"Is my cherry ChapStick too much?"

I shook my head. "It's perfect. You're perfect."

"Shep, there's no such thing as perfect."

I knew she was wrong. She was my perfect in every way. My fingers tangled through her hair, and I tilted her chin up as we kissed again. But this time, I could feel her hips crushing into me, the heat between her legs, the frenzied scuttle of her hands underneath my shirt. She was ready. I pulled Lucy's shirt off, and she pulled off the rest of her outfit and tossed it on the floor as she hopped onto me. I caught her as she wrapped her legs around my waist, and I moved us to the bedroom. I'd waited long enough for this.

Lucy ripped off my shirt, and it fell to the ground as my lips brushed along her neck. I couldn't help but memorize every part of her. The little creases along her skin, the sweet cherry smell, the little goosebumps from where my hands brushed her shoulders.

We crashed to the bed in a crazy fit of passion and firsts. She let out a nervous giggle, but that wasn't before straddling me and combing her fingers through my hair. I nipped and tugged on her breasts, feeling her thighs clench around me as I flipped us over.

My mouth devoured every part of her body. My lips felt the softness of her breasts. My tongue tasted the sweetness of her nipples. Everything about Lucy was incredible. Her fingers tangled through my hair as I looked up into her eyes. My hands traveled down her belly into the V of her thighs.

"Mmm." Lucy's lips let out a little hum as she arched her back and closed her eyes.

I smiled and let my fingers go deeper into the warmth

and wetness between her legs as her body writhed in ecstasy. I'd seen this side of Lucy before, and it never failed to make me want to consume all of her. As she tipped to the edge, she opened her eyes and shook her head.

"Shep, I need to feel you inside me," she moaned. "Please."

The whimper in her voice and the need for me to be inside her nearly broke me as I slid out my fingers and pushed inside her, still teasing her with my hands.

"Oh, Shep," she hissed as I moved inside her. "Amazing."

"Yeah?" I said, nuzzling my mouth next to her neck as her body stayed on the verge with every thrust. I brushed my thumb along her thighs and between them as I dove deeper and felt her legs wrap around me.

"Please don't stop. I love . . ."

Please say 'you'.

"This."

Her small hands ran across my back as her breathing turned ragged, and she spun me into another galaxy as I savored every part of this woman. I felt her clench around me as her body shuddered and her moans of pleasure rang through the air.

I couldn't last any longer. Pushing into her and feeling

her let go sent me into a frenzied world of dreams, and just when I thought it couldn't get better, she looked up at me with her beautiful green eyes and smiled, whispering,

"Can we do it again?"

I smiled, realizing Lucy would always be full of surprises.

Chapter Thirty-Two

Too Good to be True

Lucy

A flimsy sheet covered me while I stayed sprawled in Shep's bed as the sunlight splashed across his bedroom in a dizzying array of sparkling dots. The smell of coffee permeated the air, and I was absolutely starving.

And a puddle of confusion blurred into a simple fact that I couldn't shake.

I had fallen for Shep.

Okay, a tad more than that . . .

Oh, my gosh. What had I done? Where had I dared let my heart go?

Everything about last night was magical. I couldn't have asked for anything more, and it confirmed my worst fear. I wasn't falling for Shep. I already fell, and I fell hard.

The way he held me so tenderly last night after we'd had sex created a space I'd never experienced before. There was an unspoken vulnerability shared between us where I no longer felt as worried about the unknown. We'd face it together. We'd go as slow or as fast as we needed.

Just thinking about Shep made my chest swell to twice its size.

He understood my vulnerabilities and had no reason to expose them.

"Good, you followed orders," Shep teased, walking into his bedroom with a food tray. "Since we never got to dinner last night, I made the quiche, and you get some leftover salad."

I scooted right up in bed and pulled the sheet over me as he walked toward me.

He smiled at me. "You don't have to do that, you know."

"Do what?"

Shep chuckled, placing the breakfast tray over my lap. "Cover up."

"Right. Nothing like a pair of boobs dangling over some quiche to be uber sexy."

Shep shook his head and sighed. "You have no idea what it would do to me, actually."

I laughed, taking a sip of the fresh coffee as he spun around. "Where are you going?"

"I'm kind of hungry too."

I rolled my eyes and flashed a dopey smile. "Oh, right."

"Be right back."

My phone dinged, and I realized I'd never read the gossip text from Mae last night, but Shep wandered in just as I saw another text from Mae. I tossed my phone on a pile of pillows and took another bite of quiche.

"You know, I've never done this before," I told Shep.

He eyed me as he crawled onto the bed with his own tray. "Had breakfast?"

I loved the lightness about Shep.

"You know what I mean. I've never had breakfast in bed. I've never had the morning after be so relaxed and . . ." I shrugged, shoveling in some salad. "I don't know, just plain awesome."

I saw the same tenderness as last night touch Shep's eyes, and my entire body warmed. How did he completely disarm me?

"Your chef is incredible, by the way."

Shep took a bite and shook his head. "I don't have a personal chef. I just called a service."

"Ah, right. Well, you know of a service to call." I grinned, stabbing more lettuce and a piece of steak. "I'd have no idea who to call for a chef."

"Another confession." He eyed me.

"Yeah?"

"I had to call my mom to get the information. She uses them a lot." He shoved his salad around the plate and smiled. "I told her about you too."

My eyes widened. "You did? What did you say?"

"That I've found someone who knows how to keep me on my toes."

I snorted on accident, and he laughed. "What? You know it's true."

"I also told her you made me realize what I've been missing in life."

"Which is?"

"You." He took a bite of food and kept his eyes on me while a wicked swirl of emotion zipped through me. "Lucy, I wasn't kidding when I said I was falling for you. I can't imagine you not being part of my life."

I nodded slowly, letting his words wash over me. The problem was that I felt the same way. The idea of not getting to hang out with Shep terrified me. He'd become the bright surprise in my often uninspiring days filled with the demise of relationships and vendettas. I had built my career on the notion that all good things come to an end, and I'd be the one to help pick up the pieces for the victim.

But what if it were my pieces that needed to be picked up?

Shep's apprehensive laughter filled the room. "That certainly made you go silent."

I laughed, realizing I'd been self-reflecting too much, and shook my head quickly.

"No, it's not like that. I swear. I'm just so confused. I never thought I would be able to open my heart up to someone, and with you, it's been easier than I imagined. That alone freaks me out."

"No. I get it." He nodded, flashing his beautiful smile in my direction. "I certainly didn't make things easier by presenting myself as this goofball who could never turn down a bet. But I'm trying to show you that's not the only side of me."

I touched his cheek and nodded. "And I see that every day."

He put his tray down, and I slid mine over. "On that note, my mom invited us over next Friday."

My mouth fell open. "Like meeting your mom at her house?"

Shep smiled and nodded. "I'd imagine she'd be there since it's her house. I bet she'd even use the same chef from this weekend."

Even though every nerve was on edge, I grinned and nodded. "Then, you've got a deal."

Shep backed up teasingly. "I don't want another deal. I want a date."

I couldn't wipe the happiness from my soul as I nodded quickly. "Fine. You've got a date."

Shep moved slowly toward me and caged me in with his arms, softly running his lips across mine right when a loud thud crashed through the hall. He shot up from the bed and reached for a pair of joggers.

"Stay there. I don't know who would be in my house." His eyes locked on mine for a brief second before he left the bedroom. I quickly scanned the room and found a T-shirt of his that I slipped on and a pair of boxers in the top drawer of his dresser since all of my clothes were strewn about the great room.

My pulse pounded with every second that Shep was gone. We were essentially in the middle of nowhere, and since he wasn't expecting anyone, my mind raced wildly with frightening scenarios. He'd said no other woman had been here before, so if that was true, it shouldn't be a crazy ex out there, but Shep wasn't coming back, either.

A sharp male voice drifted down the hall, and my heart stopped. I dashed over to my phone to call 9-1-1 before sneaking out to the hallway.

I didn't see any sign of Shep, but I finally heard his voice. His tone was extremely agitated and heated. A side I'd never heard or seen before.

With each step closer to the voices, my hands trembled until I reached the end of the hallway, where I could peek around the corner.

I drew a deep breath and slowly craned my head ready to see a shirtless Shep arguing with a man who looked exactly like him, only older. My eyes strained to see the stranger closely as Shep's arms flailed in the air in disgust. I kept my phone steadied in my hand to call emergency services.

The man stopped looking at Shep and saw me immediately. A cocky smile spread across his lips as Shep stopped talking and turned around to follow the man's gaze.

Shep's expression turned from anger to worry in an instant.

He rushed over to me, attempting to smile, and scooted me back down the hallway.

"What's going on?" I asked, shaking my head and frowning. "Why are you pushing me away? Do I need to call the cops?"

Shep stopped himself, realizing we were far enough away, and shook his head. "No. Sorry. It's not like that. It's my father."

Shock registered through me. That explained the strong resemblance.

"Okay," I said slowly.

"I've never invited my dad here, but Winter did once." He ran his hands along his temples like a pounding headache had just invaded his brain space. "Apparently, he remembered how to get here, and the lady he's been sharing his home with kicked him out."

"Oh, no." I bit my bottom lip and stared at Shep. "I should probably get going, then. I don't—"

Shep reached for my shoulders and squeezed them gently. "No. I'm not letting my dad ruin my perfect weekend with you. Everything was going right, and then this. I told him he had to find somewhere else to crash. This is all too common for him, but he's never tried this before."

"You can't do that to him."

"I'm pretty certain I know why his girlfriend kicked him out, and I'm not going to be around to help him out and enable his bad behavior. It's like a slap to my mom." Shep groaned and rubbed his temples. "I can't believe this happened."

"How did he get in?" I asked since he wasn't ever welcome here.

Shep rolled his eyes. "I forgot to close the garage door, and then I got so swept up in you . . ."

I smiled, feeling the memories from last night flood me.

It suddenly seemed like a long time ago.

"Anyway, just hang tight, and I'll get my dad to leave."

"I'm not going anywhere, Shep." His dad's voice crawled up my spine. He reminded me of someone I'd face in court while the ex was left to pick up the pieces.

I peeked around Shep's broad shoulders to see his father standing at the end of the hallway. "We're all adults. You won't even know I'm here."

"All due respect, Dad. That's not happening." Shep shook his head.

"Oh, come on. We know how these weekends go. You probably won't even leave your bedroom."

I recoiled from his father's words. He seemed so . . . just ick.

His dad tried to get a better look at me and then pointed his finger in our direction. "Hey, wait a minute. She's still with you after everything?"

I cocked my head in confusion.

Shep and his dad weren't close, so I highly doubted he knew about our rough start.

"She's the attorney, right? The one that just got duped or something?" His father shook his head, looking at me with some weird admiration. "Divorce attorney, I think I read."

My eyes flashed to Shep, who looked as confused as me.

His dad snapped his fingers. "What is the name? I got it. I got it. Lacy? Linda?"

"Dad, I don't know what you're talking about, but I'd like you to leave my residence now."

Shep's jaw ticked, and I saw anger rise slowly.

"What's your dad talking about?" I whispered, wondering if maybe Shep had told him more than I thought.

"I have no idea, but I'm not going to wait around to find out."

His dad's hands went into the air. "Wait a second. You don't have a clue what I'm talking about?"

Shep slid his father a withering look, and a sickening feeling spread through my belly.

His dad shrugged and continued, "It's why I thought this place would be empty, or at least just you up here. I thought we could be two bachelors wallowing in our mistakes."

"Shep, what is he talking about?" The sternness of my features strengthened with the practiced ease I'd been accustomed to displaying in the courtroom.

The nagging voice in my head made me nauseous.

"You're the woman from the dare," his dad answered. "The footage from the bar across the street from my son's place. I recognized it immediately. His best friends were there in the video."

I tore my gaze away from his dad and looked at Shep.

"What footage? What bar?" I knew Shep, and I had made an anonymous mark on the pages of the Seattle gossip machine with the photo of me reaching over the table to strangle him at the matchmaking event, but I was never identified. Maybe that had changed.

But it wasn't a bar. My stomach clenched as the gnawing feeling inside me intensified.

"I . . ." Shep shook his head. "I don't know."

My phone buzzed in my hand again, and I brought it up to see another text from Mae.

This time, the link showed an image of what looked like Mae and me. I opened my phone and zoomed in on the image before hitting *Play*.

Shep groaned as he looked at my phone. "Oh, no."

"Shep, what? Tell me before I see it play out."

But it was too late.

The sound of a crowded bar filled the hallway with Mike and another guy hanging onto Shep, placing a bet.

I squinted my eyes to focus as Shep accepted the bet.

"It's not what it looks like," Shep said softly.

My eyes flicked to his before landing on the screen again.

"Oh, and if you can get her to sleep with you, I'll pay you double." The words rattled around my brain like a grenade about to go off.

"So I was just a bet?" Anger flashed through me, filling every cell with a fire I'd never felt before.

"No. It's not like that. I didn't even remember it."

"Why is this footage out there?"

Shep shook his head. "I don't know. Mike was recording it for posterity, but I don't—"

"For posterity?" I shook my head as my body trembled.

I'd been a joke, a wager to Shep this entire time.

I shook my head and shouldered past Shep and his dad into the great room, where I picked up my things from last night and grabbed my suitcase.

"Lucy, don't. I swear to God that it's not like that."

My mind was running wild with things I wanted to say and do to Shep. I could feel my steely resolve rise as if I were in the courtroom. He'd humiliated me in a way that couldn't be explained away.

And yet the only person I had to blame was myself because I'd ignored the red flags. I pretended that a leopard could change his spots. The worst part was that it wasn't like I hadn't been part of one of his bets before.

I gripped the handle on my suitcase and rolled past Shep and his father straight to the powder room, where I stripped off his boxers and shirt and pulled on some clean clothes before sitting on the toilet to call for help.

My mind buzzed with anger, but the sadness etched away at my fire as I dialed Danni's number. Every part of me felt hollow and as if I were nothing more than a shell of who I was yesterday.

What would my firm think? Would I even have a job?

The moment Danni answered, I sniffled into the phone.

"You okay?" she asked. "I take it you saw the video."

"You mean the one where I was just a bet?" I sniffled again as I heard Shep and his father arguing down the hall.

"I'm so sorry."

"Me too." I wiped my nose with some tissue. "The worst part is after last night, he can collect on the grand instead of five hundred bucks."

Tears flooded my cheeks as every bone ached in my body. This was exactly why I'd vowed to stay away from relationships, feelings, and men.

"Oh, Lucy. I'm so sorry," she said again.

I balanced my head on my hands. "I know this is a horrible imposition, but—"

"Tell me the address, and little Lucy and I will be there."

Hearing my best friend's words warmed me, and I realized I already had my little family, and that was perfect.

"I'm not going to make you drive up to the mountains. I think we're almost to Silver Ridge. I was going to call Mae for that, but I was hoping that maybe I could stay at your place for a few days. I don't want to deal with Shep showing up and trying to win me back. I'll even take night duty."

Danni giggled. "Music to my ears. Absolutely."

I sniffled again and said a quick thank you before hanging up as the images from last night slammed into me. It had felt so real with Shep.

A knock at the door alarmed me, and my entire body went rigid.

"Lucy, please let me talk to you. I swear I never did anything to hurt you. I was just being . . . dumb."

His words hung in the air as I texted Mae, who responded immediately.

"My dad left."

"What's your address?" I asked.

He recited the numbers, which I quickly texted to Mae.

"Please, Lucy. Everything between us is real. I promise you that. I would never do anything to—"

"You already did. Please, just leave me alone until Mae gets here."

"I can drive you back."

Fury replaced sorrow as I clenched my eyes shut. "And what makes you think I ever want to see you again, let alone be trapped in a car with you for hours?"

Shep sighed on the other side of the door. "I deserve that."

And his footsteps padded down the hall.

Chapter Thirty-Three

Dinner Party

Shep

"Where is your girlfriend?" my mom asked, glancing over my shoulder.

"We broke up." My mom frowned and shook her head. "But I invited Winter over since her husband and Hunter are skiing all day."

"Good. Because I had the chef make a ton of food." She studied me. "Your face looks gaunt."

I smiled at my mom, but I felt completely and utterly destroyed. I'd barely slept all week. I couldn't eat. All I could think about was losing the one woman I'd finally fallen in love with. I was going to tell her that Saturday. The night I'd spent with her was unlike any I'd ever had. I swear to God, our souls touched.

"You don't look good, honey."

I slid onto a grey barstool at the kitchen island and nodded. "I don't feel good. I screwed it up with Lucy. Big time."

My mom swallowed down a gulp of wine and stared at me. "You didn't cheat, did you?"

"Mom, you know I would never do that, but I almost wonder if what I did was worse."

She shook her head from personal experience. "Doubtful."

"Did you see the video of me placing a wager with Mike and Brendan that went around?"

She shook her head and slid me a glass of wine. "No. I don't pay attention to any of that. It's all noise."

"I used to think that too."

"What? You believe the gossip?"

I laughed coldly. "I am the gossip."

"Hello in here," Winter's voice rang out from the hall. "Everyone in the kitchen? I've got something awesome for Lucy."

My sister wandered into the kitchen with a belly that had somehow expanded substantially since I last saw her.

I stood and gave her a big hug before taking a seat.

She looked around the kitchen. "Where is she?"

"We broke up."

"Oh, no. Was it the video?"

"Okay. Somebody needs to tell me about this video," my mom muttered.

I folded my hands together and cracked my knuckles. "It's not just the video. The problems go back a bit."

"Problems? Isn't it a fairly new relationship?" My mom's brows knitted together in concern as Winter piled some nachos on a plate. "You shouldn't be riddled with problems so quickly."

I laughed and shook my head. "Okay. Fine. I'm the problem."

Winter giggled and took a bite of nachos. "Now, that I can believe."

I flashed her a wicked stare, so she stuck out her tongue at me.

"The very first night I met Lucy, I happened to have accepted a bet from Mike and Brendan about attending a matchmaking event in Seattle."

My mom nodded. "Okay."

"But I had to go there not as Shep. The reasoning behind it doesn't even matter now, but I met Lucy, and we hit it off. The moment I saw her, it was like my world stopped, and the only way to get it going again was to bring her into my orbit."

Winter crunched on another chip.

"I confessed right away that I wasn't Perry on my nametag. I was Shep."

"Oh, dear." My mom stared at me. "How'd she take it?"

"She reached over the table and tried to strangle me."

"Don't blame her one bit."

I nodded. "I know. Anyway, months later, she happened to arrive at the bar across from my condo when I was having drinks with Brendan and Mike. They didn't know it was the woman from the matchmaking event, but they saw my reaction to her and placed a wager, only this time, it was on video. Mike recorded the whole thing. They figured that Lucy would ignore me, but I knew our history, and I was certain she wouldn't ignore me. She might throw one down, but she wouldn't ignore me. I thought it would be a good icebreaker. She ignored me."

"This is horrible," Winter said, shaking her head. "You never told her about the bet?"

"What does any of this matter?" my mom asked, leaning over the counter.

"The video went viral," Winter informed my mom.

"Thanks to Lucy's sister, I got in contact with her, and

we started dating. She's a divorce attorney, so it was hard for her to get past the incident without thinking it was a big red flag. But I finally convinced her that I wasn't just one big prank to happen. We went up to my house in the mountains, and out of the blue, Dad showed up."

My mom gasped while Winter nearly choked on a chip.

"Why?" Winter asked.

"His latest kicked him out because she found him cheating on her. Surprise. Anyway, he mentioned the video at the same time her sister texted her the footage, and my life has basically imploded, and I will be single and miserable for the rest of my life."

"Well, you're right about one thing," my mom said. "You were the problem."

"Yeah, and I get to live with that for the rest of my life. Not only did I screw up my chances with Lucy, but I also screwed up her chances at love. She was finally learning to trust, and given her profession, that isn't an easy thing to do."

"What's she do for a living again?" my mom asked.

"She's a divorce attorney."

My mom's eyes widened. "Whoa."

I nodded.

"No wonder she saw you as one big red flag."

"Thanks for that, Mom."

The chef wandered into the kitchen holding a tray of flautas. My mom did very well in my parents' divorce. Good enough that she had a second working kitchen behind the one we were all sitting in.

"Flautas. My favorite." Winter hopped up and down, holding her belly, and my chest tightened.

It was so hard to believe that less than a week ago, I'd actually caught myself daydreaming about little Shep and Lucy munchkins running around.

My throat tightened, and I cleared the lump.

No. This wasn't going to go down this way. I needed to fight for her.

It didn't matter that she ignored my texts, calls, and emails. Or that all the bouquets of flowers I left on her doorstep were still there. I needed to see her again or at least let her know that she was never a bet or a joke to me.

"Your frat boy ways have caught up to you," my mom said as the chef placed refried beans, rice, a platter of tacos, and a tray of enchiladas next to the flautas that Winter had already dug into.

"Thank you, Chef," I said, smiling while ignoring the sting of my mom's words.

But I felt empty and vacant.

I took a bite of the taco and couldn't taste a thing.

"Maybe this showed you that you actually want to settle down and give me little grandbabies like Winter. Colton thinks he might have found the one."

That was news to me.

Winter shook her head. "I don't think that's the best advice for Shep right now, Mom. Can't you see he's like a shell of a human at this point?"

My brow quirked. "Well, I wouldn't say that."

But Winter knew me better than myself.

"Really?" She took another bite of flauta. "You look like crap. You sound like crap. Your eyes are vacant."

I waved my hands in defeat. "Okay. I get it."

"Well, I was really looking forward to meeting the woman who'd finally swept my son off his feet." My mom put a taco on her plate next to some beans. "But I guess I'll have to wait for that."

I nodded, taking a sip of wine and wondering what Lucy was doing. Sliding my phone out, I sent another text to her and realized she'd blocked me.

My shoulders slumped.

"What now?" Winter asked, taking a seat next to me.

"She's blocked me."

"How do you know?"

"I just tried texting her again."

"Why do you keep texting her?" Winter asked. "She's obviously . . ."

"Done with me?"

"Sounds like it," my mom said softly. "You will meet a woman who is your match, Shep. You'll need a special one who can take care of herself and put you in your place. You get a little rowdy sometimes."

I nodded, knowing Lucy was just that person.

She never let a second slip where she didn't remind me of who I was and that she didn't need me. She just liked me. And I liked her.

And then I fell in love with her.

I'd planned on telling her that day. I knew during breakfast that I was going to confess everything I felt, and then . . .

My dad showed up.

The guy I'd tried to impress from a distance. The man I wanted to prove I wasn't, but I suddenly felt like the spitting image of the dude.

A bachelor with the ability to break someone's heart over a senseless act.

"How's Mike taking things since it was his phone that got hacked?" Winter asked.

"Not well, considering he had a lot of photos and videos of Skylar and him."

"Like together?" Winter's brows rose. "As in compromising pics?"

I nodded. "They're newlyweds. I guess he wanted to document that."

"Oh, my gosh." Winter grimaced. "I am so glad I'm technologically challenged lately. I was doing fine with social media and my phones, and then the next thing I know, there's like a million more apps and phones that take 3D video and filters that make Hunter look like an alien, and I just tapped out."

"Good plan," my mom said, nodding. "It's obviously not doing wonders for your brother, either."

"I blame you for this," I said, pointing at Winter but teasing.

"Me? What did I do?" She feigned innocence.

"You told me to go ahead and do the spread for Seattle's Most Eligible Bachelor."

She laughed and shook her head. "How does that have anything to do with this?"

"It just does."

"I got an idea." Winter stood up from her stool and reached for more beans.

"What's that?" I asked.

"How about I text her?"

"And what would you say?"

"That my brother's an ass, but he has a heart of gold and never meant to hurt you."

"I tried that already, but without the ass part, and she didn't take the bait."

Winter rolled her eyes. "That's because it came from you. Listen, we all make mistakes. Sometimes, it's easier if things are explained by someone other than the perp."

I scowled. "Perp?"

"Sorry. I've been on a true-crime binge. All I'm saying is that maybe if she hears that your heart was in the right place, she'll listen."

"I'll try anything, but I don't think she'll believe anyone who's connected to me." My chest tightened at the thought of Lucy losing all trust in not just me but humans at large. I did that to her.

She'd finally broken down her walls piece by piece to imagine a life where she could be free and vulnerable, and that was all stripped away by a completely juvenile act that I hadn't even remembered.

I shook my head, thinking back to a night at my apartment. The whole thing had popped into my head, and I was going to mention it, and then I forgot.

Because that was what Lucy made me do. When I was with her, all I cared about were those moments of us together so I could memorize her little smirks or her snarky comments to hold me until the next time I got to see her.

"I'm just saying that maybe it's not you who needs to carry the first message." Winter stretched toward the ceiling, and my mom nodded.

"It's worth a shot." My mom shrugged.

"Would either of you respond to Winter if you were in the same place?"

My mom laughed and smacked the counter. "Absolutely not."

"Great." I rolled my eyes and let out a deep sigh, thinking about what I'd done to destroy Lucy, and I realized that whatever message she received from me couldn't just be about me.

I wanted her to know that she shouldn't lose everything she'd gained this last while. Love could still exist for her, even if she wasn't in love with me.

Chapter Thirty-Four

Deal is Done

Lucy

I stared at my best friend sitting across from me in the office. The fire from the breakup with Shep led to amazing things in my career. Every ounce of fury I felt, I put right back into my cases. Danni's ex rued the day he'd messed with her heart, and his legal team was on its knees.

"You ready to sign the deal?" I asked, feeling the charge run through me. "I don't think we'd get any better by getting into a courtroom. They're nervous and don't know what other cards we have to show."

Danni smiled as relief etched her features for the first time since little Lucy's birth.

"I didn't even know he had some of these properties," she whispered in disbelief.

I grinned. "It's amazing what a forensic accountant can dig up."

"So, I really get two apartment buildings, three rental houses, and the home I'm living in?" she squeaked out. Her hands slid to her mouth.

"You're also entitled to half of his 401k, pension, and IRA. Not to mention spousal support for the next seven years to get you on your feet and child support until little Lucy turns eighteen."

Danni's eyes glazed over in disbelief.

"Aren't you happy?" I asked, clapping my hands together.

Danni nodded and swallowed hard. "Of course."

"But what? He also has to pay for little Lucy's education, so we have a new trust set up for that."

"No. I know. This is more than I ever could have hoped for from this disaster of a marriage. It's like you're our fairy godmother, but it's just . . ." She bit her bottom lip and straightened in the chair.

"Come on, tell me. If you want to go to court, I know we can rip him a new one there too." I nodded, letting my best friend know I had her back. I always would.

"It's not that, and you're going to think I'm super weak, especially after the whole debacle you had with Shep."

Just hearing his name made my stomach gnarl. Sure. Good things came out of it. My rise in cases hit new heights because technically, I was merely the woman who'd ignored Seattle's Most Eligible Bachelor on film. That was all that was caught on video. No one knew that I fell hard for him. That I slept with him. That Shep earned that grand from his buddy.

My spine stiffened at the thought, but it brought great things for my career.

So, I guess if I ever saw Shep on a sidewalk, I could tell him thanks because everyone wanted a divorce attorney who didn't believe in love, and of course, the firm played that up.

I'd even made partner.

"You're the strongest woman I know, Danni. Don't think for a second that it's not true. Tell me anything." I reached for her hand and pulled it into mine across the desk.

"I wish my marriage had stayed together." She let out a sigh as tears ran down her cheeks. "I just don't know why I wasn't enough. Why was Lucy not enough?" Danni's eyes met mine, and a new wave of fury ripped through me.

"Cheaters are selfish in nature. They think about their own gratification by taking the easy way out." I shook my head. "I've seen it time and again. Rather than work on the marriage and try to build those connections, they fall for the guy at the copy machine or the woman at the bar who winks at him. It's never about the person who's been cheated on. Ever. It's not that you weren't enough. It's that they weren't enough. They don't like themselves. They seek that approval from everyone else in the world rather than sit down and focus on what is making them search for something they'll never find."

I squeezed Danni's hand. "It's not you, sweetie. You are a catch, and your baby is the sweetest Lucy I've ever met."

Danni chuckled. "That's because you're the meanest. I mean that in a totally good way."

"I prefer ruthless," I teased, feeling like my old self again.

But that was the problem. I kind of enjoyed my new self. Getting to have fun and laugh was like a new freedom, and there was no legal win that made me feel that way. Even this one for Danni. I was delighted and felt victorious and knew I'd kept my promise to make her ex pay, but I didn't feel personally uplifted.

I just felt tired.

And if I truly admitted things to myself, I might admit that I missed Shep. I longed to feel the way he made me feel again. There was a reason he was where he was at in life, being chosen as Seattle's Most Eligible Bachelor and living up life without much worry.

He had that carefree spirit that I craved so much, but I knew it wasn't in me. I liked stability. I knew what was expected of me at this firm. I understood what I had to do to keep it going. I couldn't just take off for weekends or early evenings. I had clients waiting for me to help alter the course of their lives.

"Do you, though, Lucy?" Danni's eyes met mine, and she smiled. "I know you're an amazing lawyer. And yes, I do want to take the deal, but you seemed so much lighter when you were with Shep. Like you could still do great legal work while not being miserable personally."

I frowned. "Who says I'm miserable? I'm like on a high skewering that bastard who cheated on you."

Danni laughed. "And I thank you for that, but I just don't know what ten or twenty more years of this life will do to you. At least when you had Shep in the background, he made you smile and chuckle at his shenanigans."

My brows rose, and I felt the familiar tightness in my chest. "Until I was the focus of his shenanigans, Danni. I totally fell for his lines. I thought he was falling in love with me. We shared secrets and dreams and insecurities, and then—Bam! It was all so he could win a bet." I shook my head. "Unfortunately, I just let hormones and lust get in the way of what I knew I was getting myself into from the beginning. The man was one giant red flag. I even called him Mr. Flirt."

"Maybe it's not exactly like that."

I stared at Danni and wished I could say what I wanted to say, which was that I wasn't the one sitting on the opposite side of the desk, and I never would be because I decided to stick to my original plan and never marry. Maybe someday, I'd try the fling thing, but after the devastation from falling for Shep, I truly knew my heart couldn't handle doing it twice.

The mere thought of Shep made my body want to crumble. If I focused too long on thoughts of us, my arms turned heavy, my breaths turned shallow, and all I wanted to do was hide from the world.

So, I couldn't even imagine what it would be like to be in a relationship for years with someone I loved, and then they ripped the rug out from under me.

Me.

That was who I needed to worry about.

And it was a lot easier since I blocked Shep's number.

"What did he do that was so bad, Lucy? Really, what?" she asked softly as I slid a pen over for her to sign the first set of documents.

"He teased vulnerability out of me. He stretched me out of my comfort zone." I cleared my throat, vowing not to start crying. "And then he handed me back a mess of emotions that were anything but real when I found out it was all pretend. It was all for a bet."

"Shep totally forgot about the bet because all he wanted to use it for was an excuse to talk to you again."

I focused on my best friend. "How do you know?"

"He called me. We spoke for hours. I feel bad for the guy."

"You feel bad for the guy? I'm the one who got played." I shook my head. "That's how these players work it. They become the victims."

"Oh, no. He doesn't think he's the victim. He thinks he's the biggest douche out there."

"That's something, at least." A bitter laugh rolled off my lips.

"It's not like he even collected on the bet." Danni's eyes widened, and she dropped her gaze to the document and quickly signed.

I waited until she dated the page.

"Is that supposed to make me feel better? That he suddenly grew a conscience and decided against getting his thousand dollars for sleeping with me?"

Danni shrugged. "I don't think he even thought about the bet. He just wanted an excuse to get you to speak with him. He told me the night he met you at the matchmaking event was the night his world stopped. Did you know he didn't even go out with any women between the time of that matchmaking event and the moment you two went out for coffee?"

"How commendable," I said flatly.

"Well, I mean . . ." Danni waggled her brows. "It kind of is, considering he can get anyone he wants, whenever he wants."

"Which is why being the center of his bets and practical jokes more than once hurts more than most things would."

Danni let out a deep sigh and nodded. "No, you're right. I'm just being ridiculous because I knew how happy he made you."

"So, now you can just focus on how mad he made me."

"Right." She nodded and dropped her gaze to the stack of documents she needed to sign.

After two cups of coffee and over an hour later, Danni collapsed back into the chair. "We did it."

I smiled at my best friend and shook my head. "No. You did it. You stayed strong. You stayed brave."

"And I can finally breathe again." She chuckled. "Maybe I'll even date again."

"I know a guy," I teased.

Danni rolled her eyes. "He's not my type, but thanks."

My phone beeped, and my assistant came over the speaker. "Your next appointment is here."

Danni stood and smiled. "That is my cue to exit. Thanks again for everything. I just couldn't have gone through this without you, but I still wish I never had to do it, Lucy. I wish my family stayed intact more than I want all the property and money I landed."

"I know, and that's what makes you an incredible human being." I gave her a quick hug before she made her way to the door, just as my next appointment appeared in the doorway.

My mouth dropped open as my assistant stood behind him, and Danni walked by, saying goodbye to me one last time.

"What are you doing here?" I asked Mike.

The infamous best friend.

Another guy came up behind my assistant and flashed a cocky smile.

What was it with these men?

My eyes tightened. "And who are you?"

"I'm Brendan, Shep's other best friend."

"Oh, he had to send two of his best friends to do his dirty work?" My arms folded over my chest as a prickly sensation spread over me.

"Can we have a seat?" Mike asked. "I paid my retainer already."

I scowled at him. He obviously knew my hot buttons from talking to Shep.

"Fine."

Mike and Brendan walked into my office, and each took a seat as I handed them each a box of tissue.

Brendan scowled and held it up. "What's this for?"

"Most of my clients leave here in tears after their first meeting."

Brendan grimaced. "I have to confess I would never have thought Shep would fall in love with someone who could make a grown man cry."

In love? Ha!

"Well, you guessed right because Shep didn't fall in love with me. Only his bank account did."

"You're wrong about that," Mike said flatly.

I looked at the clock. "You have fifty-seven minutes before my next client comes in."

"And at these rates, I intend to use every second,"

Mike shot back.

Brendan smiled at me. "Shep doesn't know we're here."

I realized these two were playing the good cop-bad cop.

"So?"

Brendan shifted in his chair and shook his head. "I know on the surface that things don't look ideal in terms of how things started with you and Shep."

"And how they ended is even less ideal," I said calmly.

But the truth was that all this talk about Shep was turning me into a hot mess of clammy palms and damp underarms. Even the base of my spine was sweating into a puddle of nerves.

The last four weeks had been hell. Sure, I threw myself into my cases and worked even longer hours than before, but it was all so I could forget about the one man I'd fallen in love with.

Shep.

The guy who could flash a smile in my direction, and I suddenly felt like the luckiest woman in the world. The one man who could convince me to take a weekend off and spend it on a getaway. The one man who knew my body more intimately than I did. The person who could make me laugh when I didn't think I could.

The guy who'd destroyed every ounce of confidence I'd finally created.

"The bet wasn't his idea. In fact, it wasn't truly a bet." Brendan leaned his elbows against the desk.

My brows rose. "Which one?"

"The one that mattered," Mike clarified.

"Well, they both matter, seeing how things turned out. The first one should have given me enough pause not to allow myself to endure a second prank. But I failed myself." I pursed my lips together. "And I won't let that happen again."

"Whew." Brendan shook his head. "You're a tough nut to crack."

"Then don't wear yourself out trying." I sat back in the seat and crossed my legs, praying I wouldn't start sweating anywhere else like my hairline.

Never let them see you sweat.

A great law school motto that I never had to worry about.

Until Shep.

Thoughts of Shep were slamming into my mind at an unstoppable pace. Just being around his friends made me miss him.

"I know you're here to tell me he is sorry and what a great guy he is, and he'd never ever do something to hurt someone." I smiled. "I get it, and some other woman will be lucky enough to have him after he learned some very tough lessons about being an adult."

Mike laughed and shook his head, glancing around my office for the first time. "No. We're not here to tell you that at all. He effed up. He knows it. He doesn't expect anything good to come from it."

"Then why are you here?"

Brendan's gaze saddened. "He fell in love with you, Lucy, and it was our dumb mistakes that made him lose you. He wasn't the one always placing the bets. He just never knew how to tell us to buzz off. He didn't want to hurt our feelings." Brendan shrugged. "But that's not why we're here."

Mike leaned forward and took a deep breath. "The thing that has absolutely killed Shep out of all of this was losing you and you losing your ability to love and trust again. He doesn't just feel like he killed the relationship you two had. He bears responsibility for your inability to trust again. He talks nonstop about what a horrible person he is."

I stared at these two men and didn't say a word.

Loose lips sink ships.

"He knows he'll never find a love like you again. He's

told us as much, but what kills him even more is to think that he hurt you so badly that you won't be able to open up again."

"Jury is out on that. But you can let him know that I'll be just fine." I smiled curtly as the words sharpened in my soul, bleeding me out, making me weaker.

Because he was right.

I'd lost my ability to trust again.

The walls went up so fast, and this time, they were stronger and impenetrable.

"Shep is destroyed," Mike said softly. "I've never seen him like this, and it's all our fault. We'll have to live with it and deal with it."

"True." Brendan nodded in agreement. "But I wish you would believe that you weren't a bet to him, Lucy. You were his match. He knows it, and he realizes he'll never have that connection with someone like you again. He will never forgive us if he thinks you don't have the ability to love again."

I thought back to that moment when Shep said he couldn't bear to teach me how to flirt and attract another man. He wanted to be my only one.

An unexpected smile touched my lips, but I pushed it off my lips immediately.

"Shep is a great person. He will find an amazing

woman who is more fitted to his personality and lifestyle. It wasn't merely the bet that made me see things clearly." My heart pounded so hard I swore I could feel it between my ears.

"Fine. We get it." Brendan nodded. "He doesn't have a chance with you. But our friendship with Shep is everything to us. We already screwed up his chances with the one and only person he's ever fallen in love with. He barely speaks to us."

"And that's my problem how?" I asked curtly.

"This is a completely selfish request," Mike began. "But maybe he could start to forgive himself if he could see that you could be happy again."

His words shocked me into reality. "What are you even asking?"

Mike cleared his throat. "There's a guy back at the bar who I guess you bumped into one time when you were with Shep."

I shook my head, not remembering.

"He heard about you and Shep breaking up and gave me his number to give to you."

Fire lit my ass right off the chair. "You're trying to hook me up with someone else so your best friend will talk to you again?"

Brendan hopped over the back of his chair while Mike

stood up.

He put the number on the desk and stared at me. "My guess is you still have feelings over Shep or you wouldn't be willing to murder us in your own law firm. So, my proposition is simple. Set him free by letting him see that you can move on. Save our friendships." He glanced at Brendan. "And go on being the person you truly want to be."

Even though the rage dove deep when I thought about what had been done to me, I couldn't bear to think that Shep hurt too. It wasn't his fault that I chose this profession or that I chose to put my walls back up. He was merely a reminder that all good things must come to an end.

But it wasn't fair to him. He deserved a woman who could make him happy without complication, and if all it took was him seeing me out with another guy to prove that I wasn't broken, I could manage that.

I looked up at Brendan and Mike.

"Fine. Consider your friendship saved." I stared at the two men in front of me and let out a deep breath. "Tell me when and where. I'm not reaching out to that guy. You do the hard work."

Mike smiled and swooped the number back into his pocket. "Deal."

I nodded and watched them both nearly skip out of

my office, and I realized I'd somehow just made a deal with the devils themselves.

Chapter Thirty-Five

Fall Off a Cliff

Shep

I hadn't been to the bar across the street for at least a month and a half, maybe longer. All I knew was the last time I was here, Lucy was trying her lines on some poor, unsuspecting victim.

The memories made me smile until my eyes met up with Brendan and Mike. I'd managed to ignore them this long, but I figured to shut them up, I'd agree to come over for drinks and set them straight. I needed time to reevaluate my life and the choices I'd made to get me here.

Holding a cold beer wasn't going to help things along any. In fact, choosing this joint only made things rawer and turned my anger up a notch at my friends. No, it wasn't their fault that I was in this situation. I was the idiot who wasn't really thinking about the ramifications of what my friends said or did. I was solely focused on seeing Lucy again.

But I was the man who lost the love of his life because he couldn't help himself around his friends. I didn't want to be a jerk. I'd been lucky in life. Mike had been lucky in love. Poor Brendan was still waiting for his luck, so I never wanted to be the sourpuss. Now, I wish I'd been the sourest of them all.

The bar bustled with the afterwork crowd as the happy hour drew to a close, and Mike and Brendan sat across from me. We were at a table next to a window, so I managed to stare outside more than at my friends. It was April first, and I'd prayed that I wasn't in store for some practical joke, but being that I wasn't speaking to them much, I was pretty certain this was just a coincidence.

"How's it going?" Brendan asked.

My eyes met his. "Been better."

He nodded. "I can imagine. Actually, I can't because I've never met the *One*."

"Right," I said flatly, unsure of whether he was trying to make me feel better or not.

"So, what did you guys want?" I asked, taking a sip of my beer. "You got me out, so shoot."

"Well, we wanted to talk to you," Mike started. "We

know you're mad at us for roping you into some really ridiculous things. We've all been acting like we're twenty for far too long."

"And we wanted to apologize." Brendan frowned. "We really do."

"You both have. Many times, through text. That's plenty."

Mike raised his brows. "Except you don't respond."

"I've been busy." I shifted in my seat and scanned the bar. It was nearly filled to capacity.

"Wallowing around over a woman." Mike stared at me like he wanted to challenge me and push my buttons on purpose.

"You should understand," I said pointedly. "Imagine if it were Skylar the jokes played out on."

Mike nodded. "No. I hear ya."

"I don't think you do." I took a sip of beer and noticed one of the regulars in a booth by himself. It was Cliff, the doctor who'd fallen over his tongue that one night Lucy was here practicing flirting. Seeing him made me smile. When she'd come back to our table, Cliff couldn't keep his eyes off Lucy, and she was blissfully ignorant of the attention. My heart squeezed just thinking about her.

How beautiful she was.

Her intelligence . . .

The sparks . . .

"What can we do to rebuild our friendship?" Mike asked, point-blank.

"Our friendship is fine," I growled. "I just need time, okay? It's not your fault I'm here. I'm a big boy. I should have remembered the dare and told Lucy about it, but I just let it slide."

"You're our best friend." Brendan pressed his lips together for a few seconds. "And we can see the toll it is taking. You look like shit. You're holed up in your condo. You won't even look at another woman."

I scowled and shook my head. "Why would I? Lucy is who I want. Lucy is who I screwed up. Do you think I should just start sleeping around to forget about her? It won't work."

"You've said a million times how you know you've broken her heart just when she'd finally opened up to someone."

"Right." Like I needed to be reminded.

"So, you're just going to punish yourself for the rest of time because she might have decided to give up on finding love." Mike shook his head and took a drink.

I shrugged. "What's it to you?"

359

"We want to see you happy. We want you to quit blaming yourself." Mike shook his head and looked at Brendan, but he didn't say much.

"What?" I asked Brendan. "You're suddenly quiet."

"I honestly wish this didn't happen to you. It's made me grow up a lot really quickly. It's made me realize how ridiculous putting friends first is, and I'm just sorry this happened to you. I mean, I'd like to find that special person someday. I don't want to wind up alone." He took a swig of beer. "And seeing you like this freaks me out."

"You don't want it to be you." I laughed. Brendan was always a bit nicer than Mike and a bit more thoughtful. He was a good guy. He'd always been lucky with the ladies but really unlucky with love, but I knew he'd wanted a big family. "Don't worry. You didn't jinx yourself by throwing some bad karma in my direction."

Brendan's brows quirked up slightly, and he shrugged. "We'll see. I just want you to be happy again."

"Show me a happy Lucy, and maybe I'll be able to smile again. Until then, let me flounder by myself while I pity my choices in life. Simple as that. I ruined myself, and I ruined the girl I fell in love with."

Brendan and Mike traded glances just as I saw Lucy bound down the sidewalk.

She looked stunning.

Incredible.

Dynamite.

My heart started beating fast, and I glanced at my buddies.

"Was this why you brought me here?" I asked, suddenly feeling like I could breathe again.

Brendan frowned and shook his head, following my finger. "Oh, Lucy is coming here?"

I looked at them. "What do you mean? You didn't know she was coming?"

"I didn't invite her," Mike said, but Brendan had a funny look on his face.

The doors burst open and in walked Lucy. She stopped and scanned the bar. I stood up, but she didn't seem to see me.

Instead, she beelined right to Cliff. He lit up the moment he saw her, and he stood to greet her.

All the blood drained from my face. My body felt limp. My arms refused to move. My legs wouldn't budge. I just watched Lucy as she laughed and hugged Cliff.

The doctor.

And she slid into the booth where a drink was waiting for her.

Lucy's infectious laugh filled the air, and my pulse didn't soar. It slowed.

My world went into slow motion as my two buddies seemed elated that Lucy had already moved on.

"That was fast," Mike said, smacking Brendan's shoulder.

Brendan scowled at him before turning his attention to Lucy and Cliff.

It was as if I'd been put in a trance. I couldn't rip my eyes off the booth where Lucy's mannerisms seemed so freeing and her laughter tickled the air. Cliff looked like he'd won a million bucks, and he was right. He had.

I brought in a deep breath, but it felt shallow and as if I weren't getting enough oxygen.

I wanted her to be happy.

That was all I wanted.

And here she was, in a bar with a man who wasn't me, and she was happy.

She was laughing.

Her body swayed as their conversation continued. Her smiles lit up the booth as the server brought their order.

My friends kept talking, but I had no idea what they were saying.

I just wanted it to be me sitting across from Lucy.

But I screwed it up.

And I had to deal with that. I had to realize that Lucy wasn't mine.

She never was mine. She'd told me that time and again.

Yet that morning, when I'd brought her breakfast, I felt that connection. I knew we'd put down our fears and opened up our hearts that night when we'd finally had sex.

I ordered another beer and a chaser while Mike and Brendan traded worried glances.

"Dude, you've basically shredded that napkin to pieces." Brendan scraped the bits into a pile. "You okay?"

"Does it look like I'm okay?" I asked, laughing as my fists bound tighter with every passing second watching Lucy and Cliff.

The truth of it was that Cliff was the better match for her. The better man.

He was responsible, acted like a grownup, and didn't involve himself in ridiculous bets.

Cliff had always been honest about why he showed up here so often. He wanted a wife and had tried everything under the sun, from joining clubs to online dating.

Whenever he'd told me about his adventures, I just thanked God I wasn't looking to get married.

And now, here I sat with my two best friends while the woman I loved sat with Cliff.

The server brought over the beer and chaser. I chugged the beer in mere seconds and followed it with the shot. I smiled at the bartender, and he nodded, readying another round for our table.

When he brought over the tray of drinks, I raised my beer to my friends. "To Lucy."

My friends looked at each other and lifted their drinks. "To Lucy."

"May she find love and true happiness with the doctor."

Mike smiled. "To Lucy," he repeated again.

I took another drink of beer and heard Lucy's voice drift over.

That could have been me.

Damn it.

I stood, leaving my unfinished beer and shot, and glanced at my buddies. My stomach roiled with nausea as I glanced toward Lucy. She looked like she was really enjoying herself.

Good.

She deserved the best.

I cleared my throat and dragged my eyes back to Mike

and Brendan. "I'm going to leave you two ladies to finish your drinks, but I'm headed home. I've seen enough for the night. Buy yourself some dinner."

I slid a couple of hundred bucks onto the table and smiled. "And don't worry. Good Ol' Shep will be back in no time. Seeing this was good."

Brendan eyed me. "Seeing what?"

"Lucy. Seeing Lucy . . ." My voice trailed off, and I glanced in her direction one last time, knowing I'd probably never see her again.

Chapter Thirty-Six

What Else Can You Ride?

Lucy

I didn't have to see Shep to feel him in the bar. His gaze burned into me, and my cheeks warmed instantly.

Damn it.

He looked insanely good. Maybe lost a little bit of weight, which he didn't need to do, but he looked incredible. It was like my mind had been playing tricks on me the last six weeks, trying to conjure up a different image of him so that I wouldn't be so attracted to the man I couldn't have.

I swallowed down the ache erupting in my entire body and inching its way up my throat when I spotted Cliff and made my way over to the booth.

He was a nice guy, and I was kind of flattered that he'd figured out a way to get ahold of me through Shep's friends. That took perseverance, which was something I totally commended. Cliff's dark hair tumbled across his forehead as we both took our seats in the booth.

"You're beautiful," Cliff said, smiling. Small wrinkles edged his eyes and cheekbones as he continued to grin at me, his eyes roaming along my body.

I snuck a peek toward Shep's table. He wasn't looking this way any longer. Maybe it had all been in my imagination.

So, life had basically gone back to normal for Seattle's Most Eligible Bachelor.

Fine.

Good.

His friends were mistaken.

"You're an attorney," Cliff began.

"I am. I specialize in family law, mainly divorce."

Cliff grimaced. "How does that bode for relationships?"

"Well, I know how they end most of the time."

Cliff didn't know whether to laugh or run.

The server came over and offered us drinks. I chose a double martini.

"Thanks for letting me take you out tonight. I'm sorry it was through some off channels." He closed the menu as his eyes stayed on mine.

"Absolutely. I'm thrilled at the chance. I remember meeting you here quite a few weeks ago."

He beamed. "I wasn't sure if you'd remember."

"Of course." I laughed, thinking back to Shep that night. The evening had been filled with such lightness, and I think that was the night I finally started to crack my heart open for Shep a little. "You were kind of bummed that I wasn't alone."

Cliff nodded. "Things work out."

I smiled as the server brought over our drinks, and Cliff ordered appetizers. I took several sips of the martini while the server stood at our table, and I bobbed my brows up and down to signal for another drink.

Since I hadn't eaten much during the day, the liquor was hitting me hard, which was good since I had the love of my life sitting across the bar with his best friends while I sat across from someone I really had no interest in.

But I knew Cliff was supposed to be who I was interested in. He had the looks, the degrees, the career, the dry sense of humor, and an overwhelming sense of responsibility with every syllable spoken. He was my ideal guy on paper.

I flicked my gaze to Shep and saw him staring at the table next to us.

Figured.

It was a group of three women.

I brought my gaze back to Cliff's.

"So, you're a physician?" I remembered Shep telling me he was a doctor all those weeks ago.

"Trauma surgeon." He nodded, taking a sip of wine as the server brought me another martini.

I took the last two sips of the first one so the server could take it away.

"Wow. That is incredible." My head spun a little from the alcohol.

"The martini or being a surgeon?"

I laughed, feeling like the room was spinning, as I brought my eyes back to Cliff. "That you're a surgeon. A trauma surgeon. Wow. That has got to keep the adrenaline flowing, right? Phew."

He frowned at me. "Yeah. I suppose it does."

Our appetizers came, and I snuck another look at Shep's table. He was downing a shot.

How could he not even notice I was here?

"So, you must keep really long hours?" I asked, taking a sip from my new martini before eating a fried artichoke leaf.

"They aren't the most conducive for dating." He nodded. "But I can't imagine being a divorce lawyer is exactly forgiving when it comes to billing."

I pretended to shoot him with my index finger, which made him jump back a little. "Right you are. My evenings are pretty much eaten up by work, and I might get a few free hours on the weekend."

Cliff smiled. "Sounds like we might be a match made in heaven."

"You think?" I laughed again, but this time I wasn't sure why.

I noticed Shep look in my direction, and for a brief second, I wondered if he had seen me.

My body stiffened, and I took another sip of my martini. Heat drifted through me from the mix of alcohol and overall bad decisions as I swallowed my pride and stared at Cliff.

"We've both established that we're workaholics," Cliff said, smiling. "But what do you like to do in your off-hours?"

I thought about it for a second and smiled. "Well, I love playing Jingle Berry Balls. In fact, it's kind of my addiction."

Cliff looked at me like I had three heads. "I have no idea what that is."

I smacked the table so hard Cliff looked like he almost

had a heart attack. "Oh. Sorry. It's only the best pay-to-play game in existence. They have monthly expansions. In fact, I got to see what's ahead before everyone else."

Cliff didn't look the least bit impressed. "Oh, wow."

"It's awesome. A real stress reliever." I eyed him and nodded before taking another sip. I was past tipsy, but I didn't care. "And when I'm not playing mobile device games, I'd say I love to read. I love eating." I twisted my lips into a speculative pout, realizing Shep and I had never played this game. We never needed to do this dance. We just existed. We just were right.

God, I missed Shep.

I pushed down the crazy, drunk feelings and brought my attention back to Cliff.

Cliff was responsible. Serious. A physician. Stable.

God, was he stable . . .

I smiled at Cliff as an unsteady bubbling arose from my belly. I took another bite of artichoke and smiled even wider as my body swayed.

"What do you love to do, Leaf? I mean, Cliff?" I held in a hiccup and snuck a look at Shep.

Shep was wearing a graphic T-shirt that made his biceps look all bulgy.

Wait. Was bulgy a word?

I chuckled to myself. It was when you were in my condition.

I brought my gaze back to Cliff. His navy suit jacket covered his lengthy arms nicely. He probably had agile fingers. I stared at his hands. Long and lean.

Shep's digits were muscular. Everything about Shep shouted strength and masculinity.

And flirting.

And jokes.

And dares.

I scowled at Cliff.

"Did I say something wrong?"

Realizing I had absolutely no idea what he had said, I shook my head. "No. Sorry. Not at all."

"So, sailing is always a fun treat," he continued. "And sometimes, I'll take Mama out riding. Do you like to ride?"

My eyes widened. "As in horses?"

"Are there other things you can ride?"

I polished off my martini. "Well, yeah. There are snowmobiles, four-wheelers, jet skis, and motorcycles."

If I were still dating Shep . . . then Shep.

I hid a smirk. What had gotten into me?

Oh, yeah. Two double martinis in under an hour.

Cliff frowned as if I'd said something ridiculous.

Good thing he didn't know what I was thinking.

He folded his hands and set them on the table as if I were about to get a lecture. "I'm a trauma surgeon. You think I'd get on a motorcycle?"

"Well, I mean, horses aren't exactly safe either. They are huge creatures."

"Safer than ATVs and motorbikes."

I shrugged. "Depends on the situation, I suppose. But if we are to look at life as a set of variables that range from liabilities to assets, then I'd have to assess that most things would fall into the liability category, right? So at that point, you just have to evaluate what your risk level is. Your risk level is horses with a mind of their own."

He looked confused. "Yeah, I suppose. Do you ride?"

"I've ridden horses, but I don't do it a lot."

His eyes glinted with excitement. "When was the last time?"

"Umm . . ." I ate another bit of artichoke. "I'd say about the fifth grade or so."

"That doesn't count." Cliff looked like I'd just socked him in the gut, and I found myself giggling uncontrollably.

"But I can learn."

"No, I just . . . I'm not sure."

The server came over and took our orders for dinner,

along with another martini for me, but this time a single.

"I would love to take riding lessons," I offered. "I've just never had any reason to think about it."

He looked relieved, as if maybe there was some common ground after all. "Really?"

But I knew there wasn't.

"Totally."

"I love to snorkel and dive too."

I nodded, thinking back to his earlier statement about never having time off. "You dive a lot?"

He shrugged. "It goes along with sailing."

"Makes sense."

I looked at Shep clanking his bottle with his friends and scowled. I wanted more than anything to be there with him.

But I knew better. I knew it was the alcohol. I knew what I needed in my life for happiness, and that included stability. Always had.

Shep was an unknown.

A bit of a live wire.

A loose cannon.

God, I missed him. I'd been doing sort of fine staying away from him, but seeing him in person made every cell in my body ignite with longing.

I missed him.

We never had this getting-to-know-one-another phase because we just clicked. Things just came out naturally. There were no I-like-baseball-do-you-like-baseball? conversations.

But he needed to grow up. He needed to be responsible.

Shep was a million red flags balled up into one giant red flag with a big red bow on top.

Cliff was a physician who took his mom out horseback riding for fun. He worked a lot. Spent a lot of time at this bar for Shep to call him a regular. And he probably had some pretty unreasonable expectations.

I gasped at the sudden realization that finally hit me like a dead fish in the face.

The server brought over my umpteenth drink of the night, and I took a small swallow as Cliff watched me carefully.

"You know, Cliff. You are amazing. I have no doubt that you're a highly skilled surgeon with a kind heart and a vast amount of interest. But that's not me. I'm a little bit rough around the edges, and I don't mind staring at my phone playing games in between court cases or finding myself curled up in a ball reading my latest romance."

He kept his eyes on me. "Okay."

"I am not perfect, and I need to find that person who's not perfect with me."

"And that's not me."

I shook my head. "I'm afraid it's not, and I don't want to waste your time. On paper, we're perfect, right?"

Cliff laughed. "A doctor and a lawyer. Can't get much better than that."

"But you'd bore me to death."

Cliff's smile only widened. "The moment *Jingle Berry Balls* left your lips, I panicked."

"So, you're okay that we're not okay?" I asked, feeling my pulse soar a little more with each passing second.

"Absolutely."

I patted the table. "Good."

"Good."

Our meals were delivered right then, and I glanced at Shep's table. He was watching me, and the very act sent a thrill of the unknown through me.

I turned my attention back to Cliff as we dug into our burgers.

"I'm glad we got this straightened out," Cliff said, licking his fingers. "Because this has to be the most awkward date I've ever been on. You're beautiful and super awesome. Don't get me wrong."

"Same for you. Very handsome fellow." I took a bite of my cheeseburger and tried to come up with how to approach Shep.

Light and funny.

Angry and scrappy.

I just didn't know, but when the tab came and we split the bill appropriately, I couldn't wait to walk over to Shep.

Cliff stood and wandered toward the door as I took a deep breath and smoothed my hands over my skirt. I'd polished off the last of the martini because I knew I needed all the liquid courage I could muster.

But when I looked over at Shep's table, he was gone.

Chapter Thirty-Seven

I Fell for It

Shep

The knock pounded through the entire apartment like a brigade of firemen were outside. I grumbled a few curse words as I trudged to my front door, where I could chew out my best friends. I didn't need any more bright ideas that they'd come up with. I needed peace and quiet and time to lick my wounds.

Seeing Lucy tonight only solidified what I'd screwed up for myself. Right when I got to the door, more raps on the door rippled through the condo.

"What the hell do you want this time?" I growled as I opened the door to see Lucy staring at me with her bright green eyes and dark hair falling below her shoulders. She shivered a little and kept her gaze focused on me.

"Lucy!" My heart raced with confusion. Her glassy eyes and the wobble in her stance made me want to fold her into my arms.

"I'm not perfect," she said softly.

"Yes, you are."

She shook her head. "I'm not, and I shouldn't expect you to be, either."

The smell of alcohol drifted toward me.

"You're drunk," I said quietly.

The gravity of the situation felt like a lead weight.

"So?" She smiled. "I told you I'm not perfect."

"I never wanted perfection."

Lucy took a step forward, and I pulled her inside, shutting the door behind us.

"I've missed you so bad." Her voice trembled as she took a step back from me to keep the space.

The absence made my chest pull, but I didn't want to do anything I'd regret.

"I've been so worried, Shep. Just downright scared. The feelings I've had for you are completely new to me." She peeled off her coat and dropped it on the floor. "I've been looking for a way out since I met you."

Her words stung me like falling into a nettle bush. Each little prick damaged my already frayed ego.

"We are both afraid."

She leaned against the foyer wall. "I'm tired of being frightened, Shep. I don't want to wind up with a Cliff."

"A Cliff?" I asked, confused.

"I was on a date with him tonight. You know, Cliff?"

"Oh, right. I thought you meant a cliff, as in like falling over."

She chuckled. "See? This is what I'm talking about. I miss you."

I swallowed down all the emotion running through me. She was drunk.

"I didn't want to go on a date with him, but I kind of had no choice," she confessed. "Some might call it a dare or a veiled threat. Not sure."

I tensed. "Of course, you had a choice. Just like I did all those times that I didn't tell my friends enough with the bets."

She laughed and shook her head, bringing her eyes to mine. "Actually, I learned just how persuasive your friends could be."

"What are you talking about?"

"Nothing." She shrugged. "Do you have anything to drink?"

"Like water?" I suggested, eyeing her.

I didn't understand what brought her here tonight, and it felt like one wrong move, and she'd flee into the night, never to be seen again.

"I guess water will do." She pouted and followed me into the kitchen, where I handed her a glass of H2O.

"I've never seen you this drunk."

"You're not exactly sober," she bit back, and I had to smile.

"Why are you here, Lucy?"

My heart tugged to be with her, to pull her into me, kiss her, and feel her once more.

But she was drunk, and by morning, I knew she would regret whatever had happened.

At least now, she could just hate me for doing what I did. She didn't need to wake up hating herself too. I didn't want to open the floodgates and unlock emotions that couldn't be locked away again.

"I was wrong. I was selfish." She took a few more sips of water before setting the glass down. "You were just being Shep. You had no way of knowing that I'd develop feelings for you. That your dare had escaped the bounds of reality."

I nodded, unsure of what to say.

"You alarm me, Shep. The thing we have between us freaks me out, and I think I was looking for any little thing to be able to cry foul and jump ship."

I studied her, trying to unwrap whether this was coming from the alcohol or her heart.

"Your friends explained to me that—"

My hand flew up. "Wait. What?"

"Your friends. Mike and Brendan came to my office."

"Why? When?"

She bit her lip, which looked deliciously sexy, but didn't answer my questions.

"They are extremely convincing, and as I was sitting with Cliff tonight, I realized a lot of things. Can I have a seat? The room is kind of swerving. Or maybe it's me. Maybe I'm swerving."

I laughed nervously and sat her on the couch while my mind ran wild with thoughts about Mike and Brendan.

"Your friends told me that you just needed to see me happy with someone else." She drank more water. "And I tried to fake being happy tonight. I really did. I wanted you to see it and be able to move on and forgive your friends. There's nothing more that I want than for you to be happy."

"You knew I was there?" My heart hammered in my chest. There was so much I wanted to say to her, but I could see she wasn't completely focused.

"I snuck a look at you every chance I could get," she

confessed.

"I never saw you look in my direction."

"That's because you were busy scoping out the table of women next to us," she teased.

Her words burned. "No. I wasn't. I didn't even see any table but yours, and the more I saw you enjoying yourself with Cliff, the more I realized that I needed to get out of there."

And this was the problem. She saw me as the womanizer, the player.

Mr. Flirt.

I wasn't like that any longer. Not since I'd met Lucy, but I didn't know if I could ever get her to see the real me. Tonight was showing me that, and it killed me.

"I wasn't enjoying myself with Cliff," she continued.

"You laughed a lot."

She smiled and sighed. "Because I was thinking about you and how you'd react to the things we were saying and how little I had in common with the perfect man on paper known as Cliff versus how much I had in common with the silly and fun CEO who'd never want to settle down."

"You see the Shep you want to see, Lucy. I wasn't looking at other women. You're the only woman who exists in my world. But you see what you want to see because of my past actions, and that worries me. I don't think a future can work when it's buried in the past."

She nodded. "You're right. Absolutely right."

My heart caved into confusion and worry and everything in between. I loved Lucy more than I could even put into words, but she wasn't exactly sober enough to let my hopes soar.

"I made some foolish mistakes. I'm sure you read all the texts I sent. I never thought of you as a dare. The moment my friends uttered those words, I forgot them. I didn't even remember the added part about sleeping with you. There was a brief second where I remembered the whole thing and thought about telling you, but one thing led to another, and we spent our time doing other things. There's no excuse, and I know what it looks like. I know how I'd feel if I were in your shoes, but from the bottom of my heart, I never meant to hurt you. I fell in love with you, Lucy."

Her mouth parted, but no words came out. She drew a blue pillow toward her and hugged it. She looked so vulnerable and like the Lucy I knew better than anyone. The same Lucy I'd managed to singlehandedly crush. The ache spread through my body quickly. It was the same pain that had burned through me for weeks. Now, she was sitting in front of me, and I felt completely at her mercy.

"It's true," I repeated, pulling her hands into mine. "I apologize for everything."

"You didn't do anything wrong, Shep." She shook her head. Her words slurred slightly. "Client after client comes streaming into my office telling me truly horrendous things about what their partners did to them, and somehow, I internalized all that and placed those things on you. I'm tired. I'm exhausted. I see my future, and it scares me. I don't know what I want in life anymore. I thought I craved stability, but the thought of picking up everyone's pieces for the next four decades worries me to death. You're not the problem. I am. I need to figure out what it is that I truly want in life."

"I get it, though." I shook my head. "You saw me as a liability. If I lied about who I was when you first met me, I'd imagine that doesn't give a lawyer a warm and fuzzy feeling."

She smirked and nodded. "True, but then I had to remind myself of the context. I had to quit being the super serious attorney and remind myself that someone still has fun in the world."

"When was this?"

"Tonight, when I was having dinner with Cliff. He was so dry, and I've missed the fun of being with you."

"Wow. I owe Cliff a lot."

Lucy smiled. "Can we start over?"

I shook my head. "I don't want to start over."

Her expression fell, and her voice quavered. "You don't?"

I smiled. "I want to start right where we left off."

Her eyes brightened, and she scooted closer. "Yeah?"

"Absolutely." My eyes steadied on hers as longing pushed through me. "Do you forgive me?"

"There's nothing to forgive, Shep. Nothing at all." She climbed into my lap, and I took in every single second in case she woke up tomorrow and forgot it all. "But I don't think I want to be a divorce attorney anymore."

And she passed out in my arms.

Chapter Thirty-Eight

Called in Sick

Lucy

I stretched my hands above me, knocking into a headboard I wasn't expecting. My eyes blinked open, and I looked around to see an unfamiliar bedroom.

Shep's bedroom.

Panic set in as the fuzziness from last night pummeled its way into startling clarity.

I was at Shep's condo. It was a workday. I bounded out of bed, tripping over the sheets that were tangled between my ankles. I was fully clothed in the same outfit I wore yesterday.

We didn't have sex.

Or did we?

As I peeled myself off the floor, Shep wandered into

his bedroom with a cup of coffee and quickly swooped his arm around my waist to steady me.

"I'm late," I snapped unexpectedly.

He shook his head. "No, you're not."

"It's after eight, right? I'm late." My head pounded with the mistakes of last night walloping through my brain.

"I took the liberty of using your phone and texting your assistant. She's got it handled."

I stopped in my tracks. "Has what handled? I have appointments."

"Actually, she texted that you only had one appointment this morning, and the woman canceled. Your client is actually trying to reconcile with her husband or something crazy like that." The right corner of Shep's mouth lifted, teetering into a sexy smirk as he steadied me and handed me the coffee.

"For you."

I rubbed my temples and let out a deep breath.

"Wow. Well, that's a first for me."

"You've never called in sick?"

I shook my head. "Never. I need to get to the office."

My thoughts felt fuzzy, but I needed to get back to my routine. What happened last night was obviously a mistake.

This wasn't how I needed to present myself after

finally being offered partner.

I looked around the bedroom, trying to avoid Shep's gaze. His side of the bed looked made as if I'd slept in it alone.

Taking a sip of coffee, I reluctantly brought my eyes to Shep.

"Did we?"

Shep smiled and shook his head. "No. You fell asleep in my arms, and I carried you to the bed. I slept in the spare room."

My chest squished into an emotional mess of longing and annoyance. Why did he constantly have to do the right thing?

"Well, thank you. I'm sorry about intruding last night. I'd obviously had too much to drink. My head is thanking me today." I rubbed my forehead and took another sip of coffee.

"Do you remember anything from last night?" Shep asked as his brows quirked. His long, lean, and muscular body stretched in front of me as he rested his elbow on a dresser.

"I remember Cliff and seeing you at the bar and then coming over here," I mumbled, not wanting to admit how much I remembered.

Because it had all been a big misunderstanding of epic proportions. We were on separate tracks apart and leading away from one another, which was the smart and stable thing to do. And then I had too many martinis and fell at his doorstep, professing my feelings.

I scowled. What had I been thinking?

Weakness.

Something I loathed.

"Anything else?" The mischievous sparkle in his eyes made me smile before I pressed my lips together into a frown.

I gave him a dirty look. "Well, you obviously didn't have your way with me."

Shep chuckled and shook his head. His eyes locked on mine, and I felt goosebumps spread across my skin. The chemistry was undeniable.

"We both said a lot of things last night," he started. "And I want you to know I meant every single thing I said."

The conversation had started flooding through me, and I stiffened. I bit back a defeated grunt of frustration.

"But it feels like your guard is already up again." He drew a breath and nodded. "Yeah. Pretty sure it's like last night never happened."

"It's just that a lot has happened in recent weeks. I made partner. I closed the deal for Danni. I'm focused on my career." I almost choked on the last word, and without warning, tears pricked my lids.

He took a couple of steps closer. "Congrats on making

partner. That's a huge deal."

Butterflies in my belly crashed into one another as he reached his hand over and touched my chin. "I hope you're as proud of yourself as I am."

I tried taming the insect belly and laughed nervously as every piece of stone surrounding my heart crumbled.

"Shep, thank you. I needed to hear that. Mae couldn't care less. Danni has a mini-Lucy brain. My mom never returned my calls, and my assistant just asked about a raise. So, thank you." Tears rimmed my eyes as I swallowed down my embarrassment. I essentially had no one, and I'd pushed away the someone who'd made me happier than anything or anyone.

His words from last night fluttered into my soul, and I wiped away the tears in my eyes.

"Did you mean what you said last night? All of it?" I asked.

"All of it." Shep took a step closer. "Lucy, I love you."

My body rumbled from his words, and my throat tightened. I swallowed down the lump of tears that no longer buried my heart in loneliness.

"And I'm sorry. I'm sorry for making really ridiculous mistakes. I'm not falling for my friends' dares or pranks any longer. It's not worth it because even the most innocent of dares somehow turns into life-altering occurrences around you."

A little guilt snuck into my psyche as I closed the gap between us, nodding and looping my arms around his waist. I looked into his eyes and flashed a meek smile.

"I have a confession, Shep."

"Your name isn't Lucy?" he teased, looking into my eyes.

I chuckled and shook my head. "I was essentially on a dare last night. I don't even know how it all worked out, but the next thing I knew, I agreed to meet Cliff at the bar to make you happy and keep your friends."

"What? How would that ever make me happy? Seeing you with Cliff put me at the end of my rope. I seriously contemplated selling the company and living out of a shack on some island."

I giggled, knowing Shep was more of a cabin-in-the-freezing-snow type. I set my cup of coffee down on the dresser.

"It doesn't make a lick of sense now, but when Mike and Brendan were in my office babbling about how you'd only be happy if you saw me happy because you'd broken me, and—"

"That part is true. The thought of destroying your trust killed me." He shook his head and sucked on his bottom lip for a split second. "But I don't ever remember lamenting to my friends about wanting to see you hook up with someone else."

I breathed him in, loving the smell of soap and Shep. "And yet, it worked."

"It sure did." Shep laughed and pulled me into an embrace. "I don't know whether to hug 'em or punch 'em."

"Maybe both," I said, resting my head on Shep's chest.

The steady rhythm of his heartbeat created a sense of calm I craved.

"I have a confession, Shep."

He loosened his hug and looked down at me.

I drew a breath and smiled. "I love you, Shep. I think I fell in love with you weeks before we even slept together, but I was too busy trying to build a case in my head as to why you were wrong for me in every way."

Shep chuckled. "Oh, the old Mr. Wrong trick."

I traced a heart on his chest with my finger as his arms slid along my back. "You make me laugh and remind me that life isn't so serious."

"Maybe a little too much."

I shook my head. "I wouldn't want you to change. I love you the way you are."

"So, you don't hate love any longer?" Shep asked.

"I don't hate love. I hate endings."

Shep's fingers ran through my hair as his lips hovered close to mine. "Then how about we never end?"

His words created a hum within my body that vibrated my world into one of pure need.

"Being with you is like implosion therapy. I didn't have a chance. I only knew that wicked side of love where hearts tore each other apart and demanded things no sane person would ever ask for. But with you, I couldn't shut off my heart. There was no other option than to fall in love with you, and I went in head first when I should have gone in heart first."

Shep kissed me softly, and my body heated instantly from his touch.

"I love you so much, Lucy. I hope you know that I'd never intentionally do something to hurt you, but if you see red flags, tell me, and I'll try to change them to white."

"Because you surrender?"

"Wholly," he whispered.

"How do you always know the right words to say?" I asked, smiling as his eyes stayed on mine. It was like he was taking me in just like I was to him. I didn't want this moment to end.

"I'm Mr. Flirt." He grimaced. "Too soon?"

I rolled my eyes and laughed. "Always will be."

He slid his hand into mine. "I don't know if your stomach is up for it, but I made scrambled eggs and bacon."

"It sounds incredible."

"Ah, the words of a true hangover patient." He squeezed my hand as we walked into the dining room. Even though it was a gloomy day outside with clouds lingering low, it felt like the brightest day I'd experienced in a long time.

I felt free.

As I sat down, he scooped up some eggs and placed some bacon on a plate for the both of us before sitting down next to me.

"You know, I want this to work more than anything in the world," I said, feeling my breathing change as my idea solidified in my head. "And I don't think it can keep doing what I do."

"You mean crucifying people on the witness stand?" Shep teased, taking a bite of bacon.

"Spouses, more so." I grinned. "I kind of feel like everything happens for a reason, and I'm just going to see where this next stage takes us."

Shep smiled. "Did you actually say *us*?"

I nodded, feeling dizzy with the excitement of the unknown.

I'd always thought I craved stability, but maybe all of this was for one purpose—to help my best friend, Danni. That part of our lives was finished now. Maybe there was something else out there that would challenge me without feeling like I was losing my soul in the process.

Shep reached over the table and held my hand. "I never knew I could be so happy, and I'm really proud of you for making partner. They should have done it a long time ago."

I smiled and nodded. "You're right. They should have."

Chapter Thirty-Nine

Partner Up

Shep

Lucy marched out of the office building with nothing more than a box. She had a spring in her step as I rushed over to help.

"How'd it go?"

"Just as expected." She winked at me.

"They were shocked that I'd leave when I'd just made partner, but they understood that I had an offer I just couldn't refuse."

I put the box in my car, not the DeLorean this time.

"Oh, yeah? What was that offer?" I teased.

"Oh, some big-shot CEO offered me an opportunity of a lifetime, and all I have to do is sleep with him."

My eyes almost fell out of their sockets. "Lucy. There

are people around."

She giggled and shrugged. "Ah, who cares?"

"God, I love you." I laughed, looping my arms around her and kissing her.

"But remember, there is no work scheduled on the weekends or my team will hate me for bringing you on."

"Well, we can't have that."

Her expression changed, and she nodded. "You know, Shep, I can't thank you enough for bringing me on."

"Lucy, I just nabbed the best contract and trial lawyer in the city, and you want to thank me?"

She smiled and shook her head. "You know what I mean."

We climbed into the car, and I pulled onto the street. She thought we were headed back to my condo, but I had a little surprise for her first.

She'd been working insane hours these last six months and basically crashed at my condo every night just so we could see one another, but it was all for a good purpose.

Lucy had decided she wanted to give up being a divorce lawyer, at least for now, and focus on more pro-bono work and lead my legal team four days a week. In order to make a clean break, she worked her butt off to tidy up her workload and shift cases where they needed to go.

The firm didn't want to see her take any clients, which was fine with her since she didn't feel like ending any more marriages for now. Instead, she wanted to focus on bringing families back together again and found a great volunteer position at the community center that dealt with homelessness and child welfare.

I couldn't be prouder of her.

"So, they took the news okay?" I drove about two blocks before spotting the parking garage to the Fairmont Olympic Hotel.

"If I'd told them I was leaving to go to a competing firm or wanted to take some clients, it could have been a very stressful event, but the firm loves nothing more than retaining clients and patting themselves on the back when one of their own stars decides to do good for the world because it means they don't have to."

I chuckled, knowing she was right.

"This isn't our place." She glanced at me as I pulled up to the valet.

"Nope. I thought we should enjoy a celebratory dinner."

"You always know the way to my heart or in my pants or . . ."

"Lucy, seriously. I've really rubbed off on you too

much."

She chuckled as the valet opened her door and helped her out of the car. I followed her to the doors and felt a jolt of nerves thread through me like I was on fire.

This could go one of two ways, and I was really hoping for the positive one. The more time I spent with Lucy, the more I realized I couldn't live another day without her.

As we made our way past the restaurant, she glanced at me and furrowed her brows. "Aren't we supposed to go there?"

I held her hand and walked toward a small ballroom and opened the doors to a private reception area with one long table overflowing with white roses and hydrangeas. Towering floral arrangements flanked the corners of the room, and Lucy looked at me with eager eyes.

"Shep? Why do I feel like something big is about to happen?"

I chuckled as we took a seat. "Define big."

"Umm. Perry is here?"

I laughed and shook my head, pulling her hands into mine. I knelt down, and her eyes widened as I pulled out a ring box.

"Yes!" she screamed before I had a chance to say anything.

Her hands trembled, running up to her face as she laughed and shook her head. "I mean, sorry. I just wanted to go on record."

I chuckled, shaking my head. "You're not in the courtroom anymore. I promise."

Lucy leaned over and kissed me.

"Lucy, you are the best thing that happened to me. I always thought that love was too fragile for a guy like me, and then I met you. And I realized that I'd finally met my match. I wasn't the only one who was scared of loving with all their heart because we knew what that really meant if we failed."

Lucy sniffled, still trembling, and I smiled. "Lucy, I promise to love you for the rest of my life. I promise never to accept another dare or participate in another prank for as long as I'm on this earth. I want lots of little Lucys and Sheps running around. Lucy, will you make me the happiest man on earth and be my partner, my wife, my everything?"

Tears streamed down Lucy's cheeks as her hands came up and clutched my cheeks.

"Yes, Shep. Yes. I thought you'd never ask."

The doors opened, and in trickled Mae, Danni, little Lucy, Winter, Hunter, Colton, and the rest of our friends and family.

My mom clapped her hands and dashed over to hug

Lucy, who couldn't stop crying.

Mike slapped my back, and Skylar chuckled.

"I told you so," Mike said, laughing. "It just takes finding your match."

"That easy, huh?" I looked over at Brendan and smiled as his eyes caught mine.

I wandered over, and he gave me a great, big hug.

"So, should I pretend I didn't just catch you looking at Danni or . . .?" I teased.

Brendan laughed and shook his head. "Just focus on your big day, fella. I'm in absolutely no rush."

He patted my shoulders, and I looked over at Lucy, who made her way over.

"You know, I really need to thank you and Mike, Brendan."

"Why's that?" he asked, surprised.

"If you hadn't dared me to go to that bar that night to date Cliff, I probably would have kept Shep blocked forever."

"Oh, yeah?"

Lucy nodded, looping her arm around mine.

"Then you're welcome." Brendan smiled, glancing at Danni again.

"Just let me know if there's ever any favor I can do for you, and I'll try my best." She looked over at her best friend holding her baby. "Maybe I'll even dare you to do something out of your comfort level."

Brendan nodded and smiled. "I'll remember that."

I shook my head and laughed, realizing that Lucy had come over to our side. Or maybe she was always one of us.

"I finally finished that article about you," she whispered.

"Yeah?" I brushed some loose strands from her cheek.

She chuckled nervously. "I should have finished it sooner."

"You don't say," I teased.

"I love where they quoted you as saying that the moment you find someone willing to be as vulnerable with their heart as you want to be with yours, love might be a possibility."

"It's true."

"So, you *did* believe in soulmates," she said, smiling.

"I was stretching out on a limb there until I met you. Then I became a believer."

"Thank you, Mr. Flirt, for always knowing what to say and how to treat me."

Lucy looked into my eyes, and I scooped her into my arms and kissed her, knowing she was the best dare of all.

***

Thank you so much for reading Shep and Lucy's story! I had such a fun time with this romance. It had started out as a short novella, but I couldn't help but fall in love with Shep with each word I typed. Before I knew it, I just had to let their story unfold into this book! Lucy and Shep absolutely needed one another. Hope you enjoyed!! If you loved this story, a rating or review would be so helpful on Amazon. I appreciate them so much, and I appreciate you for reading my stories! It's a family endeavor, and we're just so grateful to my amazing readers. Thank you!! Feel free to join my Facebook group (Karice Bolton Book Buzz) where we chat about books, recipes, relationships, upcoming stories, cover reveals, and more!

If you're interested in reading about Winter or any of her friends, the *Mr. Mistake Series* is out now on Amazon. Also, my latest series is the *Sunshine Breakfast Club* and begins with *Dash of Love*. It has been such a fun series to write. Each book is filled with laughs, romance, and a matchmaking club disguised as a book club. I highly recommend it, if I do say so myself. But I have over sixty books to sink your teeth into, so feel free to scan my book list for something that might catch your eye.

Keep reading for an excerpt from *Dash of Love* and from *Mr. Mistake*!

And thanks again for making my stories a part of your world!

~Karice

BOOKS BY KARICE BOLTON

THE SUNSHINE BREAKFAST CLUB SERIES
DASH OF LOVE
PINCH OF LOVE
SPRINKLE OF LOVE
CHRISTMAS OF LOVE

CLOUDBERRY INN SERIES
IMAGINING YOU
REMEMBERING YOU
LEAVING YOU
LOVING YOU

MR. MISTAKE SERIES
MR. MISTAKE
MR. ACCIDENT
MR. WRONG
MR. RIGHT
MR. FLIRT

ISLAND COUNTY SERIES
FINDING LOVE IN FORGOTTEN COVI
LOVE REDONE IN HIDDEN HARBOF
TANGLED LOVE ON PELICAN POIN'
FOREVER LOVE ON FIREWEED ISLA
TEMPTING LOVE ON HOLLY LAN]
CHANCE AT LOVE ON MYSTIC BA
IRRESISTIBLE LOVE AT SILVER FA
LUCKY IN LOVE ON HOUND ISLA
MISTLETOE MISCHIEF

ACCIDENTAL LOVE ON MEADOW COVE LANE
DISCOVERING LOVE ON CRANBERRY LANE
CHRISTMAS ON FIREWEED
IMAGINING LOVE ON WILLOW ROAD
CHRISTMAS CRUSH ON FIREWEED ISLAND
WAITING LOVE AT HAWTHORNE AVENUE
FOREVER CHRISTMAS ON SUGARPLUM LANE

BEYOND LOVE SERIES
BEYOND CONTROL
BEYOND DOUBT
BEYOND REASON
BEYOND INTENT
BEYOND CHANCE
BEYOND PROMISE
BEYOND the MISTLETOE

SILVER RIDGE SERIES
A HAPPY TRUTH ABOUT LOVE
A LITTLE SECRET ABOUT LOVE
A FUNNY THING ABOUT LOVE
A SURPRISING FACT ABOUT LOVE
A SIMPLE WISH ABOUT LOVE
CHRISTMAS AT SILVER RIDGE

LUKE FLETCHER SERIES
HIDDEN SINS
BURIED SINS
REDEMPTION
MIA

V MAFIA SERIES

BLAKE
DEVIN
JAXSON

THE WITCH AVENUE SERIES
LONELY SOULS
ALTERED SOULS
RELEASED SOULS
SHATTERED SOULS

THE WATCHERS TRILOGY
AWAKENING
LEGIONS
CATACLYSM
TAKEN NOVELLA (A Watchers Prequel)

AFTERWORLD SERIES
RecruitZ
AlibiZ
UprisingZ

BLOOD TORN DUET
BLOOD TORN
BLOOD CURSED